Wild Card

Feathers tickled his ear, a sensation that was oddly familiar. No, not feathers – a tongue – it was the tip of a tongue that was exploring the rim of his ear, just the way he liked it. She giggled, a light little sound, not throaty, like Victoria. Wet fingers circled his left nipple, then his right. Another hand slid between his ass and the mattress, against the flat of his left buttock. Impossible.

He opened his eyes. Black. He felt her – Victoria – gently coaxing him to erection with her mouth. Then he heard her – *not* – Victoria – whisper in his ear again and he knew he was awake.

'Who are you?' he whispered. He raised his hand to his blindfold but she caught his wrist, holding it lightly in fingers that were longer than Victoria's.

'Don't you remember me, Ray?'

Damn! He almost blurted out Lonnie's name but stopped himself in time. It couldn't possibly be her, anyway. He wasn't thinking straight, and no wonder, with four hands and two mouths teasing him.

Wild Card
Madeline Moore

BLACK LACE

Black Lace books contain sexual fantasies.
In real life, always practise safe sex.

First published in 2006 by
Black Lace
Thames Wharf Studios
Rainville Road
London W6 9HA

Typeset by SetSystems Limited, Saffron Walden, Essex
Printed and bound by Mackays of Chatham PLC

ISBN 0 352 34038 X
ISBN 9 780352 340382

1

Victoria had waited so long to see Ray again that when she opened the door of her hotel room to his knock she was speechless. For a moment they simply stared, as if each dared the other to make the first move.

'Is it true, Victoria? Are you really dying?' The concern in Ray's voice didn't quite make up for the lack of a friendly hello, never mind a passionate embrace. It did, however, break the spell.

'Dying to see you, anyway.' Victoria grinned at him.

Ray Torrington leant against the doorframe, still not quite inside her hotel room. 'Cheap shot, even for you.'

Victoria pouted. 'I'm not well and I can prove it. Please – come in.' She turned and left him in the hallway. Her lilac-coloured shift whispered as she sashayed into her room. Would he follow? It was good that she'd said 'please' so 'come in' hadn't sounded like a command. He didn't like to be told what to do. They both knew it was dangerous for him to enter her domain. Would he? Please?

The door clicked shut behind her.

'It's not like I was happy to get the news.'

'Were you glad to hear from me?' She was so happy to have him there that her voice shook, so she shut up. She picked up a sheaf of papers from the coffee table and sorted through them. Damn. Now the papers shook because her hands were shaking. Her heart hammered in her chest. Inhale. Victoria took a deep breath. Exhale. Victoria blew out a silent stream of air. Better. She squinted at the papers in her hand, pretending to concentrate. It was important to be cool – crucial that he make the first move.

'Sort of. And sort of terrified,' he said.

'You, terrified of me? I don't believe it!' Victoria twirled on her high heels and handed him a few pieces of paper. 'Here are my angiogram results and my ECG read out ... and my blood tests.'

Ray studied them, as she'd known he would. It was in his nature to be suspicious, though he liked to pretend otherwise.

'Note the negative STD results,' she said. 'HIV free – that's me.'

'Such a good girl,' he said.

She batted her lashes to acknowledge the compliment. 'What about you? Still giving blood every few months?'

Ray nodded. 'I'm the universal donor. My blood flows in the veins of half the world.'

Victoria arched an eyebrow. 'Only half?'

'I'm still young!'

She looked him up and down. Six feet of handsome, chunky man. He had one of those boyish faces that made a woman feel safe, but his pale-blue eyes, if you looked into them for any length of time, were veiled with deceit, or danger. He had a disarming grin, which could be sincere or phoney, depending on the depth of his dimples. Oh, she knew him so well. On the whole, he made a woman feel safe but disassemble him a little and it was clear a gal could get hurt. 'Aren't you forty?'

'Just. Which makes you thirty, I believe.'

'Almost. But, unlike you, my heart is broken.'

'How do you know mine isn't?'

'I mean literally. See?' Victoria handed him more medical papers. 'Idiopathic cardiomyopathy. When my dad died suddenly they discovered he had a congenital heart disease. The older you get, the worse it gets. I got tested and I have it too. Just think, Ray, I could go at any time.' She snapped her fingers. 'Like right now.'

'Isn't there something they can do?'

'Or now.' She snapped her fingers again. 'Or now?' Snap.

'Cut it out, Victoria.' He gave her a warning look. Bad behaviour would not be tolerated.

Victoria whispered, 'OK.' She let her subservience linger between them for a moment, then banished it with a brave smile. 'I'm on medication to help regulate my heartbeat. Other than that ... I've decided to live my life to the fullest! I'm not going back to Canada when I leave London the day after tomorrow. I'm off to the Caribbean!' She pulled her airline itinerary out of the sheaf of papers she held and handed it to him. 'I won't be back.'

'You don't know that.' Ray glanced at the packet and then focused on her. 'Isn't there anything else to be done?'

She basked in his charisma for a moment before answering. God, it was positively addictive to have the full attention of a man as desirable as this one. If only he didn't know it! 'I'm trying some alternative approaches. Stick around for a bit and I'll show you what I mean.'

Victoria posed – five feet six inches of cool blonde beauty. She could see herself with his eyes – her heart-shaped face, the chin tilted bravely, almost defiantly, as if to say 'Don't feel sorry for me.' Yet her features were so delicate, her moss-green eyes so vulnerable. She let her lips, which he'd once declared 'the most kissable ever', tremble just a little. He'd found her irresistible in the past. Her plan depended on him still finding her so now.

Their eyes met. She saw need in his but it might be her own desire, burning so brightly that it reflected back at her. 'Hey! It's 'tini time. Join me?' She crossed the parquet floor to a bar in the far corner, swinging her hips with every step. 'Do I still walk like a stripper from the Canadian prairies?'

'Yes, as a matter of fact.' Ray set down the papers and joined her at the bar. There was a round table with two sleek leather chairs tucked in front of the glass doors to the balcony but he remained standing.

'Now let me see, ice in the shaker, dribble the gin over it, now the vermouth . . .'

'You look like you know what you're doing. What gives?'

'I've learnt some new tricks. Look how nicely I bruise the booze.' She capped the martini shaker. Victoria held it in both hands and shook hard, deliberately making her breasts bounce and letting her bum wiggle.

Ray laughed. 'You're so funny. I forgot.'

A gleeful Victoria poured two drinks and topped them with olives already skewered by miniature red plastic swords.

Ray discarded his garnish and sipped his drink. He closed his eyes, lightly smacking his lips as he judged its quality. He clutched his throat with both hands. His eyes opened wide, frozen in a horrible stare.

'If I were planning to kill you I wouldn't use poison. Too quick,' said Victoria.

Ray stopped feigning death. 'Actually, it's not bad.' He sipped his drink again.

Victoria held her martini glass up. 'A toast! To perfect martinis . . . and imperfect love.'

Ray tipped his glass to hers. Again, their eyes met. This time, Victoria was sure the desire she saw in Ray's gaze was his own, responding to hers maybe, but originating within him.

'I've missed you, baby,' he said.

'I could tell by the barrage of letters and the torrent

of phone calls.' The words were out before she could stop them. She bit her lip.

Ray frowned. 'I'm out of the country more than I'm in it. Anyway, I thought it was better to stay away.'

'You didn't even call when Gordon died, for God's sake.'

'I sent a card.' Ray leant his elbows on the bar.

'Did not. I kept waiting for one to arrive addressed, "To the Widow Victoria from her Long-gone No-good Love", but alas...'

'I truly meant to send a card.'

'It was over a year ago.' Victoria shrugged and sipped her drink. 'It doesn't matter now.'

'Sure it does. You've been mad at me for much longer than you were ever happy with me, you know.' Ray exhaled heavily. He rested his chin on the palm of his hand and gave her a rueful look.

Victoria pretended to count on her fingers. 'By gum, I think you're right!'

Ray laughed. 'I should have married you way back when, instead of running off to learn how to start a revolution.'

'You really wanted to be armed and dangerous,' said Victoria, 'but I believe what you left me for was another woman.' She gave him a sulky look, with lots of biteable lower lip.

'No ... I left you to work in Cuba ... didn't I? It's a while ago now.'

'It is, isn't it? I've decided that your approach to life is the best one, after all. We have to seize the day. That's all I want now. Another day, or another few days, with you.'

'*Carpe Diem*, pretty pussycat.' Ray raised his hand to caress her cheek. She leant into his big fleshy palm. 'Beauty Puss. The old question arises once again ... what to do with you.'

'The same old answer ... whatever you want.'

He stepped away from the bar and wrapped his arms around her from behind. She leant back against the solid length of him and relaxed with a sigh.

'I was mad at you too, you know, when I came back from Cuba and found you'd got married,' he said.

'Boo hoo. I should wait forever in case you get tired of chasing women and saving the world?' Now that she was in his arms it was hard for her to concentrate on their flirtation. Bitterness mustn't creep into the banter. The only thing that made sense was that he felt the same eager euphoria that she did. But, if that was true, how could he ever have given it up? And, now that they were together, how could he keep it so light when their mad attraction could consume them both?

'It's the other way around. I save the world first and then I chase women.'

'I wish we had married. I'd love to be your ex-wife.'

Ray chuckled. 'Isn't there a chance we'd have lived happily ever after?'

'Not the slightest. But it really doesn't matter. I just want to be with you now. One more time.' Victoria wriggled. She felt him stir against her ass. Ray's cock wasn't what made him so irresistible, but it sure didn't make him any less so. He knew what to do with it, too. 'I've planned everything,' she purred. 'I've got snacks and champagne and toys in case we want to get kinky –' She bit her lip. Damn. She'd gone too far.

'Victoria, as long as you're here, I've got everything I need.' Ray spun her in his arms so she was facing him. 'I'd love to make love to you.' He captured her mouth with his.

Oh, the delicious taste of him, flooding her mouth again, at last! Delight mingled with relief. Victoria practically swooned. He tightened his grip on her and she let herself fall into their kiss. He was igniting sparks all over her body, making her weaker by the moment. At the same time, she was ravenous for more.

The kiss dissolved into a thousand little kisses. He kissed her cheekbone; she nuzzled his earlobe; their lips met again, soft on soft, tongue touching tongue, and then moved on; his lips to her eyelid, her mouth at the crook of his neck.

He leant away slightly to put his hand between her knees, and then drew it slowly up her dress until his fingers cupped her sex. She widened her stance to accommodate his big hand. He laughed at the wetness of her panties. She unbuttoned his white shirt and buried her face inside it, embarrassed that her need was so obvious.

'You can't hide from me,' he whispered. His middle finger pressed against the silk of her panties, relaxed with the other four, then pressed again, rhythmically, as if it were a pulse that exerted pressure with each beat of his heart. He licked and kissed the nape of her neck. 'Don't be embarrassed. Come out.'

'I don't want you to know how much I want you,' she murmured. Her cheek was hot against his cool skin. Still, she did as she was told.

'Why? Does it make you feel weak?' He hooked his finger under the crotch of her panties and stroked her slippery slit.

'Yes,' said Victoria. It was awful, awful to want him this bad. It was as if the clarity of her academically trained mind had abandoned her head to take up residence in her erogenous zones. Her thinking was muddled but her need was sharp and clear.

He pulled her against him and held her with his strong left arm, kissing and releasing her mouth at his whim but never changing the rhythm of his thrusting finger.

'Killin' me,' she murmured. Her knees buckled, and it

was lovely to sink down on his hand as he pushed up. Lovely to be supported by his arm so that she didn't even need to be concerned with standing.

'Beautiful wet baby,' he murmured reassuringly. 'Take your dress off.'

'I can't, not with your hand inside my panties.'

'No?' His grin was adorable, guileless. It was terrible how innocent he could look when there was nothing innocent about him at all.

Victoria bit her lip. 'Nope.' She shook her head, as if helplessly unable to perform the simple task of removing her clothes. She could look innocent, too. At any rate it wasn't far from the truth.

Ray slid his finger out of her panties and his hand out from under her dress. Victoria was grateful for a moment's reprieve from the onslaught of sensations his intimate touch inspired. She unzipped her dress and let it fall. She stepped out of it clad only in her heels and white satin panties. Victoria twirled, plucking at a ribbon over her right hip and then a ribbon over her left and tugged the triangle attached to them from between her legs.

Her body was as curvy in the breasts and butt and slender in the waist and thighs as ever. Victoria would never have let herself go, not as long as Ray lived. She knew her body was the only home he'd ever had, even if he didn't. He was the only one who'd ever made her hot and wet with lust over and over again, the only one she'd ever truly welcomed inside every single time. It was her *job* to stay beautiful for him.

'Still a naturist?' she asked.

'You remembered not to say nudist! So clever.' His words were teasing but approval was obvious in his facial expression. Ray grabbed her around the waist mid-twirl. He bent her back in his arms so that her breasts were thrust upwards, her pink nipples hard in anticipation of his touch. He took the left one between his teeth, nibbling with exquisite control.

'I remember everything, Ray . . .' Each tiny bite sent a current through her body that culminated at her clit. Victoria was already well past hopefulness. She knew it was just going to keep getting better and that fact was electrifying.

He released the nipple from between his teeth. 'Me too, baby. But I think I'd better be extra gentle with you, now that you're an invalid. No rough stuff.' Ray captured her nipple with his lips instead, sucking it and tickling it with his tongue.

Gentleness was as exciting a torture as pain because it was firebrand Ray exhibiting such restraint. She was flooded with a need to respond. Victoria reached for his belt and he released her so she could unbuckle it and unzip his pants. His cock was hard against his leg, trapped by his underwear. She tugged it free and gripped its impressive shaft with her fist.

'Marvellous,' she purred. Victoria started to sink to her knees but Ray stopped her.

'Not here,' he said. 'To the bed.' Ray gave her a little spank on her bottom and she sashayed to the king-size bed. He followed, shedding his clothes.

Victoria stretched out on her side. She shook her blonde hair out. Her feet kicked off her high heels and she struck a courtesan's pose for her ardent lover. This was going to be so much fun, worth all the time and effort she had put into making it happen. 'Come get me, Ray.'

His cock jutted proudly from the black thatch of hair between his muscular legs. His hairy chest was hard and his stomach was still flat. So was his ass – his broad back curved ever so slightly at the bottom before it became his butt. She loved that in a man. First, she'd loved it in *this* man and then she'd loved it in *all* of them. Ray had influenced so much of who she was, who she'd become. He'd formed her tastes when she was young, and then he'd wandered off without staying to see what she did with what he'd taught her. It hadn't seemed fair, or right, when it happened, but in the ensuing years she'd come to understand his point of view. Maybe it was just a matter of maturity but eventually, whether you were capitalist or communist, atheist or Deist really was beside the point. The mystery lay in whether you were male or female. If it worked, be happy. If it didn't, move on.

'I never imagined this would happen again,' he murmured, sliding up between her legs. He placed his hardon on her belly and licked her breasts. 'It's been bad out there without you.' He rested his weight on his elbows and kissed his way up her neck to her mouth. 'My world is a big bad place without you in it.'

She stroked his face. 'I'm here, darling. Right where I belong.'

'I like you to be beneath me. I could kiss you forever.'

Forever. She wanted him to mean it. But, if he didn't, she wanted to have her fill of him before she left London. The problem lay in the voracity of her appetite for Ray. What if there could never be enough to satisfy her? 'It's just as good as it ever was,' she moaned.

'Yes. You haven't changed a bit. Beautiful body. Beautiful face.'

She wriggled beneath him. She'd waited years for this, planned it for months, and now she was so excited she couldn't stand it. It had always been like that between them. She'd never understood how he'd been able to discard a relationship like they'd had without a backwards glance. But she wouldn't make the mistake of asking, not now. What she wanted now, more than clarity or closure, was climax. 'I can't wait any longer, please, Ray.'

'Of course you can,' he said. He smiled at her but his eyes were fierce. He slid down until his face was between her legs. He rested his big head on her right thigh and gazed into her. 'Beauty Puss,' he murmured. He blew short hot breaths that stirred the damp curls of her pelt. 'I see you,' he whispered, flicking his tongue out to taste her.

Victoria moaned; she was starved for him, starved almost to death for his touch. 'I might cry,' she said.

'Mmmmm.' He kissed her like he was kissing her mouth, lips to lips.

Her clit was the 'on switch' to the current of her body. Every time he so much as flicked it, electricity coursed through her, making her shudder. It would have been embarrassing if their love was new but it was ancient. Sexually at least, she was safe with him precisely because he knew how deeply he affected her.

'I'll come,' she complained. Now that it was really happening, she wanted to delay her orgasm as much as she wanted it to happen. The exquisite combination of Ray-and-Victoria was a rare and wonderful dish that needed to be savoured, not gulped.

'Is that a problem?'

'Yes.' She pouted at him. 'I don't want to come yet. I want to suck you first.'

'Suck me later, love. I'm going to fuck you now.' He knelt between her legs and pulled her up into his lap. He leant closer, sliding a couple of inches inside her. He paused; then, instead of impaling her further, slowly drew back until he was almost out.

Victoria was as powerless as if she had been bound. She found she didn't dare move, much as she wanted to tilt her hips to capture the prize. Ray was in charge, as always, and the only thing she could do was beg. The words tumbled easily from her mouth. 'Don't come out, please, Ray, please fuck me . . .'

He obliged, slowly leaning into her again. With a quick thrust he was all the way in, then out before she could wrap her legs around his hips. 'Mewling becomes you,' he said in response to the moans that escaped her lips. She started tossing her head from side to side but that, too, elicited no mercy. He pressed his thumb to her clit. His fingers were broad, like his hands and his back and his forehead. His thumb exactly fitted her clit and when he rubbed it slid against her pubic bone like a stripper sliding a pole and if he kept doing it at this pace for more than a couple of minutes she would have to come. She closed her eyes and sank into the sensation.

'All right,' she murmured, then, 'I can't . . .' (which he laughed at) and 'Please, Ray . . .'

He knew the trick to her was rhythm. Even more devastating, he knew which rhythms accomplished what. He could hold her like this for a long, long time if he wanted to. Apparently, he wanted to.

It was torment, trying to 'decide' if she could stand it and knowing that the decision wasn't up to her anyway. It made her thrash from side to side and cry out 'No!' as if she were being taken against her will when she was not. It wasn't something that had happened with the other men she'd known and that was just as well because most men couldn't handle it, nor should they be expected to. But it had often happened with Ray and he'd always known that it was her invading thoughts she was banishing with her words, not the act they were engaged in.

Still, it had been a long time for him, too, and he took pity on them both by sliding all the way inside her again. They both moaned. Ray established a rhythm of long, slow thrusts as he continued to torture her with his thumb.

Victoria shuddered as tiny spasms raced through her

body. They were coming faster now, and building in intensity. It was as if all there was to 'Victoria' was her sex, a wet slut riding him bareback. She was panting, willing herself to yield even as she ached to stay on the edge.

'Good,' he grunted. He thrust harder, faster, leaving his thumb pressed against her, increasing pressure on it with his belly each time he pumped.

Victoria wrapped her legs around his hips. She couldn't get enough of him. She wanted him to pierce her to the core and he did; he entered that empty, lonely little space in the centre of her and filled it with joy. Victoria tumbled into orgasm.

Tiny spasm upon tiny spasm blurred into one complete, clenching paroxysm. Victoria opened her mouth and let it out – a sound as much one of pain, or release from pain, as of pleasure – a low loud delirious groan. Her eyes flew open. The encouraging look on his face made her want to smile but she was panting and then groaning again as he made her keep coming with his punishing thumb and his rhythmic thrusts and the lovely approval in his eyes.

'Enough!' she yelled and she almost meant it. He laughed and she did too, clinging to him as he rode her to the end of her climax.

Victoria was limp. Ray started pounding into her, faster than ever. Now that it was approaching, she remembered the furious pace he liked to set right before he came. He'd told her some women couldn't handle it, even though he always made sure the woman was sated before taking his own pleasure. She'd handled it all right, back when they were both younger, and by God she'd handle it now.

He grunted. Victoria knew he made no noise until he was close to orgasm, so it meant he was going to come now too. She tilted her pelvis up to him, taking him deep. She urged him on with sex talk. 'Yes, darling, fuck me hard, come inside me, Ray, come hard, fill me –'

'Quiet,' he hissed through gritted teeth. For Ray, orgasm was as much an admission of defeat as it was a triumph. He hated to lose control, even for the few moments it took to reach the height of his own pleasure.

Most women would shut up but Victoria knew Ray just as well as he knew her. She knew his words were just like her 'No!' – evidence of mounting passion.

'Shush, don't say a word,' she murmured, intent on spurring him on. 'It's OK, hush, darling. I won't tell –'

'God!' Ray roared as he came.

Victoria kept her voice low, though she, too, could have roared. 'Yes, oh, it's good, it's so good . . .'

'I – need – it!' His words were a simple loud statement of fact, neither demanding nor explanatory. He was the Alpha Male and she was the female he desired. Ray collapsed on top of Victoria and for a second she couldn't breathe. He rolled off and threw his arms out to the sides. 'Yeah!'

Victoria breathed in deeply, inhaling the heady scent of their successful sexual union. Their mutual satisfaction was intoxicating. She curled up against Ray with her head on his shoulder and kissed the sweat that beaded at his temples. 'King Fuck,' she purred.

It really couldn't have gone better.

2

They'd been playing no-limit Texas Hold'em for almost twenty hours. The 'flash' players had been eliminated after three. Penny'd known George the Greek's style before the game began; she'd been studying him since he'd walked away from the Grand Prix de Paris with just over a million euros. He had a habit of drumming his fingertips on his stacks of chips but it didn't mean anything; he just did it to distract. Penny wondered if he knew that, when he saw a card he liked, a muscle in his cheek tightened.

There was no way to read Goldie's face. It'd been botoxed to such a point that her expression wouldn't have changed if her hair had been on fire.

On her part, Penny'd faked a couple of 'tells' during the course of the game, but only when the pot was petty. When she'd been about to bluff, she'd touched a fingertip to her left nipple, where it prodded through her thin shirt. Overt flirting or sexuality was frowned upon but the touch had been a subtle 'unconscious' one. A few times when she'd had a really good hand, she'd let the tip of her tongue show between her teeth.

A close observer – and all poker players in this class were close observers – would think he had a way to read her. She knew she had George fooled but wasn't so sure about Goldie or Brandon Nigrenna, a hot newcomer to the scene. He'd thrown in this hand, so he didn't count for now. She'd get the arrogant upstart later.

She had Ace-Queen of hearts down. When the dealer'd turned the first three cards of the 'flop' he'd revealed the ten of hearts, Queen of diamonds and four of spades. That gave Penny two Queens to the Ace. George hadn't reacted to the Queen but his cheek had tightened when he saw the ten. Chances were he didn't have a Queen in the hole. Brandon, a wiry young man with short-cropped sandy hair and a goatee, hadn't got one either, or he'd never have thrown in. His weakness was that he hated to sit a hand out.

Penny'd seen five cards and didn't think two of the other three players had either Aces or Queens, so she calculated the odds that there was another Queen or Ace in the unturned cards and decided they were 57 per cent against her having the best hand. Still, there was a hundred and fifty thousand pounds in the pot and it would only cost her fifteen to twenty for a shot at it.

She touched her nipple to make George think she was bluffing and pushed a stack and a half of chips in.

George's cheek twitched. He pushed all his chips into the pot. Damn! She'd hoped to provoke him into a simple raise, not to go for broke.

Goldie threw her cards in. Penny matched George's gigantic bet. The dealer turned the nine of hearts, making Penny's stomach sink, and then, hallelujah, the deuce of hearts. Penny's calculated risk that there'd be a Queen or Ace had come to nothing. Instead, against much greater odds, she had a nice little winning flush!

Penny threw in her next four hands, then folded three after making minimum bets. Goldie, never much of a player once the game passed eighteen hours, quit. As she retired from the table she gave Penny a wink. Goldie probably hadn't been fooled by Penny's new mannerisms. She joined Penny's friend Bill and the other ex-players who were sticking around to see who'd be the big winner.

Brandon appeared taut. He'd won seven hands in a row, penny-ante each time, without opposition. Aggressive players like him would rather lose than win too easily.

Brandon and Penny fed the kitty and each of them was dealt two 'hole' cards. Brandon was on the button so Penny bet first. Her two cards were nothing to write home about, a five of diamonds and a seven of clubs, but she bet big anyway. Brandon was happy to contribute a matching pile of chips to the pot, calling her bet. The first two cards of the flop were the ten of spades and the two of diamonds. When the third card in the flop showed the five of hearts, Penny let the tip of her tongue stick out for a second. If Brandon noticed and had been taken in by her false 'tell', he'd think she had three fives, not two.

Penny cut her bet from her stack of chips in three quick precise movements, ten thousand pounds per stack. She pushed the three piles of chips into the centre of the table, letting the tip of her tongue show again.

Instead of folding, Brandon shoved his own stack of chips into the pot, matching her bet and raising an additional ten thousand. Damn. Either he hadn't noticed her tell or he'd guessed it was false.

Penny met Brandon's bet with ten thousand in chips and the round ended.

A fourth card, the turn, was dealt face up. After such a string of low cards Penny expected a face card, so she wasn't surprised when it was a Jack of diamonds.

Penny kept her dark-blue eyes carefully clouded. She needed sleep almost as much as she needed to vanquish the upstart seated across from her. Her upper lip tingled with perspiration but she ignored it. The room was hot and her opponent had sweat beaded on his forehead. It meant nothing.

Brandon Nigrenna's brand-new reputation as a card shark was about to take a kick in the teeth from 'The Fire of London', as she'd been dubbed by *Card Player*

Magazine when she'd aced her first World Series of Poker championships three years ago. It was a pity that all she had to vanquish him with were two fives and a poker face that was a legend in the making. Even more of a pity, this was a cash game. But Penny'd been in tight spots before. She slid another thirty thousand pounds in chips into the pot.

Penny sat back and sipped her drink. Now the tingling on her upper lip was gone while the beads on Brandon's forehead had begun to trickle down the sides of his face. She blinked at him, showing the tip of her tongue again. This time she was sure he'd registered the tell, but would it matter? Hopefully, her opponent was locked in a battle with his own aggressive instincts.

Brandon still hesitated. He slowly shook his head and slapped his cards on to the table face down. 'Fold,' he barked.

Penny grinned. She leant in to scoop up the pot with both hands, knowing that her top was just low enough to give him a glimpse of her gorgeous cleavage. This time, she didn't do it to distract him, just to soften the blow. 'That's it for me,' she said.

'We just started!' he protested.

'Twenty hours ago by my watch,' she replied, shaking her too-long auburn bangs out of her eyes. 'We agreed this was our last hand.' She started gathering the cards. As Penny reached for his, she 'accidentally' flipped her hand over so that her lowly pair of fives was exposed. Brandon and the other men in the room groaned when they saw that she'd bluffed. Quickly she scooped up her cards, adding them to the pile. She rose from her chair, stretching her lean, five-feet-ten form. She was wearing low-waisted custom-designed denim jeans and when she stretched her top rode up in front so her smooth lean belly was exposed. Brandon shook his head again.

There was no point in crying foul now. Penny'd been the model of decorum during the game and any whining about feminine wiles would be taken as just that, the whinging of a loser.

Penny relaxed her facial muscles and let a huge smile cross her face. 'Feels so good.' Suddenly, she was beaming.

Her former opponent gnashed his teeth. 'How about a friendly game of snooker before you go, Penny?'

Penny's grin grew even wider. 'Gosh, Brandon, how long do you suppose it would stay friendly? Nope, I've got to get moving. People to see and all that. Lend us a hand, Bill?' Bill was a poker pal from way back and Penny could always rely on him to have her back. He helped her scoop up her chips with a minimum of fuss, and they left the table together and headed towards the cashier.

When they were out of earshot of Brandon Nigrenna, Bill shot her a sly proud look. 'You're a bright copper penny, you are. Pair of fives.' He snorted.

She shook with silent laughter. 'Don't get me started.'

'If you want to join us for snooker, I'll make sure you get out in one piece,' Bill offered.

Under normal circumstances, Penny probably would have gone along. She knew she wouldn't be able to catch any sleep without a wind-down but this weekend was special; Penny would be lucky to get any shuteye at all before her big date. She had to try.

'Not this time, Bill. Listen, you won't be seeing me for a while. I'm taking a vacation.'

'Funny time to quit, when you're at the top of your game. You know, "The Fire of London Scorches Another Tournament!" and all that.'

'I'm *always* at the top of my game.'

They turned in her chips to the cashier.

'You don't always have movie actors trying to track you down so they can hire you to teach them the tricks of the trade.'

'Please! That's nothing but a hoax. Someone's trying to put me off my game.' Penny snorted derisively. 'At any rate, I don't teach. Bill, I just need a break, for personal reasons.'

'You're not sick?'

Penny rolled her eyes. 'See, that's just the kind of thing I don't want floating around the tables. Although I guess it'd make it all that much easier to bankrupt you boys once I got back, tanned and in tip-top condition.'

Bill laughed as he slung his arm around her waist and gave her a squeeze. 'I'll make sure no one starts worrying about you. But tell me, what's up?'

She disentangled herself from his arms. 'An old friend is in town. A lover.' She growled the words in a voice that said she smoked a pack a day, though she didn't. She grabbed Bill's face with one hand, pursed his lips with her fingers and planted her lips on his for a big smacky kiss.

'He's a lucky fellow,' said Bill.

Penny accepted her winnings from the cashier. She tucked the cheque into the front pocket of her jeans. 'I suppose I'm the one who's lucky at cards and he's the one who's lucky in love.' Her navy-blue eyes misted. She shook her head impatiently. 'I need sleep.'

Bill nodded sympathetically. Like her, he was acquainted with the buzz that came from a big win at the end of a long game. But Penny suspected he wasn't the type to grow weary of it or notice the price it exacted from winner and loser alike. She knew 'when to fold 'em', as the Country and Western song admonished. She was making pots of money as a player but physically and emotionally she was numb to the bone. She needed catharsis; she needed to scream and shudder, wiggle and yelp. Serious shagging, raucous laughter, hot hamburgers and cold beer. She needed sunshine after eons of drizzle and grey clouds that eagerly crowded each other to fill the sky.

All that was about to happen if plans unfolded as they should. In truth, Penny didn't have a date; she had a date with destiny.

3

Ray pissed long and hard, then flushed the toilet and bent to turn on the shower. His body felt fantastic, virile and sated at the same time. Every muscle in his body felt relaxed but ready for whatever he demanded of it. Victoria could do that to a man or, at least, she could do it to him.

He stepped into the steaming shower and let the water hit the top of his head. It was good to be alone. Victoria had always been high maintenance. She was the same fantastic beauty she'd always been, though. More so, in fact. Since he'd last seen her she'd filled out just a little, becoming perfectly voluptuous, whereas before she'd been a little too girlishly skinny. Her skin was alabaster, dotted with a few velvety, exquisitely located moles but otherwise as smooth and pale as bridal silk. She hadn't wrinkled one bit; even her hands, those betrayers of age, were young.

Ray shampooed his short crop of black hair. Victoria's hair had felt like soft fur in his hands. In his case, his hairline had just begun to recede but if she'd noticed it she hadn't said anything. Of course, she wouldn't; she was a good girl that way.

He closed his eyes as he rinsed his hair. Victoria's eyes really were the intense shade of green he'd always remembered; they were the colour of some shiny plant that grows so deep in the woods most people never see it. Their hue made her misty gaze entrancing. God, he'd love to spank her bum until the mist became a fog and she disappeared so completely into pleasure that endorphins turned her pupils into pinpoints.

Ray shook his head, banishing the vision. He soaped his pubes, ignoring the erection that thoughts of playing rough with Victoria had caused. The last thing he needed was to give her a heart attack. Anyway, there wasn't time – as it was, he wouldn't be able to stop by his room at the Plaza before his dinner date. He started to rinse off.

The Plaza was where he'd been that morning after an exhausting and unproductive four-day International Symposium on Housing. He'd been the keynote speaker the previous night. Wowed 'em, as usual, but, again as usual, when the hat was passed around the take had come up pitifully short.

It was hard not to get disillusioned when your job was to house the homeless of the world. Time marched on and nothing ever really changed.

Ray, a modern man in an expensive suit, had been watching a hotel employee dismantle the convention display that featured his smiling face on a poster. He doubted anyone could have told from the smirk on his face as he watched how much he wanted to tear the poster to shreds with his bare hands. He was tired of being civilised about something that was fundamentally wrong with the world.

The receptionist called to him in her delightful English accent. It was a relief to turn his attention to her. She handed him a scented pink envelope with his name scrawled across it in the precise, childlike handwriting of Victoria Ashe. At the same time, she reminded him that the organisers of the just completed symposium had scheduled a series of 'fun-filled events' for those participants interested in staying on for a few days. He barely listened until she asked if he'd be checking out.

He'd replied, 'No and likely not tomorrow, either,'

even before he read the letter. So if he was honest with himself, and he liked to believe he was an honest man, he had to admit that it wasn't the contents of her letter – she was in town as well, finalising the sale of her husband's European holdings, before leaving for the Caribbean in a couple of days and, by the way, 'dying' – that had made him decide to stay on in London. Sure, he'd come running, just as any concerned friend might do, but deep down he'd known that if she and he got together they'd end up in bed.

Ray stepped out of the shower. He towelled off, taking a moment to inspect his body in the clouded full-length mirror. He was in great shape; he had to be, to keep up the good fight.

'King Fuck.' Ray grinned at his reflection. And why not? He was damn proud of his equipment and his prowess in the sack. It gave him the confidence to approach beautiful women. Victoria was one of the hottest pieces of tail in the prettiest package he'd ever known. As far as he was concerned her looks were flawless. He honestly had no idea why every man she met didn't fall at her feet, but she claimed it just wasn't so. Some, sure, but not all. He combed his hair with his fingers. Still, the same could be said of him. Victoria thought he was handsome as well as heroic. She said he was like Hercules, which was ridiculous. He was a man of the people, not a Greek demi-God. He flexed his pecs again.

When they first met she'd still been a student, labouring away on a degree in dusty old poems and their new-age symbolism, or something. He'd long ago abandoned formal schooling for meaningful work. Ray had wanted to save the world then and he still did. He just didn't advocate saving it by means of a bloody revolution any more, as he had then.

He'd been having drinks with the members of the Young Communist Party when she'd come into the

Student Union bar at the University of Toronto. Even then he was a cool cat but he remembered his jaw dropping at the sight of her. She seemed to have a light around her, maybe a new-age aura, that proclaimed her vulnerability. He'd wanted to rip her skirt and blouse off and bend her over the bar then and there. Take her. Make her be his. It was nuts. If he'd had more to drink he'd have dismissed his reaction as drunkenness, but he'd only had one beer.

'Yeah, sure,' was all he said to the eager youths that had gathered to share their thoughts with someone already established in the outside world as a leftist mover and shaker.

He slid off his bar stool and approached her before she could join the group of girls she was waving to. 'May I talk to you?' he asked, gently taking her elbow.

She met his eyes with hers; sea green on a sunlit day, fantastic peepers. 'Huh?' she said, as if this sort of thing didn't happen to her every day, which she later claimed it did not.

'I'd like to buy you a drink. Or, if you're free, dinner.'

'Who are you?'

'An admirer.'

'Since when?'

'Since now.'

She seemed as surprised as he was when she said yes. Later she told him it was because he reminded her of Hercules. Fine. The intensity that scared off some women, no matter how carefully he tried to keep it under wraps, must have attracted her.

That very first night he'd wooed her with every ounce of charm and every penny he had. After their 'date' he'd taken her to his apartment and made love to her.

From the beginning they'd fit together perfectly. Somehow he'd known, maybe from the rhythm of her walk, or the cadence of her voice, that slow and steady was the key to her passion. When, in the throes of ecstasy, she'd thrashed her head from side to side on the pillow and cried out 'No!' it hadn't even occurred to him to stop. He'd known for a fact she meant 'Yes'.

They'd talked about it later, how much of a chance he'd taken, but he'd been right. She'd wanted him never to stop and he'd made her come three times. ('Twice more than ever before,' she'd admitted.) Then there was that lovely period of post-coital cooing and praising and sharing of information.

She was an arts student so she was a bleeding heart liberal. He toned his own politics down for the time being. Of course, she was happy that he was dedicated to helping the world. She hadn't known, then, that women who love men of destiny lead a lonely life.

After twenty minutes and another glass of wine, Ray had looked at her, naked and dreamy, curled up in the sheets of his bed, and known he had to have her again. This time he was masterful. He knew what made her moan and she knew he knew it, so he could be unyielding in his demands.

He kissed her and licked her until she was panting again, and then he flipped her over on her tummy. He stretched out on top of her, his weight on his elbows, and tickled her ear with his tongue. 'Have you ever?'

'What?' Victoria gave him a puzzled glance.

Ray grinned at her and wriggled against her bum. This was the part where he had to be his most innocent fun-loving self. It was imperative that she see the adventure in what he was suggesting.

Victoria gaped at him. 'Of course not!'

Ray had to laugh at her indignation. 'Why not? It's fun.'

'I'm not gay!'

'No? Funny thing, me neither. I guess that's how we managed to end up in bed together, eh?'

She saw his point. She wriggled beneath him, gently trying to buck him off. He stayed put. She stopped wriggling.

'Think about it, Victoria. You sucked me with your mouth. Your pussy welcomed me. Why would your ass be any different?' He rested more of his weight on her. His hard-on nestled in the crease between her cheeks. His voice lowered to a whisper. 'Spread your legs a little.'

'I'm scared. What if I hate it?'

'If you hate it I'll stop. Where's the fun in making you do something you don't want to?'

Beneath him, her lithe little body shifted as she spread her legs. The way she was trembling almost brought tears to his eyes. 'So brave,' he whispered, 'such a big brave girl...'

'Will it hurt?'

'It does at first but then it's nice. I think you'll like it. Really sensual women do and that's what you are, a really sensual woman. Say "OK".'

'OK, Ray.'

Ray's cock nudged against her. She moaned. Joy exploded in his gut and rushed through his body to his fingertips, his toes and the head of his dick. She liked it. He *needed* his women to be anal. He pushed, just a little, edging his way inside. She gasped.

'Wait!' she pleaded.

'Do you want me to stop?'

'No...' she said, sounding a little unsure.

'You'll like this,' he promised, as he jutted his hips and entered her.

'It hurts!'

'I know, sweetheart,' he murmured, his lips against her ear, his soft voice belying the hardness of him as he forced his way in, inch by incredible inch. 'You can do it, though. I'm going nice and slow, aren't I?'

'Yes but –'

'Just think what a bad girl you are. A *good* bad girl. None of the other girls in your Comp Lit class do this, do they?'

'I doubt it.'

'Little Victoria's virgin ass. What a beautiful gift. Nobody ever gives me anything, you know, I have to fight fight fight for every little thing. And now this. Thank you.' He pulled out a little, then forced his way back into her, a little deeper this time.

'It hurts!'

'Thank you!' he gasped into her ear.

'I can't.' She was breathing in short shocked bursts.

'You can. Almost there.'

When most of him was inside her he paused for a moment, letting her get used to the sensation. Then he buried himself to the hilt.

Victoria screamed but that was OK because he screamed too. The sensation of her tunnel as it surrendered to him was almost more than he could stand. On his second stroke she was still as tight as she'd been on the first, but by the third he was riding her more smoothly.

'See?'

'Yes.'

'Relax.'

'OK.'

'I'm opening you with my cock.'

'Yes.'

'I'm making your ass fuckable. What do you say?'

'Thank you, Ray.'

They laughed a little and he felt her relax beneath him. He plunged into her again and this time she didn't scream, she moaned.

That little strangled sound of lust that he'd drawn from her by taking her virgin ass made his cock, already rock hard, pulse to a greater rigidity.

'Touch yourself,' he ordered. He loved it this way. Ray Torrington, by day a champion of all mankind, fighting for a dignified life for everybody. Leftist. Feminist. Secular Humanist. But by night he was the supreme commander of his own particular dark desires, subjugating women purely for the sake of his private selfish needs. 'Do it.'

She obeyed. Ray's thighs tightened and his teeth clenched and he knew he had a limited number of strokes left in him.

'You're so good,' he whispered in her ear. Her head turned slightly to catch his comforting words. 'Such a good pretty puss, letting mean old Ray fuck your ass.'

'More . . .' she gasped.

'So tight and smooth . . . it's the tunnel of love, baby.'

'Oh, Ray, I'm going to come.'

'Good – go for it, sweetheart. It's yours Victoria. Take it!'

She threw back her head and started yelling. Ray whooped with delight. He thrust hard and stayed put as the force of her orgasm rhythmically clenched and released him.

'Beautiful,' he whispered. He kissed the wet from her cheeks, whether it was tears or sweat he didn't know. 'Now me . . .'

Ray started pumping again. He knew it was going to be a good one; all he needed was a good head of steam. Half a dozen frenzied strokes were all it took before he climaxed suddenly. His orgasm was like fireworks or bombs exploding in his head and his gut at the same time – like he'd been hit. Ray roared like a lion, coming so hard he almost passed out.

That had been some night, all right.

Ray started to pull on a terry robe, then changed his mind and let it fall to the floor. He preferred to be naked whenever possible; he was an animal, comfortable in its skin. He liked his women best naked too, especially this one. Her skin was creamy everywhere, softer in some places than others but nothing less than silky anywhere.

He picked up a big bottle of pills that sat beside her hairbrush on the counter. Was it possible Victoria was really as sick as she claimed to be? The pills looked legitimate. He read the label. They were some kind of heart medication all right, to be taken twice daily. He set the bottle back down.

Ray hated to leave before he'd fucked Victoria's ass but it would be the right thing to do. Then again, he was always doing the right thing these days. Always dressed up in a monkey suit, playing the civilised man. He'd done the right thing when he'd let her go, almost a decade ago, after she'd come to understand his dedication to revolution as the answer to the world's ills. In truth, he'd become kind of bored by the intensity she showed for metaphors and literary conceits. He was the kind of guy who called a spade a spade, or sometimes a goddam shovel.

Now that he thought about it, maybe Victoria was right after all. Maybe there *had* been a girl he'd spent a few months with before his work papers for Cuba were in order. But then he'd spent years in Cuba, learning first hand how communism works. He'd met a few fabulous women there, too. He chuckled at the memory of the 'kinky' games he'd introduced Victoria to, before his trip. In Cuba he'd met a woman who'd introduced him to real rough sex, and it involved a lot more than the spankings and bondage he'd believed made him a dominant. What was her name – Marita? Marina, that was it. Marina had been a fantastic lover except for her need to be whipped for hours at a time. His arm got tired and he began to wonder if she was crazy. He'd been lucky when his expiring visa gave him an out.

On his return to Canada, Ray had decided to fight the good fight from within the system. He might even have married Victoria if she'd still been single but she wasn't. He got used to moving around, working for all the people most of the time and making love to some of the women in his spare time. He'd resolutely stayed a bachelor all these years. He was no Hercules, or hero of any kind, but he was, he had to admit, 'King Fuck'. Ray pointed at himself in the mirror and winked. It was high time the King left the building.

4

Victoria slipped into a pink and orange chiffon 'robe', if you could call something as translucent as tinted mist a robe. She ran her fingers through her hair, freeing the strands that had become matted at the nape of her neck by the heat of their lovemaking.

She hadn't come like that since the last time she'd been with Ray. Good Lord, he was good in bed. A rush of pleasure shuddered through her belly to her clit. Gordon had been a great husband but he'd never grabbed her attention the way Ray did. Her husband had been a mild man, dependable and wealthy and older. Victoria had had many lonely nights in her life, even before she'd been widowed. But all that was in the past. Victoria and Ray were together again, living in the now.

She freshened up her 'natural-look' makeup. Ray, like so many leftwing types, insisted that he loved women as they were, without high heels and bustiers and stockings and perfume and makeup. But that just left him all the more defenceless when faced with a beautiful woman who knew how to enhance everything she had to make it that much more irresistible. She added a second coat of mascara.

Victoria ran her hands over her body, pausing to caress her nipples. They were delicate little pink nubs. She coaxed them to harden a little. She knew Ray's love for her lasted precisely as long as their encounters did and she wanted to be desirable to him for as long as possible.

Victoria straightened the bedclothes. She laid a black leather blindfold on a pillow and a thin black crop at the end. She was attaching the last of four velvet-lined steel cuffs to the last of the four posts of her king-size bed when Ray emerged from the bathroom.

'Hi, honey, have a nice pee?' Victoria chirped.

He eyed the manacles. 'Someone hasn't been listening. I said no rough stuff. Unless there's something you want to tell me about your heart condition?' He sat at the end of the bed.

'I can have all the sex I want. Anyway the crop and the cuffs are just in case.' Victoria crawled across the bed towards him, letting her breasts sway.

He tousled her hair as she rubbed against him like a domestic cat. 'Just in case what?'

'Just in case I'm a bad girl.'

'We have to talk,' he said.

'I love to talk. May I pick the topic?'

'No.'

'My topic is, why do atheists always yell "God!" when they come?'

'I mean it, Victoria.'

'Because "Maggots!" just doesn't have the same ring to it.'

'Very funny.'

'Not only funny, but true.'

'Do I yell "God!" when I come?'

'Yup. Are you still a devout atheist?'

'Of course.'

'So you see, I'm right.'

'Little Victoria is always right.' He straightened his shoulders, bracing against her reaction. 'You know what – I have to go.'

Victoria gasped and her eyes filled with tears. 'No, please, I was just kidding around. I thought we were having fun.' The colour drained from her face. 'We still have things to talk about. I want – I want to invite you to go to Cuba with me.'

'What? You said you were going to the Caribbean.'

'Cuba is in the Caribbean, honey.' Victoria laughed even though two hot tears were trickling down her cheeks.

'I know that! It's just not what I – why are you going to my favourite place?'

'You always made it sound so fabulous. I want to see it for myself. And I have two tickets, Ray. You didn't even look when I showed you my itinerary. *Two* tickets. Please come.' The promise Victoria had made to herself not to appear desperate was forgotten.

Ray began getting dressed. 'I don't know about this.'

'Will you think about it?' She tugged at his sleeve.

'I don't think I can just take off for Cuba – although I'm not due anywhere for a while now.' He paused with a sock in his hand.

'Yay! Imagine! Just the two of us, together in paradise.' Victoria plucked the sock from his fingers. She hid it behind her back but he ignored her.

'Are you sure it's a good idea? I might fuck you to death.' Ray pulled on his pants.

'I told you I can have all the sex I want – even rough sex. I talked to my doctors. I have my own nurse. I can afford such things now. I'm rich, Ray.'

'I can't go to Cuba with you.' Ray sat down on the bed, pulled on one sock and held out his hand for the other. 'And don't you dare try to buy me, either.'

'Don't leave. At least spend the night.' Victoria couldn't seem to stop herself from begging, now that she'd started. It was humiliating but also exhilarating, like finally biting into a truffle after denying yourself chocolates for years. Reluctantly, she gave him his sock.

'Sorry, cupcake. Duty calls.'

'Will you come back?' Victoria threw herself across

his lap, clinging to his waist. She raised her face to him, showing him the tears that were now pouring down her cheeks. 'Please say you will!'

He kissed the wet from the sad corners of her eyes, then crushed her against his chest. 'I love you,' he growled. 'I promise you I'll come back, and you know why?' He licked the impossibly fragile contours of her ear. 'Because I've always loved you, Victoria, and I always will.'

'Me too, darling,' she whispered back. She was light-headed with relief. 'For as long as I live.'

5

'Would Mademoiselle care for an hors d'oeuvre?'

'No, thank you.' She drummed her red-lacquered nails impatiently on the linen-covered tabletop and squirmed on the banquette. He had five more minutes and then – Ah! The sight of him made her pulse quicken. Ray was one handsome – how do they say it? – handsome drink of water. Even if she was a lot younger than him.

Ray hurried to the table. 'Bai Lon. I'm sorry I'm late.'

'I was about to leave.' She pouted, an expression that was well suited to her Cupid's bow lips. They were painted as red as the shiny ornamental berries on a Christmas wreath.

'No! Bai Lon, that would have been a tragedy.'

'Call me Lonnie.'

'Lonnie, your presentation at the conference was remarkable. I'd have been devastated not to have managed to spend a little more time with you.'

'Are you always so hyperbolic?' She half-smiled, though she was careful not to let him suspect that he was already forgiven for his tardiness. When she was travelling, she detested any kind of wait; there was enough of that when she was at home in Hong Kong.

'I'm not exaggerating. I mean every word.' Ray slid on to the banquette opposite her. She followed his movements with her eyes, bright and dark like almonds with a glossy black candy coating. Her flawless face was focused on him like a miniature spotlight. It began its job of melting his heart.

Ray picked up his napkin and snapped it in the air,

then dropped the open cloth on to his lap. She watched him gravely, not letting on that she was aware that he was unnerved by her steady attention and was over-compensating by being goofy.

Ray launched into his 'Comrades in the War on Homelessness' speech and Lonnie let her gaze drift from his face to find out what he would do and, of course, his gaze immediately dropped from her face to her breasts. Why not? He was a red-blooded man and the way her breasts subtly pressed against the satin of her jade cheongsam was splendid. The style of the dress suited her diminutive curvy body and its colour complemented her black hair and eyes and luminous skin.

Lonnie returned her gaze to his face and once again he locked eyes with her. It was fascinating how well he could talk jargon with his generous mouth and at the same time flirt with his pale-blue eyes. They were the colour of the sky around a mountaintop. Ray was a very handsome man and at least a foot taller than her. She liked Caucasian men who were big and solid, and it was nice that, like her, he cared about the plight of the world's homeless people. It was just that, after a four-day conference at which she too had been a speaker, Lonnie was bone-weary of the topic.

'It was terrific to get the perspective of someone with your background as a girl in Hong Kong during the merge with Mainland China,' he continued. 'I was so inspired by your decision to embrace the socialist perspective regarding basic human rights like housing and healthcare. Your point of view is unique and absolutely invaluable to –'

'I'm hungry.' That shut him up fast. Lonnie's lips parted as she started giggling. She hastened to cover her mouth with a dainty hand. His face seemed very big and his eyes were wide with surprise. 'Even crusaders must eat sometime. Wouldn't you say so, Ray?'

'Of course. Sorry. I'm famished, myself. Or maybe I should simply say I'm peckish.'

'I like that. *Peckish*. It means sort of hungry?'

'Yes.' Ray snapped his fingers and the waiter, who had been hovering at a discreet distance since his arrival, hurried forwards. 'Drink?' he asked Lonnie.

'I would love a cocktail, as it happens,' she replied.

He ordered drinks for both of them. She liked it better when the man ordered for the woman. It made each drink an adventure and also gave her information about him. In this case Ray ordered extra dry Beefeater martinis, which meant he was a sophisticated leftist, not a lout, and perhaps that he would like to see her get just a little bit tipsy.

Lonnie sat ramrod straight, though she wasn't using the banquette for support. She was perched on the edge of the leather seat. When her drink arrived she picked up the beautiful V-shaped glass and tipped it to her lips. The liquor flowed into her mouth; an exquisite combination of taste and sensation that at once burnt and soothed her throat. She set down the glass and licked her lips. 'Mmmmm.'

'Tasty?' Ray grinned at her.

'I am not a socialist at heart, Ray, so much as a sensualist. Very different things.'

'I absolutely agree.' Ray steepled his fingers and concentrated on her. His charisma was intoxicating.

'My beliefs are the same as my emotions. I can't always say what is right or just or decent, but I can feel it. That is why I do what I do. Because I am compelled. I think you know what I mean.'

'I burnt more fiercely when I was younger, Lonnie. I have to keep it at a simmer now, most of the time.'

'I am young. I burn fiercely. That is why I must sometimes stop and say, "Lonnie! See the beautiful glass your drink is in. Taste the liquor. Touch the handsome man."' At this she reached her slender arm across the table and stroked the tiny hairs on the back of Ray's big hand. 'I don't want to burn out.'

He caught her hand with his. 'Suddenly I'm not so hungry,' he growled.

'Are you in a hurry? Do you have to get back to whoever it was who made you late?'

'No,' he replied.

'Then let us get to know each other more intimately while we eat.' Lonnie tilted her chin down and looked up at him through her lashes, as if hiding half her face behind an imaginary silk fan.

'Of course.' Ray flipped his menu open with such force it bounced on the tabletop. He scanned the entrees with an intensity that made Lonnie laugh. It was as if he could make their meals appear on the table by sheer force of will. She loved the eagerness of North American men, even the ones that insisted they were 'laidback Canadians'. They measured the age of their countries in terms of hundreds, not thousands, of years and it showed in the way they approached everything.

Lonnie liked to tease such a man by coming on slowly and then, just when he resigned himself to a night of polite courtship, dropping a bomb like 'I'm a sensualist, Ray.' With her dark little naively tilted eyes and crease-less lids, her gaze suggested she didn't quite know what her words implied, as if she had slightly misunderstood the definition of 'sensualist'. She would retreat behind her mask of Asian coolness, then dart out again when least expected and boom! Drop another bomb! 'Lonnie the Bombshell.' She giggled again.

'I'm glad you're amused,' muttered Ray, clearly flustered. Lonnie could guess the source of his discomfort. 'Water, for God's sake!' Ray frowned as Lonnie burst into peels of laughter. 'What?'

'You are calling for water? Is that Canadian for waiter?'

'I called for the waiter. Didn't I? You minx!'

'You are calling "water, water", like a parched man in a desert.'

'I feel like a parched man. Inches from the oasis, I perish.'

The waiter appeared by Ray's side. Again Ray ordered for the two of them, entrees only, no soups or salads, and a bottle of chardonnay to complement their pasta dishes.

Lonnie fished the olive from her glass with a brightly lacquered nail. She waited until their martini glasses had been removed and the wine poured before she dropped her next 'bomb'.

Ray was talking about Cuba, where he'd apparently lived for a few years. Lonnie had never been to Cuba but naturally she knew all about its politics. She'd also heard about island rum and hot sun and white sand and Latino lovers. She slid her high heel off her stocking-sheathed left foot. He didn't notice the subtle wriggling she did to get into position, but he definitely noticed once she slipped her dainty foot between his legs. As she'd suspected, he was already stiff inside his trousers. It felt like a big one, too. Ray's voice trailed off in mid-sentence.

'No, keep talking, please. Unless you want me to stop?' Lonnie pressed the pad of her tiny foot against his balls and wriggled her toes, lightly massaging them.

'Don't stop.'

'I see you lean to the left,' she said. She giggled, hiding her laugh with her hand again.

'No surprise there,' he replied with a straight face.

'Unzip your pants,' Lonnie whispered, suddenly fierce. 'I can make you come into your napkin with my toes.'

'The things they teach at Beijing University.' Ray complied with her command. Her foot wiggled against the pouch of his underwear until he reached beneath the table again and slid himself free of his jockeys.

'Ha! I did learn this at university, too, but it was at the University of British Columbia.' Lonnie sipped her wine, her face unlined by emotion. It was so much fun to toy with him like this, in public, where he would be forced to keep a lid on it. For her, to keep a 'straight face' was a simple thing. It was part of her culture, a necessity of life in a crowded country. She suspected that for Ray, though he might insist high and low that he was merely one of many, it would be very hard to be thought of as unremarkable.

'Kinky Canadians.' Ray's voice was even but, sure enough, he was struggling to fix an expression on his face that didn't announce to the room that he was experiencing something new and thrilling and sexual in nature. He shrugged and gave up, grinning foolishly at her.

Lonnie watched her companion's face light up with joy. She was a lifesaver, honestly. When she wasn't busy trying to make the world a decent place for everybody, she was spending her spare time saving sad Alpha males by making their hearts soar. It was a good thing that turning men on was such a turn-on for her. The warmth of his crotch against the tips of her toes and her silk-sheathed instep made her tummy tingle with delight. 'That's right.' Lonnie licked her lips. 'A kinky Canadian and a kinky Chinese. Won't we have fun?' She tilted her head at him, the picture of modesty, while the enticing words dropped from her lips like exotic jewels.

'Yes. Yes.' Ray was panting now. Her foot pressed harder against him. The sole was soft around his sheath and then her foot rolled across his cock like it was rolling on a log until the pads of her toes played his length like a flute. He stifled a groan just in time.

'You were thinking I can't make you come with my foot,' she whispered. She slowly licked her lips again. 'You were thinking you are too jaded for the girl in the jade cheongsam to make you come and now you are thinking, maybe I was wrong about it. Am I right?'

Ray gave a curt nod. He licked his lips in unconscious imitation of her, and then gulped from his glass of wine.

'Consider. No fingers. No lips. No vagina. No anus. I can make you come with just my toes, Ray.' She let her mouth go lazy on his name. So cute. Her nimble toes continued to toy with him. So nasty. 'Consider how good it would be to have all of me.'

'I want you, Lonnie. More than I've ever wanted anyone –'

'Don't lie to me, baby, not now that we've become so close.'

Ray tilted his pelvis, yearning to capture her foot in his lap and somehow hump it to a climax, but it was impossible. Her foot danced over him, tickling and softly pummelling, all the while eluding capture.

'Wonderful! Here is our food, Ray!'

'Great!' Feigning enthusiasm, Ray picked up his fork.

Lonnie kicked off her other shoe. Her present mission meant just as much to her as any of her other causes. She was going to show this big man that *she* was the unique one in their twosome. He wouldn't be forgetting her overnight, like he was probably used to doing with his women. A single straight man his age, with his looks? Oh he must be very popular with the ladies. And a so-called 'feminist', as well? He must be used to women creaming their panties in his presence. But she was the real prize here. Young, beautiful, smart and talented, too. When she was finished with him, he would never make her wait for him again. 'I love the wheat pastas as much as the egg noodles, don't you?'

Ray seemed barely able to hear her, let alone understand.

Lonnie put her free hand beside her on the banquette and raised her right foot to join her left. The sensation of his manhood twitching and growing still larger between her ten toes was exquisite. She ate a morsel of food. It was delicious. Sometimes life could be so austere and then other times, like this one, there was an abundance of pleasure. Lonnie savoured the food, the wine and the large incredulous horny man. She leant back against the banquette and slid her bottom forwards so she could manoeuvre more easily. She cupped him with her feet, and he began to hump the narrow hollow space between her soles. Lonnie shivered as she realised he must be at least eight inches long. She steadied herself with both hands on the banquette, determined to take him all the way.

'This is crazy. Come to my room,' he muttered.

'We can do it. Concentrate.'

'Come sit beside me and let me finger your pussy.'

'Maybe later. What's wrong? Don't I turn you on?'

'Is this a test? I could come if I hadn't already –'

'I knew it! You kept me waiting because you were with another woman.'

'Sit in my lap.'

'After you cover my feet in your creamy come, Ray, I will spread my thighs and let you sink your fingers deep into my hot steaming naked cunt –' she made her words as crude as she could. The sudden revelation of her inner predator could shock a weak man into impotence but it always had the opposite effect on a strong one.

'Good God!' Ray hissed through gritted teeth. His cock jerked twice and two spurts wet the soles of her feet.

'I love the way that feels.' Lonnie grinned triumphantly. She always got her man and, in a world where things were either chaotic or mind-numbingly the same, that was the one fact that never changed and never became boring. One day, maybe, she would settle down, or at least begin to question the thrill she got from playing with a different guy every week, but for now she preferred to work hard, play hard and sleep sated.

'Wow, you're something else.' Ray looked like he didn't know if he should laugh or cry.

Lonnie batted her spiky lashes at him. She slipped her shoes back on and proceeded to finish her meal while Ray sorted himself out opposite her.

'Are you almost ready to go?' He hadn't touched the food on his plate.

'Even better, Ray,' she said, draining her wineglass. 'I am gone.'

'What?'

'I promised some friends I'd go dancing with them.'

'What about me? What about your steaming –'

'Maybe another time.' Lonnie was on her feet. 'Must run. I have your cell-phone number. Maybe I will call you.'

'Wait. How long are you in town? I'll see you out.' Ray had half-risen from the banquette when Lonnie put her tiny hand to his shoulder and gently pushed him back down. He put his arm around her wasplike waist. 'Talk to me, Lonnie.'

She bent to brush his cheek with her lips. The little kiss made her tingle. It was almost a pity to leave him now, just when she'd started to warm to him. But experience had taught her that it was best for both of them not to let things progress too quickly. 'Let me go now. I am free, tonight. You understand? Free from all my obligations. Don't become one, OK? Don't be no fun.'

Ray released her immediately. Lonnie left the restaurant with no coat, no purse and no accoutrements.

In a moment, nothing but her musky exotic perfume suggested she'd been there at all.

From the street she could see Ray, rumpled and stunned, still sitting in the corner of the banquette. A thrill ran from the top of her spine straight down to the tip of her tailbone. Fun! Lonnie whistled at a taxi. 'I am a bombshell,' she whispered fiercely. 'I am the "Hong Kong Bombshell" and tonight I rock!'

Really, when all was said and done, she was a lot younger than he was. Lonnie hopped into the cab and directed the driver to take her to Soho.

6

Victoria's eyes opened. The room was dark and for a bad moment she thought she was alone. Abandoned in the dark; it was the fear that had intermittently pestered her since childhood. She breathed deeply, slowly, letting her senses settle into wakefulness. In a moment the room was not so dark and she could hear the steady deep-sleep breathing of the big man beside her in the bed.

She rolled over to face him. Ray's posture in sleep was as self-assured as any he adopted while awake. His arms were flung out to both sides in the same triumphant pose he struck after a round of great sex. But he was lying on his belly, whereas, after sex, he rested on his back. It was only because of the size of the bed that his fingertips hadn't touched her in sleep.

Victoria propped herself up on one elbow and watched him. He'd take three deep breaths, snort on the fourth, then repeat the pattern. She counted and waited and, sure enough, there it was, the soft little snort that meant he was fast asleep. She knew him as well as anyone could know a man who refused to become familiar. It was a crime that he would not recognise the depth of their love. Hadn't the words 'I love you' tripped off his tongue before he'd left for his dinner meeting? Hadn't he come back to her room as he'd promised? Why couldn't he see that they were meant to be?

The tiny fastener on the thin silk strap of her negligee bit into her shoulder blade. She wriggled out of the negligee and kicked it out the side of the bed, vaguely irritated by everything. She needn't fear waking him; once he was out, the only way he woke up was with an alarm clock or an erection, whichever came first. Suddenly she wanted to pound his back and see if that would do the trick. 'How can you sleep so well,' she might ask, 'when millions of people have no place to rest their heads?' But she already knew his answer. While other people (like her) might lie awake at night worrying about issues that appeared irresolvable, he spent his days addressing those very issues. At night, he slept so soundly because, he would say in that self-mocking tone of his, 'My heart is pure.'

Anyway, she would never wake him violently. To act on an impulse so damaging to her own plan was the behaviour of a girl, and she wasn't a girl, not any more. Victoria struggled with her thoughts, not wanting to slip into regret about Ray when he was finally truly here. But regret seemed to be Victoria's drug. She was strong enough to resist its seductive power during the day but at night it crept up on her with the shadows. If she hadn't been such an open wound when she was young, so sensitive that she wept over sonnets and feared that the world was too cruel for one as sensitive as she, perhaps it wouldn't have been so easy for him to let her go.

There had been no question in her mind, back then. He'd probably end up a criminal, she'd warned herself. He was moving to Cuba, for God's sake! If he believed in armed revolution now, after living with all those communists, he'd probably become some kind of terrorist.

How was she to know that his passion for justice would be tempered by Cuba, not inflamed. That he would become gentle with age, even as she hardened. That she would never ever find a man as fundamentally good as he was.

It all came down to the folly of youth. There was no

point pounding Ray because she'd married while he'd been gone. No point regretting her marriage to Gordon. She hadn't disliked the comfort that his name and his money had brought her. She reminded herself to remind Ray of the good works *she* had managed to do precisely because she had money. She'd done a lot of charity work during her marriage and, if she'd managed to shed her philanthropy as easily as she'd shed her mink coat when she'd left Canada, it was for new horizons. She'd tell Ray that, too, she decided. She'd explain that she meant to do more than play tourist while she was in Cuba. He could help her find the place where her money could do the most good, if he'd only come with her. If only.

The fingers of her left hand tiptoed across the space that separated them. Surprisingly, he hadn't wanted sex when he'd returned from his meeting. Instead, they'd had a late snack and then cuddled in bed. He'd admitted he was bushed but she'd assumed he'd rally. Instead, he'd fallen asleep with his arm around her. She'd rested, her head pressed to his chest, delighting in the sound of his heart thudding steadily in her ear, until he'd grunted and thrown her off to roll over on his belly. It was only then that she'd realised he'd meant what he'd said.

She touched the spot between his shoulder blades with her index finger. He didn't stir. She ran her fingertip lightly down his spine to the slight cleft of his buttocks. She loved how flat his ass was. She did it again, this time drawing a straight line down his back to below the base of his spine. Another inch or so and the progress of her finger would be interrupted by his anus.

Ray's face was turned away from her but she heard him mumble in his sleep and she quickly withdrew the offending finger.

Victoria slipped from the bed, her cheeks flushed with excitement. She had a plan! She glanced at the clock;

he'd been asleep for five hours. Surely that was plenty of rest for a man whose heart was pure?

Moments later Victoria knelt on the bed. She'd washed her face, brushed her hair and teeth, and trimmed her nails. Her naked body was refreshed and lightly scented. She moistened the tip of her left middle finger with lubricant. She had a surprise for Ray. No, she corrected herself, she had more than one surprise for Ray.

The wet finger slid down his spine and didn't stop until it nestled between his cheeks, its progress halted once more by his anus. Victoria rubbed the puckered flesh gently until the pad of her finger was in the centre. The sensation of his skin (so delicate!) yielding to her was thrilling. He moved under her touch but his breathing remained steady. She'd know soon enough if he were awake or feigning.

Victoria leant in a little, letting the pressure ripple through her arm until it reached her finger. It entered him a fraction more, until his flesh hugged the entire fingertip, and not just the pad. She counted his breaths. At the end of the fourth, he didn't snort – he was awake.

She stifled a giggle. Men were funny. They probably all wanted a finger up the bum but none of them would say so, not even a man as sexually enlightened as Ray. It was no surprise to her that he chose the easy way out, pretending to be asleep when really he was too repressed to moan.

She thrust her fingertip inside him, up to the first knuckle. He shuddered. She withdrew slightly, then thrust again, pushing her finger up his narrow passage until her hand was pressed against his ass. They both moaned at once.

His head turned on the pillow and their eyes met. Victoria held her position and tried a tentative smile. To her relief, he smiled back.

'What are you doing?' he asked in a conversational tone.

'I wanted to know you, from the inside out, like you know me,' she said. She looked at him imploringly.

'I think you ought to ask first,' he replied.

'Sorry. May I?'

'It's a little late.'

'May I do it again?'

'Do what?'

'This.' She wriggled her finger inside him. She'd never felt anything so warm and tight before. It astounded her to have a part of herself, however small, enter a part of him for the first time.

'Ask for what you want, silly.'

'Please, Ray, may I almost pull my finger out and then put it back inside you again?'

'OK.' His eyes closed.

Victoria drew her finger from him, delighting in the sensation of his skin dragging a little on hers. When she could feel the opening struggle to close around her fingertip she thrust again, hard and fast, like he did when he was fucking her. He moaned again.

'I love it,' she whispered. She leant in carefully and kissed his mouth. 'I love it. Please can I do it again?'

'Tit for tat,' he whispered back. 'Kneel up.'

Victoria shivered at his dom-like command. She knelt up without disturbing her left hand. He manoeuvred his right hand between her thighs, spreading them wider with his fingers. His spatulate middle finger wriggled between her cheeks, seeking and finding the entrance to her back passage.

Victoria had only a second to savour the sensation before he gave her another order, made all the more delicious by his friendly tone. 'Sit,' he said.

It wasn't easy; his finger wasn't lubricated. Victoria

moaned as she impaled herself on it. It hurt as much as if she were being pierced by a little dagger, but the knowledge that she wasn't being damaged at all instantly transmuted the pain to pleasure. When she was sitting on his hand she opened her eyes and met his. They smiled at each other to soften the ferocity of their gaze.

'Ready?' he asked.

She nodded.

Victoria rose from his hand until his finger was almost free, at the same time withdrawing her own finger from his ass until it, too, was almost free. Then, just as she thrust her finger deep inside him, he buried his finger inside her once more.

Her body tingled all over. 'Exquisite,' she cooed.

'Enough fooling around,' he mock-grumbled, removing his hand from her and rolling over to free himself from her touch. 'Come sit on my face.'

Victoria giggled and scampered across the bed until she was poised above him, her knees on either side of his head. She grinned down at him. 'You just like me because I'm shameless,' she mock-complained. She pouted, but he wasn't looking at her face. His gaze was focused elsewhere.

'You're shameless all right,' he agreed and extended his tongue to taste her. 'But that's not why I like you. I like you because you have a beautiful, beautiful cunt. If I could paint . . .' He sighed deeply, as if with disappointment in his lack of artistic ability. His hot breath caressed her. He slid down the bed a little and his hands gripped her ass cheeks, parting them.

Victoria knew what he was gazing at now. She gripped the brass headboard with both hands, forcing herself not to protest. She felt his hot breath blow between her cheeks as he exhaled heavily again, this time a sigh that indicated his pleasure. His tongue touched her asshole, wet it all around and slithered inside.

Twenty minutes later Victoria was bent over the bed, her legs an inverted trembling V. She'd come twice already. Once from the shamefully exotic rim job he'd given her while fingering her clit, and once when he'd first taken her from behind. That time, she'd slipped her own hand between her legs while he'd steadily worked his inside her. It had been rough going for a few terrible strokes but now he'd reclaimed her ass.

'You haven't been fucked properly in a while,' he muttered, moving slowly to establish a rhythm she could tolerate.

'I know.'

'You're so pretty when you come.'

She laughed. 'Like you could see my face.'

'The back of your head comes so beautifully. Your blonde hair thrashes around and your ears tremble.'

She laughed again. 'My ears tremble?'

'Quiet. I'm doing my best to wax eloquent.' He leant into her for a moment, kissing her between the shoulders, licking her vertebrae. Then he resumed the solid steady rhythm. 'Tell me what you are.'

'I'm a naughty girl,' she murmured. She concentrated on the sensation of him violating her. It was such a serious thing, anal sex. She didn't want to talk silly any more. She didn't want to talk at all. But he persisted.

'Everyone knows that. Tell me something new.' He was changing the rhythm of his thrusts now, speeding up.

'Mmmmm . . .' Fear mingled with excitement in the pit of her belly. She sank to her elbows and put her head in the palm of her hands, tilting her bum up. Perfect form.

The pace was building now, as was the force with

which he penetrated her. She slipped her left hand between her legs and dabbed at her pussy, wetting her fingers, then started rubbing herself again. 'Mmmmm...' Her clit eagerly responded to her touch. She had a mother of an orgasm left inside her but she'd better be quick. She rubbed hard and fast, trying to catch up with him. 'I'm greedy,' she said.

'More.' His hips banged against her ass. He wasn't withdrawing very far any more, just enough to power a thrust that reached the centre of her.

'Mmmmm...' Victoria stalled for a couple of precious seconds, until she felt the gathering of energy that meant her orgasm was inevitable. 'I am ... a greedy ... anal...'

He groaned. He was whaling against her at a furious pace now. His eyes were screwed tightly shut, so he didn't see her glance over her shoulder and grin. She would never laugh at his come style, of course. Her own was extravagant too. But it made her even hornier to see how willing he was to risk looking ridiculous in the name of release.

'Ray? I am a greedy ... anal ... bitch!' She yelled the last word so it could be heard above his groans as he exploded into orgasm. His release triggered hers and she rocketed along with him to a place where the air was thin and the sky was electric and midnight blue. A place where two can be one, if only for a moment, and pain can be pleasure and greed can be unselfish. A place she hadn't been to in a very long time, but one that, once visited, she had never been able to forget.

She collapsed beneath him and he slumped on top of her. She couldn't breathe for a moment, but she didn't much care.

Ray rolled on to his back on the bed and flung his arms out to either side. If he saw her tears he took them to be tears of joy, which they were. He grabbed her arm and dragged her to his side. In a moment, he was out cold.

Victoria lay in the crook of his arm, listening to the solid beat of his heart. She pulled the sheet up over them both and in another moment she too was fast asleep.

7

Penny took a long drag on her cigarette and set it back in the seashell that was balanced on the edge of her soaker tub. After sleeping twelve hours straight she was sluggish and in need of sustenance but the only things she could find in her cupboards were bottled water and half a pack of cigarettes. She should have made a more elaborate plan, she realised now – one that included groceries and a new outfit and a day at the spa. Who knew that a little private game among a dozen players would take so long to win? She sighed deeply and raised one long leg from the bathwater to inspect it. She really shouldn't let her grooming slide so far, no matter how many pounds sterling were at stake. She sighed again. There was a lot of work to be done before she was ready to face Ray Torrington.

'Life is like a game of poker,' she said out loud. She stubbed out the cigarette and considered the stunning truth of her words. You're cruising along, riding a nice little winning streak, and then suddenly – bam! Life tosses you a King. Do you go for broke or back off, content to be a steady winner rather than risking being a big loser? Ah, but if the King is the King of Hearts? Then what?

'If you're me, you always go for broke.' She'd spoken out loud again. She called self-consciously for her Siamese cat, Mitzu – at least if she were talking to the cat, and Mitzu were, as Siamese are wont to do, talking back, she wouldn't feel like a crazy person. But the cat, probably curled up in the Victorian armchair they'd both come to consider hers, ignored the plaintive plea.

Was she pathetic? Penny sat up, splashing water over the side of the tub as she reached for her *Les Sylphs* shaving cream. Far from it! She'd simply been alone too long; that much was obvious. Otherwise, she was a winner! When she was at the poker table she dressed the part of a tough smart cookie. Don't mess with me, her look said, from her tousled flaming-red hair down to her killer stiletto boots. They were hell on the calves but they made gams of her legs and ensured that no slow-talking Texan ever looked too far down his nose at her. This tough-gal strategy had the added bonus of encouraging her opponents to let down their guard in terms of her femininity, so later, when she made a little moue or tossed off a quick pleading glance, it hit them harder. She knew what she was doing. All she had to do today, same as ever, was dress for the part. The only difference was her role and the etiquette of seduction required an entirely different look.

Half an hour later, Penny exited the steam-filled bathroom, properly cleansed and ready for top-to-toe lubrication. Her glossy auburn mane was squeaky clean and there wasn't an errant hair anywhere on her body. She felt glorious – like a perfect specimen of the exotic breed of woman known as 'a real redhead'. She strode like a member of the military into her bedroom.

'Note the translucent skin!' Penny announced to the room, tossing her towel on to the armchair. It almost landed on Mitzu. 'Sorry, kitty!' she called but the cat was not mollified. Mitzu leapt to the floor, then stepped disdainfully around the little wet footprints Penny had left on the hardwood. Mitzu started a plaintive meow that ended in a luxurious yawn.

Penny dabbed on some eye cream and patted age-defying lotion on her face and neck. She rubbed moisturiser on her breasts and tummy and butt and legs, taking her time, then sat to work it into her bare feet and between her toes. There was nothing more glorious than top-of-the-range skin creams, each one created by chemists and packaged by artists to seem to be the elixir of eternal youth. At last she was properly primed for the pending paint job. Penny glanced at her clock; she had plenty of time.

'Ever noticed my finely turned ankles?' Penny asked the cat. She jumped to her feet and danced a few steps on the polished hardwood floor. Mitzu replied in proper Siamese cat fashion, indicating that she had, in fact, often noticed Penny's ankles. 'Yes, Mitzu, I know,' said Penny, deciding to be generous, 'your ankles are marvellous as well.'

Penny tried to run her fingers through her wavy wet hair. She grimaced – sometimes she could still descend into an adolescent hate-on for her hair. She spritzed it with leave-on conditioner. She scrunched it gently, resisting the temptation to pull a comb through it. Best to let it dry naturally for a little while before she tried anything so radical as to style it. Like many redheads, she'd somehow survived the early years to come to a mature appreciation of the colour and body of her hair, hair so many women swore they'd kill for. But dealing with the bloody stuff could still make her crazy.

The telephone rang. Penny grabbed the receiver. 'Hello?'

'Don't hang up.'

'Who is this?' Damn, another obscene phone call! 'Listen here, you pathetic little wanker –'

'I'm no wanker.' The man on the other end of the line stifled a laugh. 'I don't even know what a wanker is. It's Bryce Stafford, Junior. I've been trying to get in touch with you for a while but I just finally got your private number –'

'From who?'

'Oh, I have my sources.'

'It's too early for this nonsense. I don't for one minute believe that a big American movie star wants to hire a poker player to teach him the game.'

'Look out your bedroom window.'

'A peeping Tom, too!'

He dared to laugh out loud. 'I promise, look out your window and you'll see Bryce Stafford, Junior. I hope you know what I look like.'

'I know what Bryce Stafford, Junior looks like,' grumbled Penny. 'Hang on.' Penny put the telephone receiver down on the bed. She pulled on an oversized black T-shirt, tugging at the hem to make sure it covered her entire bum. She took the telephone with her as she walked to the window.

When she raised the blind, she saw the real-life Bryce Stafford, Junior, the movie star, sitting in a silver Porsche convertible parked on her street. He waved with one hand, holding a cell phone to his ear with the other.

Penny's famous poker face came in very handy. Though her temples thudded with the sudden pounding of her heart, her voice was cool. 'Nice car,' she commented.

'Thanks. Want to go for a ride?'

'No.' Penny continued staring at him. It really seemed as if she were watching him in a movie, romancing his leading lady in the rosy hues of daybreak. The only problem was she'd somehow landed in the movie and no one had handed her a script. Penny blinked rapidly. He was still there. Penny asked herself if she'd had one too many nightcaps before bed. It seemed like a good question to ask him, too. 'Have you been drinking?'

'Not a drop. I don't know how much you know about me but I don't drink alcohol any more. Only water and coffee.' He fumbled for a moment and then held up a cardboard tray with two big Styrofoam cups in it. 'Coffee?'

'Hmmm.' Penny quit trying to reconcile her reality with what common sense told her was impossible. Bryce Stafford, Junior had come bearing coffee. After the poker game Penny had been so tired she'd come straight home without picking up any of the items that were essential to her wellbeing – coffee, cream and chocolate. 'Do you have any chocolate?'

'I just quit drinking. *Of course* I have chocolate! He fumbled around the dash of the Porsche. 'I've got half a chocolate bar here somewhere.'

Penny laughed. He didn't seem to need a script. He was carrying the scene all by himself. 'Where's your entourage?'

'I fired them all. I had to. Like I said, I just got out of rehab. I mean, just now. Even the paparazzi don't know where I am. It's the perfect moment for us to get together. I swear on a stack of poker chips as tall as the Taj Mahal, and I'm talkin' about the Taj Mahal in Vegas, I'm harmless.'

Penny nodded. Now that he mentioned it, she remembered reading something about Bryce Stafford, Junior entering a local rehabilitation centre. For the first time it clearly occurred to Penny that he was real. 'Wow,' she whispered.

'Please, let me come up. I'll be on my very best behaviour, I promise.' Bryce's voice was warm and sweet, like maple syrup.

'OK.' What else could a girl say?

'This is a business proposal, I promise,' he vowed.

'I'll have the concierge let you in,' said Penny. A business proposal? Not if she had anything to do with it.

The coffee was delicious. Close up, Bryce Stafford, Junior was a bit of all right, too. He was tall and buff, with brown hair and big dark brown eyes and the carefully cultivated five o'clock shadow that made handsome men really sexy and did little for men who were merely good looking. The muscles in his arms bulged slightly; the short sleeves of his tight white T-shirt hugged his biceps. He absent-mindedly patted his abs when he talked, sometimes over his T-shirt and sometimes with his hand under it. She wasn't sure if he did this to draw her attention to his rippled belly or just in an unself-consciously male gesture that said 'I love my body.'

Now that the actor had managed to track her down, she wondered why she'd been so quick to dismiss the communications she'd received from 'his people' in the past. It didn't seem so outlandish now that it was actually happening. She'd made up her mind that it was all a hoax and hadn't really considered the possibility that it was legitimate. Of course, she didn't teach poker and wasn't about to start now, but it sure was going to be fun to tell the movie star as much, in person.

He stretched out his long legs, looking confident and comfortable in his tight faded jeans and trainers, and commenced talking earnestly. In no time at all, he'd covered an apparently unfounded scandal involving him and a number of French strippers, a Grammy award-winning diva he was engaged to marry, and his recent stint in rehab. Right.

Penny pressed her knees tightly together and tucked her ankles under her chair. Her T-shirt, barely adequate to wear standing at the window, now seemed deter-mined to work its way too far up her body. She sipped her coffee and actively listened, even encouraging him to continue when he paused to ask if he was monopol-ising the conversation. She could drink his coffee and look at his fabulous famous face for hours.

'I don't know how much you know about me but I just wanted to set the record straight,' he concluded.

'I certainly know plenty about you now, Bryce,' she said. 'But I didn't refuse to meet you because of your reputation. Honest. It's just – I don't know how much you know about me but I just –' she shrugged '– I don't teach poker.' The shoulder of her oversized T-shirt slid down her arm. She felt before she saw his gaze linger on her clavicle.

'I know one thing about you,' he said. 'You have incredible skin.'

Penny blushed. She thanked the Gods she'd finished moisturising just as he'd phoned. She'd only had five minutes before he arrived at her door and, even though she'd have loved to spend them with a mascara wand and lipstick, the last of her common sense had dictated that she use the time inserting a female condom. She was a bare-faced barefoot seductress.

Penny could only marvel at the power of his attractiveness. The old tom-tom beat started up in her belly, the rhythmic tattoo of desire. She'd been planning to keep it muted until later, for Ray, but Bryce was too much of a gorgeous young stud-muffin for even her very best intentions.

Bryce persisted. 'Maybe we could just hang out together, play cards, you know, nothing formal. If you could commit to, say, five hours a day for the next few weeks –'

'I already told you, I'm not available.'

'So, OK, four hours a day –'

'Right. What about your top-secret island wedding?'

'Aha! So you *have* been following my exploits in the tabloids!'

'Everyone knows you're supposed to be secretly getting married this weekend.'

'Is that so?' He glowered at her. 'Well, I don't think that's going to happen,' he said. He rubbed his belly and sighed. 'You heard it here first.'

'Honestly, don't you think your time would be better spent with your fiancée?'

'Honestly? I dunno. I'm lying low. Man, I just got out of rehab! Anna – she doesn't know what she wants. I mean, she wanted me to quit drinking so I did. Plus, I admit, I *was* hitting the bottle far too heavily. I missed the première of my latest movie because I was in rehab.' He leant forwards. 'Did you get to see it by any chance?'

'I rarely get out to the theatre these days. What's it called?'

'*Radar Man.*'

Penny giggled. 'No, I didn't see it.'

'Hey! Movies about superheroes are big. Although *Radar Man* tanked.'

'I'm sorry, Bryce.'

'Doesn't matter. I'm thinking of returning to the stage; well, I guess it would be more like debuting on the stage, since I've never tried it before. Anyway, I had to give the superhero thing a try. A superhero gig, it's incredibly lucrative, sometimes, but it's not very fulfilling, artistically speaking, and it's goddam hard on the body.'

'I imagine your body looks marvellous in tights,' said Penny.

'Not bad, not bad at all,' admitted Bryce, 'though I bet you look even better in 'em.' He grinned into his coffee cup. 'So what do you say? Take me on for a couple of weeks and see if we can fly?' He shot her an appealing look.

'I think the best thing is for you to find out if you're getting married or not. First things first, Bryce. And is poker playing really the right move for you, right out of rehab? Poker can be habit-forming, you know.'

He laughed. 'I'm not worried about that. I can afford the habit. It's not like it's gonna kill me – not like drugs or alcohol.'

'That's for you to decide. But I decided a long time ago not to teach it. I honestly don't believe in poker players formally teaching others the game. I think you should simply play a lot and maybe pick up a book or two. There are some excellent books on poker out there now. So, you read a book and you play some more and, before you know it, you're competing in the celebrity tournaments.'

'No. No.' Bryce leant forwards and tapped her naked knee twice, once for each no. After the second tap, his finger hovered, not touching her skin but close enough Penny fancied she could feel its heat. 'You see,' he continued, 'that's just it. I don't want to be a celebrity poker player. I want to be like you, a *real* poker player.' Now he grabbed her hand and held it, rubbing her palm with his thumb. 'I realised in rehab, this celebrity thing is destroying me. Destroying me.'

Penny stared into his mesmerising gaze. It was incredible how good looking he was in the flesh. If you saw him on the streets of London, you'd stop and gape and exclaim, 'Gosh, you're so handsome you should be a movie star!' No wonder he was paid millions of dollars to act in movies. His intensity was astonishing. His eyes were so dark they were almost onyx, but they glistened. Wet onyx. Penny squirmed in her chair. Was he acting? He was young but he wasn't *that* young, probably only a few years younger than her, maybe 23 or 24. He was old enough to know that coming here alone like this was looking for trouble. She tugged her hand a little, to pull it free of his, but he held on more firmly. The electricity where their flesh connected, in their fingertips and her palm, was startling.

'I think celebrity might be destroying any real talent I have as an actor. It's already driven me to drink. I think "fame" has already obliterated any possibility that Anna and I might have had of creating something real between us. It's like something huge, something bigger than both of us, decided that she and I don't belong together. And we don't get any say in the matter. Celebrity is ruining my life.'

'It must be awful,' Penny murmured. Certainly she wasn't anywhere near as famous as a movie star like Bryce Stafford, Junior but fame had recently started infringing on her freedom. She just didn't feel as anonymous as she once had, even in the heart of London. She hadn't had a meaningful relationship in years and she hadn't even been with a man in months. She found it useful, in her business, to maintain an air of mystery, and that meant keeping herself to herself. 'I understand,' she said. 'I'm a very shy person myself, Bryce. I don't even like the celebrity that comes with being a champion poker player.'

'That sounds so great. "Champion Poker Player." That's what I want to be. This acting thing is so superficial. I want to do something real. Teach me to play cards!' Bryce leant even closer, so that his jean-clad knees touched her naked ones. She could smell him, so clean and yet spicy, like a musky breeze that had blown in with the dawn.

'I can't. I'm sorry. I've made plans. And you – so have you. Bryce, the only thing I can do is this.'

'Yes?' He pressed his voluptuous mouth to the back of her hand. Was this his tell? If so, was it real or false? He gave her a soulful look that made her nipples tingle. She had to call his bluff and go for broke.

'They say if you have sex with a poker player sometimes the luck rubs off.'

'Is that so?' His cheeks dimpled as he tried not to smile.

'Yes.' Penny slid from her chair onto his lap. 'Surely you've heard that saying?'

'No.' He juggled her on his knees as he pulled her close. 'But then, maybe it's an old English saying. We have a saying in Hollywood that goes, "Kiss a movie star good morning." Heard that one?'

'No but I like it!' Penny laughed. She kissed his gorgeous lips. She felt she could melt in his mouth, as if she was no more than a little bit of milk chocolate that was made just for him.

'Wow,' he said when the kiss ended. 'We got chemistry.' He slid his hand up the front of her shirt. 'No panties, huh? You must have been expecting me.'

'Hush. I always wear panties, but I just had a bath,' she said. Penny tugged at his T-shirt and managed to pull it off first one, then both of his arms and up over his head. She tossed it down. He was perfectly sculpted. It must have cost a fortune in trainers alone to fine tune his form like this. She ran her fingers over his rippling abs. It was like playing a harp while it was still in a buckskin case. Corresponding tremors rippled through her belly. God, she wanted him badly.

Penny twisted to face him. She wrapped her thighs around his hips, as she lowered her mouth to his. God, she didn't even have lipstick on! But his lips were as hungry as hers. He made her feel like a siren.

He cupped her breasts underneath her T-shirt. 'Nice,' he murmured, nibbling on them through the fabric.

'Jesus,' she moaned, arching her back. Her breasts were small, which made her nipples seem deceptively large in comparison, although they were no bigger than her baby finger, from the knuckle to the tip.

Penny pressed herself against the thick seam of his jeans' fly. How long had it been since she'd had a man? She didn't feel like she could wait the five minutes it would take to get him free of his fly and hard and inside her.

'You're hot to trot, huh, Penny?'

'Yes. C'mon. Right here, right now.' She was almost

babbling. Never, never ever, she silently vowed, would she let herself get this sex-starved again. She'd ignored her feminine needs far too long and now look what had happened. A handsome movie star pops in to give her a little kiss and cop a feel and she's half-crazed with desire.

He stuck his head under her shirt and lapped at her left nipple, drawing it out with his tongue and teeth until it had achieved its full size. Then he did the same to her right nipple. She hated not being able to see his fabulous face but the feel of his mouth on her nipples made it worthwhile.

Penny tore at his belt buckle. She was pressed so hard up against him that he couldn't work his hand in between his fly and her body so he let her unbuckle and unzip him and used his hands to pull her shirt up over her head and off.

'Look at this burning bush,' he said when he saw her fire-engine-red pussy. 'Hallelujah!'

Penny giggled. 'Cut it out.'

'Holy Moses! She's a real redhead!'

'Show us what you've got, then, Mr Movie Star.' Penny's hand swooped down the front of his briefs. It closed around a firm column. 'Nice!'

'Put me in you, Penny,' he cooed. 'Put me inside. Warm me up, Penny. Please.'

He was just as strong as he looked so it was no problem for him to rear up and support her weight while she shoved his pants down around his hips. They kissed ravenously. Penny took him in her hand again. It seemed Bryce Stafford, Junior was as hot blooded as she was and that he, like she, could not resist temptation for one split second longer.

Penny braced her heels on the rungs of his chair. She straightened her knees a bit and lifted herself from his lap. They broke the kiss and both looked down to see their pubes held a foot apart. It was sort of porno-graphic. Again, Penny had the sensation that she'd somehow stumbled into a movie, though this one was more X-rated than the romance she'd imagined earlier. She grinned lasciviously at Bryce. 'Fuck me right now,' she said.

He jerked his hips. The fat wet head of his dick disappeared inside her. 'So warm,' he cooed.

'Yes!' Penny clasped his shoulders. She dropped her-self into his lap as he jerked his hips again. 'Yes!' she yelled as her emptiness was fully displaced with hard male flesh. 'That's good!'

She ground down on him. Their connection was instinctive; the satisfaction she felt as he filled her with him was primal.

They couldn't seem to stop kissing each other. As if to prove that there was intimacy in this sudden frenzied coupling, they kissed and kissed whenever they weren't gasping or mumbling to each other.

'Uh huh, uh huh.' Bryce screwed his eyes shut. He was pumping into her in hard desperate strokes that were so furious she couldn't fathom how he could keep going but he could; he did – he just kept fucking her until she felt like she was lifted a little higher in the air after each thrust; as if he were driving her, forcing her, pushing her up and away. His hands gripped her hips and his dick did the rest.

'Oh baby, oh yeah . . .' Penny's orgasm ripped through her like a tear through silk.

'Ah. Ah. Ah!' Bryce was coming in spasms; he was still thrusting between her legs in the exact same stroke he'd been fucking her with since they'd started. Thank God for young men!

'You take it, baby,' she hissed in his ear. 'It's yours!' Penny wrapped her arms around his shoulders and kissed him to the end of his climax.

When they'd both stopped trembling, he lifted her from his lap. 'Wow,' said Bryce. 'What was that?'

'It was good, that's what it was,' said Penny. She picked her black T-shirt up off the floor and pulled it on.

He pulled up his jeans, zipped them and buckled his belt. 'You can say that again. There's sure something to be said for sober sex.'

'I'm happy to hear it.' Penny opened the fridge. She grabbed a bottle of water and chugged. Her hands trembled. She held the container out to him when she was done but he shook his head.

'So you really don't want to teach me how to play poker?'

'I really don't want to teach you how to play poker.' Penny closed the fridge. 'But I'll give your name to a colleague of mine. Maybe she'll take you on as a student.' She took her business cards from a drawer and wrote a number on the back of one. 'Here's my card; let me know how it turns out.'

'Here's mine,' he said. His pants were so tight he had to stretch to get his hand into the pocket, but he managed to tug a card from it. He gave it to her and took hers in exchange.

'I don't usually behave that way, by the way,' said Penny.

'Me neither,' he said. 'No matter what you might have heard about me.'

She nodded. 'I guess we understand each other, then.'

'I guess so,' he said.

'You know what else?' said Penny.

'What?'

'I'll start going to all your movies, Bryce.'

'I can't ask for more than that.'

Penny looked him up and down, memorising the moment. She picked up his T-shirt from the floor and tossed it to him. 'Nobody needs to know about this, right?'

'Right.' He pulled on his shirt. 'Hell, I might be getting married this weekend!'

'Hey! That's not what you said a few minutes ago!' Penny shook her finger at him.

'Yeah, well, I dunno. Maybe I better go find out.' He gave her a shame-faced shrug but she noticed his walk was jaunty as he headed for the door.

Penny had to laugh. She suspected that if the marriage did happen it wouldn't last much longer than the honeymoon. Bryce Stafford, Junior was a scoundrel, pure and simple. Still, she couldn't blame him if he thought the same of her.

When they kissed goodbye at the door they weren't a movie star and a champion poker player, they were just Bryce and Penny, two single lonely people who'd dallied for a few hours one morning in London.

8

Hot bodies writhed together, pressed so tight they formed the slick, surging single entity known in clubs all over the world as 'the Saturday-night crowd'. Lonnie could barely breathe but it didn't matter; nothing mattered but the music and the lights and the feel of flesh on her flesh in a public place.

She'd long since ditched her cheongsam and now wore only the neon-purple satin tap pants and matching half-cup bra she'd had on beneath it. And, of course, her high heels and opaque-black stay-up stockings. She wasn't in the least self-conscious, of course. Quite the opposite. Lots of people wore even less than she did and, anyway, they all added up to one slick primitive thing, pulsating to the beat of the music.

To Lonnie's left, there was a short plump brunette, her naked body jiggling in all directions under a black net micro-dress that didn't even provide a token of modesty. She was dancing with a tall emaciated blonde in boy-shorts with a skimpy bib front that obviously called for double-sided tape and, as she hadn't used any, exposed her raspberry nipples alternately, or sometimes simultaneously.

A pair of exquisite young men, both wearing ringlets, false eyelashes and lederhosen, were indulging in a tightly controlled mating ritual, their hands behind their backs and their hips thrust forwards.

To Lonnie's right, a boy and a girl were dancing pressed together, her hands down the back of his blue satin pants, kneading his buns; his hands were holding her tiny pleated skirt up at the back, showing off a perfect 'bubble-butt' and the wisp of silk that divided her cheeks.

The Party had warned her that England's culture was the most decadent in the West; that London was its most depraved city, and that, in all of London, Soho was the most degenerate district. She was grateful for the advice – without it, she might never have found *Absinthe*, a delightfully corrupt club that never closed.

Lonnie shimmied faster, her entire body a blur, as the song pounded to a crescendo. The wide legs of her tap pants flapped about her thighs. If anyone had been squatting close by, they'd have caught flashes of her bare mound. Disappointingly, no one was.

The music stopped with shocking abruptness. The many-headed beast shuddered as one as its heart ceased to beat, then it fell to pieces, each person leaving or arriving on the dance floor. Lonnie shimmied on the spot, turning in circles as she pinpointed the location of her companions. She waved when she saw all twelve of them at their table, collected in what they called the 'Posse'. They waved back. Unlike her friends, Lonnie enjoyed exploring the dance floor. But she always made sure she knew where they were, and vice versa. Individuality is fun but there's safety in numbers.

Now Sudang was wiggling his way towards her, holding a plastic cup above his head. He was Thai, a mad capitalist at heart who worked for a charity because of his exorbitant salary and the perks. Still, he worked hard and played hard, just like Lonnie, plus his thick hair was the exact blue-black colour she loved on an Asian man. They'd had a thing a while back and split on amiable enough terms, her idea of course. Lonnie couldn't remember the last time a man had ever lost interest first. Maybe never.

He yelled something in her ear and held the drink to

her lips. The DJ was still setting up the next set so she could have made out Sudang's words over the din of the crowd had she cared to, but she didn't. She drank greedily and liquid caffeine and soothing ginseng raced through her body. She felt a burst of affection for Sudang because he'd braved the crowd to deliver her favourite energy drink. In some ways it was nice to be known.

Above them, spotlights started swirling, bathing the crowd in weird washes of colour, blue and green and pink. Lasers flashed actinic blue, lime green and smouldering, almost-invisible vermilion. Sudang discarded the drink; he circled Lonnie and pressed up against her from behind. As the electronic beat began, Lonnie let it rise up from the soles of her feet, through her calves and thighs, to her pelvis. The throbbing became part of her and carried her away. Now that she had a partner, she let herself surrender to the grinding gyrations of dirty dancing.

Sudang writhed against her back. He was already so hard that the ridge at the front of his jeans was rubbing between the cheeks of her ass, and they'd only just begun, the horny goat. He put his hands on her hips and pulled her firmly against him, leaning forwards at the same time to shout in her ear again. It was impossible to hear him and she was a little irritated at the attempt; he should know better than to try and come between her and her music. She had a pretty good idea what he was suggesting, anyway. He was well aware of her proclivity for public sex. He knew all her pleasure points, which was good, but she knew all of his, which was not so good. Still, toying with Ray had left her more excited than she'd expected.

She broke free of Sudang, then danced a little half-step backwards so that she was pressed even tighter up against him. He wasn't much taller than she was so she fitted neatly against his groin. Maybe that's what he was trying to say, 'Remember how well we fit together?' It was true; when he'd entered her, the fit had been exact, as if his dimensions had been engineered to match hers. Perhaps that had been the problem. Lonnie liked to feel that she was being violated, just a little, when she was made love to. Still, a perfect fit had to be better than trying to accommodate a man who was oversized, didn't it? She shuddered a little at the memory of the girth and length of Ray's big cock between her feet. Lonnie wasn't afraid of much, but being impaled on a cock that size gave her pause for thought. What if, when the time came, as it surely would, she couldn't do it?

Lonnie leant way back, letting Sudang support her with his legs and torso. He licked the sweat from her shoulder and her neck, then bathed her ear with his tongue. She shuddered as he wriggled the tip of it into her tiny ear canal. She had so many spaces that only a man could reach. She tilted her head back with pleasure. His hands were at her waist now, spread wide so that his thumbs played on her ribs. They wouldn't stay there for long, she knew. Sure enough, in another moment he was rubbing his palms against the sides of her breasts. Sudang's thin fingers curled a little and found her nipples, just covered by the red lace that edged her purple bra. His nails scratched at her breasts' peaks, through the fabric. Clever man! There'd been an evening, way back when, when she'd lain across his thighs, face up, her breasts covered by a cotton T-shirt. The game had been for him to scratch her nipples gently through the cotton and to keep on doing it until either he couldn't help himself from pinching or she found herself begging him to. After an hour and forty minutes, just as Lonnie had been about to beg, his fingers had crushed her tender flesh. The sudden shock of it had almost made her climax.

Sudang jerked beneath her in a limbo-dancing move that lifted her off her feet; her legs on his muscular thighs, sitting with the burning ridge in his jeans between her bum's cheeks. It was exhilarating, a weightlessness that, coupled with the swirling lights and spacey music, gave her an out-of-this world sensation that she adored. Now she was suspended off the floor, Lonnie was able to indulge her exhibitionism a little more. Stiff-legged, she raised her feet to waist height and slowly parted them. The thin satin at the crotch of her tap pants was damp now. It clung to her sex's plump outer lips and was caught in a vertical crease between them.

Even in a crowd such as this one, her wanton display had been noticed. Three Harajuku girls had wormed their way next to Lonnie and Sudang and now clustered in a swaying giggling trio. So cute and crazy, these girls, these gothic Lolitas. They had to be eighteen or older to be in the club but they looked like depraved little girls. That, of course, was the idea of their 'cosplay' – costume play.

Probably, not all of them were really Japanese but it was hard to be sure under their layers of makeup. Maybe they were. Lonnie had been told that the club attracted a lot of Pacific Rim students.

One of the girls was dressed in a Sailor Fuku costume, like Sailor Moon's, except that Sailor Moon didn't wear her skirt so short that every time she turned it flared to show off her pink bikini panties. Nor did Sailor Moon display eighteen inches of taut bare midriff, down far enough to include an inch of her smooth pubic mound.

Another of the girls was in a parody of a nun's habit, also micro-skirted, with long garters that held up ragged stockings. She had a cross painted on one chalk-white cheek and a black tear on the other.

The third was dressed up as a bride, in white satin and lace, but ripped off one shoulder and up one leg to her hip. She'd made her face up to look bruised, with a purple and pink black eye. Lonnie thought that to be in dubious taste.

On the plus side, all three painted dolls were making an extravagant show of appreciating the intimate skin that Lonnie was *almost* showing.

Her feet touched the floor again. She twirled to face Sudang. He leant forwards, his entire body a uniform inch from hers. She leant back. Their faces were so close to touching that the sweat of his brow dripped on to her cheek. She flicked her tongue out to taste it.

Sudang grabbed her hips and lifted her up high. Lonnie spread her legs and when Sudang brought her down she wrapped them around his waist. The thin satin crotch of her tap pants pressed against the fly of his jeans. She felt him, rigid, beneath the rough material of his trousers. Lonnie gripped his shoulders and loosened the grip her thighs had on his thin hips. She bounced against him like a girl rider out of sync with her trotting horse. Yes! Yes! It was an amazingly direct assault on her clit, given that they were both still more or less clothed.

Lonnie tossed her head, purposely blurring her vision so the lights and the bodies and the faces and the shadows melded. Yes! Yes! The faces of the Harajuku girls, three perverted little dollies, uniformly wide-eyed with awe and open-mouthed with delight, blurred past. So cute!

Long before she would have liked, Sudang gripped her hips and corrected the rhythm so that they were once again moving with, not against, each other. He leant back again, gave his signature limbolike hop and her toes touched the ground on either side of his feet. She bopped backwards on tiptoe and once again she and her partner were entirely separated by an erotically charged inch of space.

The three girls crept a little closer. Lonnie didn't really understand the philosophy behind the Harajuku girls, if there was a philosophy more lofty than following fashion. Did they seek out couples, or was it Sudang they were primarily interested in? Were they content to watch or were they looking to be part of the action?

Lonnie, of course, was all for being watched. But, if it was the latter they were after, they were going to be very disappointed. Lonnie had never had sex with a woman. Not because she hadn't had the opportunity, of course, or because it was frowned upon by the Party, but because, as she'd often reminded herself, it was pointless. The point of sex, she was almost certain, was the coming together of opposites. What good was a girl to her? And why on earth have sex with a girl wearing a fake cock when you could have sex with a man who had the real thing?

She met Sudang's eyes. He jerked his head at the Harajuku girls, as if to say, 'What do you think? Shall we?' but he kept his gaze locked on her. He was panting. So was she, she realised. She grabbed a handful of his gorgeous hair and pulled him into a passionate lip lock. Their tongues danced wildly in a wet kiss that only ended when they ran out of breath. The Harajuku girls jumped up and down with glee.

Sudang and Lonnie shook their shoulders in unison and kept on dancing. Although she tried to concentrate on her handsome male partner, curiosity about the girls kept intruding. She'd never seen one Harajuku girl on her own. If fact, she couldn't recall seeing a pair. It was always three or more. How did one start? She tried to imagine herself, Japanese and maybe fifteen or sixteen, stricken with the need to dress like a Harlequin or a Raggedy Ann. Would she have to hook up with two other like-minded girls before she could show herself in public, in costume? If so, how? The Web? Was there an Internet bulletin board with postings like: 'Would-be Gothic Nurse seeks Zombie Princess or Geisha/Vampire, object, Shocking Salary Men and smoking dope, Sapphic petting optional?'

Lonnie giggled at her thoughts. Sudang raised an eyebrow and Lonnie shook her head – explaining would be too complicated and, in the din, impossible.

Sudang led her back to her Posse's table. As they approached everyone perked up, becoming more animated. It was for her, of course. There wasn't one of them, man or woman, who didn't fancy her. Three of the twelve were higher in rank than she was; seven were older than she and deserved her respect for their years. None of that mattered. Being desired beats any hierarchical structure. The highest boss is a slave to the lowliest file clerk if he's crazy for her body and she doesn't want his.

Lo Song, Lonnie's official 'minder', leant in from Lonnie's left and tried to tell her something. Lonnie made an impatient sign to tell her colleague that conversation was impossible and, anyway, Lonnie's attention was on the Harajuku girls' table, just across the way from her. Officially, Lo Song was Lonnie's boss but the power of Lonnie's personality had soon changed that. Now the plump little thing made querulous requests when she should have been giving orders.

The trio had left the floor right after Lonnie and Sudang. She couldn't accuse them of stalking her but, in a mild way, they were. They'd pulled their chairs around to the far side of their table, so they were huddled together with an uninterrupted view of Lonnie.

She gave each one of them, in turn, a long bold

eye-to-eye stare, and slowly licked her lips. They fell into a confusion of giggling and whispering in each other's ears.

Lonnie felt a rush of power. She didn't do girls, but *they* didn't know that. All she'd had to do was hint that she found them interesting and they were ready to throw themselves at her feet. Now, how to exploit it? If she hadn't already stripped down to her undies, she could have found some way to take her panties off and surreptitiously drop them in one of the girls' laps. She wasn't ready to go naked from the waist down, not with Lo Song breathing down her neck, but the thought gave her a nice little shudder.

All three little darlings were ogling her blatantly and licking their lips at her. Such adoration shouldn't go unrewarded. Lonnie turned to Sudang. 'Lend me your jacket.'

He gave her a look that said, 'I can't hear a word you're saying.'

She paid him with a smile as she unhooked his coat from the back of his chair and draped it across her lap.

Lonnie turned back to her audience. Staring directly into the Battered Bride's eyes, Lonnie ostentatiously slid a hand under Sudang's jacket. The Bride nudged both of her companions. Her eyes were wide. Lonnie turned her gaze on the Naughty Nun and let her mouth soften as if with lust. The Nun nodded so eagerly that she almost lost her wimple. All three girls bounced in their chairs and mouthed words that Lonnie couldn't make out but knew had to be something like 'Go on – finger yourself for us.'

So Lonnie did. It was such fun. Maybe Lonnie didn't do girls, skin-on-skin, but teasing these three youngsters was almost like her favourite masturbation fantasy, where a dozen men could watch her but not touch her, and they all jerked off in an agony of lust.

It got even closer to her fantasy when Sailor Fuku worked a flat palm down the front of her tiny skirt. That girl deserved a reward for her lack of inhibition. Lonnie focused on her. It was like electricity, the eroticism that crackled across the fifteen feet between them. The Sailor nodded at Lonnie, her hand was moving with an accelerating rhythm under her skirt. Lonnie could have faked that she was matching the girl's movements but that wouldn't have felt right. Moving with care, so that none of her companions could tell what she was doing, Lonnie made tight little circles around her clit.

The Sailor's lips softened and parted, and her head fell back. The girl had to have a very short fuse if she was approaching her climax already. She jerked and slumped. Well, if Lonnie ever were tempted to sample a girl, it wouldn't be Sailor Fuku, pretty as she was. Lonnie liked her sex partners to last. She, herself, was far from orgasm, but she *was* saturated, which was the object of her exercise.

When the Sailor recovered enough to pay attention to Lonnie again, Lonnie crooked a finger at her. Bemused, the girl got up and came over on slightly unsteady feet. Without a word, Lonnie took the hand the girl had been masturbating with and put it to her mouth. As she sucked the tiny fingers she discovered that girl come didn't taste at all bad, in fact, it had a delightful taste. She gave her own aromatic fingers to the girl to suckle.

Sudang noticed, of course. He turned to Lonnie and made signals. 'You, me, her, her friends? Shall we?'

It was a shame to disappoint her dear comrade but Lonnie shook her head. Sudang shrugged. He'd learnt not to argue with Lonnie long ago. She gave him back his jacket and made her way, alone, back on to the dance floor. Somewhere in the press of bodies there was a pair of gorgeous gay men in tight leather shorts. She'd noticed them earlier but they'd been so lost in each other they'd paid no attention to her when she'd flirted. Lonnie saw that as a challenge. Just because they were gay didn't mean they were immune to her charms, did it? Or did it? Lonnie wasn't entirely sure but, as she matched her footsteps to the beat of the music, she determined to find out.

9

Penny stood in her walk-in wardrobe, sliding hanger after hanger down the rack as she rejected one outfit after another. Too sporty, too sleazy, too bright, wrong season, wrong fabric, wrong wrong wrong! Mitzu was right by her side, mewing appropriately from time to time. Penny wondered if she were going mad. How had she come so far in life with so few decent clothes? For God's sake, she had no idea what to wear. Ray had never even *seen* her dressed in street clothes. Every time she'd been with him she'd either been dolled up in her dancer's feathers and sequins, or starkers in bed.

Maybe she should meet him dressed in nothing but the black T-shirt she'd been wearing when she'd helped herself to a nice slice of Bryce Stafford, Junior. He'd liked her outfit, all right. Penny stifled the girlish scream that the memory evoked. She squeaked and Mitzu gave her a mildly quizzical look.

Not for the first time, she ran through the entire event in her head. She'd (thank God!) just finished shaving and moisturising and he'd called and she'd answered and he'd said 'Go to the window' so she'd gone to the window ...

The problem was that even running it through her head in slow motion didn't take much time at all. How long had he been in her apartment? Twenty minutes? What had she done?

'I fucked a movie star,' she told the cat. The cat meowed. 'I know, Mitzu. I know. I don't do stuff like that. But I did. So we'll just have to accept it and move on. We have a plan, a real plan, a plan that's been planned, not a plan that popped into my head like the plan to have sex with Bryce Stafford, Junior. So we're just going to go with the real plan and forget about what I did, which was totally out of character for me and which had very little to do with his fame. But lots to do with his looks. OK?' Mitzu meowed agreement.

Penny grabbed a colourful Pucci shift and tugged it over her head. She looked at herself in the mirror, groaned and pulled the shift off again. The only thing she was accomplishing was the destruction of her hair-do in progress. She fled the wardrobe, near panic.

Penny threw herself down on the bed. The phone lay where she'd left it after she'd rung the concierge to tell him to let Bryce Stafford, Junior into the building. Once more she ran through the event that had transpired only this morning. He'd come up and they'd had coffee and she'd adored him with her eyes and he'd ogled her with his eyes, gorgeous limpid pools of black, and she'd said it was good luck to fuck a poker player and he'd said it was good luck to kiss a movie star good morning.

'God!' She rolled across the bed, muffling her scream with the bedclothes. She clawed at the telephone with one hand and stopped herself with the other. God, she desperately wanted to call someone and confess what she'd done, but she and Bryce had agreed that it was their secret, and anyway she was sure, she was *absolutely* sure, that part of the agonising fun of it all was keeping it a secret. Besides, she wasn't a – what did they call it – a 'star fucker'. She was a good girl. A good girl embarking on a well-planned adventure that would yield much more than a five-minute toss if she could just decide what the hell to wear.

Not for the first time, Penny wondered if Ray would even recognise her. It'd been a long time since they'd met at *La Minx*, the club in Montreal where she'd been dancing for almost a year the night he wandered in to find some 'solidarity with the working man'. Penny grinned. She'd barely been legal, even in Canada! She'd leapt across the pond as soon as she'd finished her A levels and she'd landed on her feet. She wanted some fast money to stake her claim in the New World and *La Minx* wanted a sexy young babe who could dance into the night. They were a perfect fit. Or so it had seemed for a while. By the time Ray showed up, Penny had become less certain.

She'd been in need of a firm hand and he certainly had that, even if he was prone to bouts of melancholy over the loss of his ladylove. He quoted Marx or Lenin – actually he *always* quoted Marx or Lenin – but the quote she was remembering now had cautioned against sexual attachments because they got in the way of solidarity. God, how was it she could recall jargon from ten years ago and yet she couldn't remember to pick up coffee and cream? Her stomach grumbled, reminding her that she'd forgotten to pick up bread and butter, too.

She'd kill for a big juicy hamburger right about now. She wondered if Ray were still a vegetarian. When they met, neither of them had eaten meat, which had been one of the many amazing coincidences that made them think they were well suited for a fling. Maybe, by now, Ray was a fat old man. Penny rubbed her flat belly, easing her hunger pains and showing her appreciation for it at the same time.

They'd been good together, Penny and Ray. She hadn't cared if he loved her or not so his adherence to the party plan was of little interest to her. He was cute and funny and different, and, if he occasionally got morose about having recently been jilted, so what? He'd be gone soon. He was just lying low at his parents' home in Notre-Dame-de-Grace, waiting until the paperwork he needed to go to Cuba was in order.

In public, he was her biggest fan. For a few sweet months she'd known she could look out at the sea of lechers and see his good clean sweet face. She'd known that in that bad crowd there was one man who wanted only the best for her. Yes, at *La Minx* he drank his beer and flirted with the girls and generally whooped it up with the other guys. But in private, during those times when they'd actually managed to exhaust each other with great sex, he'd talked to her about getting out before she was pressed to do more than just dance. Ray had started her asking herself, 'How much money is enough to stake a claim?' She could hear the earnest words he'd spoken, even if over the years she'd forgotten the sound of his voice.

Penny resolutely steered herself back into the walk-in wardrobe. She took a long look at herself in the full-length mirror. It was a trick she'd devised for times like this, when she suddenly found herself helplessly lost in a fashion crisis. First things first. Ray was never one for the outfits anyway; he'd pawed his way impatiently through the feathers of her costume in search of her flesh. He probably wouldn't even notice what she was wearing; he'd just want to know her position on the War on Terrorism.

Suddenly, she wondered if seeing him again was worth the risk. Ray was one of the few people who knew that 'The Fire of London' had once worked as an exotic dancer in a downtown Montreal club. If the tabloids caught hold of it, they'd probably be able to find pictures, somewhere, to prove the story. In no time the media would brand her a whore. Well, at least Ray could attest to the fact that she'd never taken a dime from him; in fact, she'd even insisted on paying half the cab fare to her flat so he'd have more money in Cuba. That might be helpful if her past ever came to light. Life had really been a lot easier back when poker wasn't a celebrity sport.

Penny straightened her stance. 'The Fire of London,' she whispered to her reflection. She struck a pose and her spirits lifted. Penny loved her bod.

She cupped her tits in her hands. They were what some might call small but which she preferred to think of as 'dainty'. If they were 'teacup breasts' then they were Royal Doulton teacup breasts. She pulled her hands away to check their bounce. They were as perky as ever. Her nipples might seem at first glance to be too big for her breasts but they didn't get any stiffer when she was excited than they were right now, and they did turn a regal shade of red. More than one of her lovers had remarked upon their beauty. She preened, running her small hands down her belly to the freshly trimmed Valentine of her flame-bright pubic hair. What was it Bryce Stafford, Junior had said when he'd seen it? 'Hallelujah, the Burning Bush!' She grinned. This time, when she replayed the morning's event, it started to acquire the misty edges of a memory. Good.

Bryce Stafford, Junior. He was such a beautiful boy. Imagine being his age and already through rehab and about to be married. She wondered what his fiancée would think if she knew where he'd been that morning, and who he'd been dallying with. Penny shrugged. She certainly didn't owe Anna Francisca anything, and anyway they'd agreed to keep it a secret, just between the two of them. Thank God she'd managed to do so, so far. It was getting easier by the minute. She'd given him the number of another card shark, not as pretty as Penny but more amenable to teaching. He was out of her life, probably forever.

Still, Bryce Stafford, Junior had been just what she'd needed to dull the sharp steel edge of her sexual need.

Penny had let that part of her life languish, for good reasons. She thought the sexual energy that abstinence injected into her game gave her a special edge. She preferred, on the whole, to be in some kind of a relationship with a man before she went to bed with him, although, since Bryce had been practically dropped in her lap, she'd made an exception for him. A tremor of remembered pleasure rippled through her body. Her ability as a poker player had attracted Bryce but it had been her physical beauty as much as his that had turned their encounter into much more than a meeting of minds.

She turned back to her pitiful rack of clothes with renewed confidence. She would pick an outfit and in it she would wow Ray Torrington from the top of his giant brain to the tips of his combat boots.

Penny narrowed it down to two choices, either the black Spandex dress with a high collar and a diamond cut-out in front that made the most of her breasts or the short white toga-style chiffon dress with the sexy gold metallic straps that highlighted her long neck and crisscrossed between her breasts before tying at her waist.

'Mitzu?' she asked, holding out both outfits for inspection. Mitzu meowed. 'I think so too,' said Penny, hanging the Spandex back up before exiting the wardrobe. 'Come, kitty,' she said. She didn't want Mitzu to be locked in when it was time to go.

She spent an hour torturing her red hair into submission, but when she was done it fell in shining waves to her shoulders, where it bounced playfully when she walked. Even her long bangs were slicked almost straight so that they fell properly into her eyes. Next she made up her face to draw attention to her dark-blue eyes and lush mouth. She polished the apples of her cheeks with rosy bronzer in lieu of blush and impulsively decided to use it as lipstick, too. After much deliberation she decided on no bra and no stockings. Her only undergarment was a new pair of gauzy white French-cut panties trimmed with dainty ruffles. She spritzed herself liberally with delicate cologne that sold by the half-teaspoonful and slipped the white chiffon dress over her naked body. The fabric settled on her skin as delicately as the perfume.

It was a little early to make contact so she sat down on the bed and enjoyed a few puffs on what she vowed would be her last cigarette of the day.

Unless Ray still smoked? It gave her a thrill to think of the two of them sharing a smoke after sex, as they had many times in the few months they'd spent together before he'd abruptly disappeared. When she'd called his parents' place and found out his papers had arrived and he'd left for Cuba without saying goodbye, she'd cried all afternoon. A few weeks later, she'd received a postcard from Cuba, on which he'd scrawled a message in his indecipherable handwriting. She'd meant to ask him what it said when she saw him again but she never did. Maybe she'd ask him tonight.

Mitzu rubbed herself against Penny's bare leg. 'Good Mitzu,' Penny said absently, scratching the cat behind the ears and along the chin. A shaft of light appeared on the floor, patterned by the shadow of a lace curtain. The sun was shining.

'I'll tell you another reason why life is a game of poker. You wait and wait and sometimes you play and then you wait some more and you play some more and, before you know it, before you can even say how it happened, a lot of time has gone by. You know what I mean? And you wonder if you're wasting your life, you know, playing a game, or ... or if it's the other way around.'

Mitzu was distracted by the end of the tasselled cord that hung from Penny's waist so she wasn't interested in replying. Or maybe she simply declined to comment on Penny's admittedly mixed metaphor. Penny sighed. She took another puff on her cigarette and then dangled the tassel for Mitzu, safely out of reach of the cat's claws.

The black T-shirt she'd worn this morning lay crumpled on the floor. Only a few hours earlier Penny had giddily decided to dub it her lucky T-shirt. But now it looked discarded, not lucky at all. What was it about her that made her so easy to forget?

Penny shook her head. It had been her idea to jump Bryce's bones and it had been her idea to surprise Ray rather than simply arranging to get together with him. He loved surprises he'd told her, back when he was still in his late twenties. He'd said that nothing surprised him any more. If he'd been that jaded then, by now he must be a real pushover for good news. And that's what she was. Good news. When that foreboding little buzz-kill whispered in her ear, 'What if he doesn't think so?' she'd just have to ignore it. She inhaled on her cigarette and exhaled again, watching the smoke curl towards the ceiling and disappear.

Abruptly, Penny stubbed out the cigarette. She tucked her fags into a metallic gold clutch and snapped the purse shut. She slid her feet into metallic gold kitten heels, then toed Mitzu with one of the fashionably rounded tips of her shoes. Mitzu, long past the 'playful kitty' stage, abandoned her half-hearted pursuit of the tassel and rolled on to her back for a tummy rub. Penny obliged. It was time to compartmentalise. The real adventure was still to come.

'Live and learn,' said Penny. If anything, the morning's event had signalled a change in Penny's luck when it came to men. With a little strategy, Penny wagered she'd be the one holding the jackpot at the end of the night.

10

The balcony of Victoria's Park Lane hotel suite faced west, so Ray could see Green Park from the café table where he sat, enjoying a second cup of coffee while Victoria conducted business inside. Last night had been fantastic. He didn't know which memory to savour most, the moment when he'd actually climaxed at the touch of Lonnie's feet, or the middle of the night anal sex he'd enjoyed with Victoria. He amused himself by mentally wandering back and forth from one to the other, sipping his coffee in the morning sunshine. It probably wouldn't last.

Through the glass balcony doors he could see Victoria, serious and efficient, chatting with her disappointingly male London estate lawyer. Her little black reading glasses and the severe bun in her hair made her look like the perfect secretary. She was probably hoping he'd play 'cruel boss' to her 'helpless secretary' later, but he doubted it would happen. Sure, he'd love to bruise her backside but he was spooked by her 'bad heart' story. Better to be safe than sorry.

He could listen in to the conversation if he wanted to, because he'd left one door slightly open when he came out on the balcony. In fact, he had listened for a few minutes before losing interest in their financial jargon; it all seemed legit. Apparently, Victoria really was a very rich widow.

Over breakfast, at least twice, he'd noticed her stop herself from asking if he'd made up his mind about the trip to Cuba. He'd like to have an answer for her but, as always, Ray found it almost impossible to imagine a time as far off in the future as tomorrow. He had stuff to do! He already felt a lingering sense that he'd forgotten something important. Anyway, in this day and age a terrorist could be lurking around the next corner, eager to take the lives of innocent folks like him and Victoria, maybe mistaking a couple of peace-loving Canadians for their more militant neighbours to the south. Even if he did give in and agree to join Victoria, they might never make it off the plane. Then there were natural catastrophes and accidents and aneurisms to consider, and her bad heart, assuming there really was something wrong with it. Worrying about tomorrow seemed silly when today had barely begun.

Ray knew this was a maddening trait of his. It wasn't like he used it as an excuse, at least not any more, and it didn't keep him from planning things like meetings and conventions – work-related things. But it was very hard for him to say, 'OK, let's holiday in Cuba. The homeless can do without shelter for a few more weeks, what does it matter?' This morning, when he'd tried to get Victoria to understand, she'd come up with a new story, something about this trip being a fact-finding mission for future good works on her part. He'd almost laughed out loud. No matter how many charities she might have amused herself with as Mrs Gordon Ashe, she was not, had never been and never would be truly socially conscious. She was much too selfish.

Contrary to others of his species, Ray didn't mind selfish women. They were usually good in bed. The female equivalent of himself, really. Make the experience fantastic and your partner will reciprocate in kind. Science, simply put. It was a pity everyone couldn't comprehend such a straightforward concept.

Ray tuned in to Victoria and her lawyer for a moment. Victoria had a lovely voice. The figures they were tossing around meant she had to be a multimillionaire at least. Add that to her looks and their sexual chemistry and he would be a fool not to make the trip to Cuba their honeymoon.

The idea of living off the avails of the capitalist old man, prematurely dead from the difficulty of thriving on the hard labour of working people, did nothing to dissuade Ray. Take that, capitalist pig. You screwed me and now I'm screwing your wife. The revolution lives. Ray grinned privately as he took a last sip of his cooling coffee.

The housekeeping girl came out of the bathroom, carrying cleaning supplies and a pile of towels. She had glossy black hair and a creamy complexion with slightly slanted eyes. Definitely not your usual English rose. Her hair was wrapped up in a twisted braid that seemed to start at her hairline and end at the nape of her neck. Ray watched as she pushed her supplies cart towards the door of the suite. Even trudging behind the cart she was graceful. Ray could tell that under her dark skirt and white shirt her body was lithe. Her curves were evident to even the most disinterested observer, and Ray was never a disinterested observer of women. His glance darted to Victoria and, sure enough, she'd noticed his interest in the maid. Damn. He hated to be predictable.

Ray rose from his spot at the table and strolled to the balcony railing, purposely turning his back on the suite. He was starting to feel self-conscious, lounging around Victoria's room in his robe as if he were some kind of leftover from the night before. He didn't much care for it.

Ray felt something vibrate against his thigh. A tinny, electronic version of 'We Shall Overcome' reached his ears. He quickly fished his cell phone from the pocket of his robe and quietly answered. The unexpected sound of the voice at the other end made his own voice thicken, so when he tried to respond to her surprising offer he couldn't speak. He cleared his throat and started over.

Half an hour later, Ray emerged from the bathroom, groomed, dressed and whistling a merry, if tuneless, melody. It abruptly became a wolf whistle when he discovered that the lawyer was gone and in his place was a statuesque model-gorgeous woman. A perky little white nurse's cap was perched on her head, anchored to her masses of chestnut hair with bobby pins.

'What the –' Ray's surprise at the presence of this unexpected visitor increased when she unbelted and removed her trenchcoat to reveal the classic white skirt and blouse once worn by nurses everywhere. But this skirt was short and the V-neck blouse hugged her ample curves.

'I hope I'm not late.' Her accent was Russian. She tilted up the pendant watch pinned to her breast to see the time. Satisfied, she let it drop. It hung directly beneath a blue pin that declared she was Veruschka Tartelova, RN.

'I get it!' Ray grinned at them. 'Victoria, my Beauty Puss, you are entirely too much. Victoria and Veruschka. Yum Yum.' He winked.

'Stop it, Ray. You're embarrassing yourself. Veruschka is my private nurse. Remember, I mentioned her?' Victoria gave him a stern look.

'But you didn't mention that she looks more like a stripper than a nurse, or that her last name is Tart-elova. Nice touch.'

'And your name?' Verushka's eyes were grey, wide apart and, at that moment, puzzled. She extended her right hand.

'I'm Ray *Torrid*-ton.' Ray laughed as he shook her hand.

'I'm serious, Ray,' admonished Victoria. 'His last name

is Torrington, Veruschka. He seems to misunderstand the meaning of your presence here.'

'Maybe it is your temperature I should take, Mr Torrington, instead of Victoria's?' Veruschka set her black nurse's bag on the bed.

'That depends on the kind of thermometer you use. Knowing Victoria, I'd guess it doesn't go under the tongue. Am I right?'

'Yes.'

'I knew it!' Ray chortled.

Veruschka opened her black bag and rummaged around inside before withdrawing an electronic thermometer.

'Ray.' Victoria's voice was cool. 'Don't dig yourself in any deeper. Veruschka *is* my nurse.' She paused as Veruschka stuck the thermometer in her ear, then continued. 'I arranged her employment through "Silver Shield Services", here in London. It provides private healthcare to its patrons, for a hefty fee of course. But, if you were listening at all when my lawyer was here, you know money is no problem for me.'

The thermometer beeped. Veruschka withdrew it from Victoria's ear and glanced at the results. Her thin black brows knitted. 'Your temperature is up,' she said.

'So you're for real?' Ray was still gaping at the woman. He snapped his jaws shut.

'I assure you, Mr Torrington, I am one hundred per cent real.' Veruschka cast him a dark, direct glance. 'So –' her Russian accent made it come out as 'Zo', the sibilant little sound and her fierce grey eyes melting his masculine heart. '– do you need your temperature taken?'

Ray shook his head. His cheeks were flaming red but that was embarrassment, not fever. It'd been a long time since he'd felt so foolish.

'Veruschka is going to examine me, darling. Would you like to help?'

'Any way I can,' he said.

'Will you get my heart medication? I'd like to show my *nurse* how many pills are left.'

'Yes, ma'am.' He skedaddled to the bathroom.

Ray was more than happy to get out of their sight for a couple of minutes. Damn! He'd called the woman he'd always dominated 'ma'am' and mistaken a registered nurse for a whore. Things couldn't be worse. Maybe he should just get the pills and get out. After all, he had a date that he definitely didn't want to be late for.

In the mirror he saw a shame-faced boy. Ray wiped his face with one of the many fresh towels the exotic little maid had just replenished the bathroom with. 'Slow down, boy,' he admonished himself. 'Think it through.' Real nurses weren't ever that gorgeous, were they? Or were they? There was that time he'd broken his arm while rock climbing in the Laurentians. Hadn't the nurse who'd tended him been ravishing? He'd always remembered her as a beauty, but he'd been young when it happened, maybe twelve. They'd given him a shot for the pain. Had that made him see loveliness in her that wasn't really there?

Ray knocked the cardboard cap off a fresh glass and filled it with tap water. Thinking like a little boy wasn't going to help him now. He'd always remembered that nurse as a raving beauty. Veruschka's looks alone did not rule out her being the real thing.

As he gulped water, Ray glanced around the bathroom. The cute little maid had been gorgeous, and she was definitely the real thing; this bathroom was spotless. He shook his head to clear it.

Veruschka's uniform was old-fashioned but the skirt was short. Real nurses didn't wear their clothes so tight. Real nurses didn't even wear uniforms any more, did they, except for green scrubs once in a while? That might mean she was a fake. Unless the expensive private healthcare company she worked for provided stylish uniforms that were still comfortingly old-fashioned and picked its nurses for their good looks. It made sense, sort of. What the hell!

Ray reached for the pills. In the mirror, he saw that his pale-blue eyes were shining with excitement. The situation was unpredictable and that gave him a thrill. There was no way he was leaving now. It was good, sometimes, just to be alive. Damn good!

When he handed the pill bottle to Veruschka she ignored him and focused on the bottle. She examined it closely, her voluptuous lips pursed. She frowned at her patient, who was now tucked into bed, the covers drawn primly to her chin. 'You haven't taken your morning pill,' Veruschka said accusingly.

Victoria hung her head. 'I had meetings with the lawyer all morning.'

'Lawyers!' Veruschka snorted in a most unladylike way.

'What part of Russia are you from?' asked Ray. He pulled up one of the sleek leather chairs and sat down. If there was going to be a show, he wanted a front-row seat. If there wasn't, well, he'd offered to help in any way he could. Maybe Veruschka would find another task for him.

'Moscow. You have a good ear, Mr Torrington. I have been in England for five years now – the five best years of my life.' Veruschka shook a pill from the bottle into a little paper cup and gave it to Victoria, then handed her a glass of water from the bedside table.

'Oh? Russia no fun any more since the Iron Curtain fell?'

'Pah. The USSR was much worse. I am happy to make my own money and spend it as I wish. As soon as I could get out I did – although I do keep up with the medical advances that come out of Moscow.' She settled the stethoscope around her neck.

'But surely some of the communist policies contributed to the good of the people . . .' Ray's voice trailed off as she plugged the earpieces into her ears.

Victoria set the water glass down. She stifled a laugh. 'Let her do her job, Ray,' she said. She lowered the sheet to her waist, revealing her big creamy breasts barely contained by a black satin demi-cup bra.

Veruschka rubbed the metal disc of the stethoscope with her fingers for a moment to warm it before she placed it to Victoria's chest. 'Breathe deep,' she ordered. She listened intently, her dark brows knitted again in that cute little frown Ray already adored. She tilted her timepiece up and glanced at it, then moved the disc to Victoria's back and listened some more.

'You seem weak,' she pronounced. She cast a long dark look at Ray who struggled not to hang his head.

'I had a big breakfast, didn't I, Ray?'

'She ate fruit and cereal. Juice, too.' Ray squirmed a little. This Russian 'nurse' was making him uncomfortable in more ways than one. Why hadn't he noticed how thickly fringed with lashes her eyes were? Too focused on her skinny black eyebrows, maybe. Or her huge, soulful grey eyes. Her gaze was devastating.

Veruschka broke eye contact with Ray and turned her full attention to her patient. 'I think too much strenuous activity. Possibly the blood is not circulating as smoothly as it should. Any pain?'

'A little,' Victoria admitted.

Veruschka leant over her black bag. Ray admired the outline of her plump ass straining against the thin white cotton. No VPL – which meant she was likely wearing a thong. She *must* be a fake! He squirmed again as his cock twitched. He knew where his blood was circulating to, that was for sure.

Victoria giggled. Ray looked at her. 'You're too much,' he said. His voice was warm with approval and she shrugged elegantly.

Veruschka withdrew a paddle from her case and placed it on the bed. She pulled the covers down. Victoria was naked except for a little black satin thong and her matching bra. Veruschka made a circular motion with her hand and Victoria turned over, kneeling up.

Ray leapt from his chair. 'I knew it,' he said. He came up close behind Veruschka and cupped her ass with his hands. 'Fantastic!'

'I beg your pardon, Mr Torrington!' Veruschka twirled to face him and free herself from his grip. Her eyes were as fierce as any warrior's. 'This is a Russian technique well known to provide pain relief and encourage increased circulation. Surely you've heard of it?'

'Come on,' Ray groaned. At the same time he realised that he *had* read about just such a technique, used by Russian doctors in certain cases, for just such results.

'Please, Ray,' murmured Victoria.

'Do you think,' growled Veruschka, 'that I would be wearing such terrible shoes if I was what you think I am?'

In fact, Ray had noticed her white stockings and sturdy sensible white shoes. He held his hands up in surrender and backed up to his chair, helpless in the face of such ferocity. She had to be an absolute tiger in bed.

Ray put his hands in his lap and gave her his most angelic look. She scowled and returned to the work at hand.

Veruschka silently piled pillows in front of her patient and gently pushed Victoria's head down until it rested on them, her face turned towards Ray. Veruschka ran her hand up Victoria's back and rested it lightly on her raised backside. Her hand rose and fell firmly on Victoria's left cheek. As the palm of her hand made contact with Victoria's bum, a little smacking sound was heard – a sound Ray hadn't heard in years. He sighed and settled back in his seat. If the visual hadn't been so superb, he'd have closed his eyes, he was so delighted to hear it again.

Veruschka was an expert at this; that much was clear. She smacked each buttock in turn, in a manner that couldn't be called delicate but was a far cry from cruel. Veruschka alternated from cheek to cheek, tinting each in turn a shade deeper, until the skin, only moments ago alabaster white, blushed a bright pink. Only then did Veruschka pick up her paddle.

Ray saw the tears in Victoria's eyes. He gave her a concerned look and she replied by wiggling her bum and giggling.

'Stay,' ordered Veruschka. For once her ferocity was focused on her patient. Victoria stopped wiggling.

'This technique can be very useful when dealing with passive subjects, like my patient here,' said Veruschka. She rubbed the smooth wooden paddle with her hand, turning it so that both sides were warmed. 'Sometimes they are so languid in nature that they must be spanked before they are fully awake. And of course it causes endorphins to be produced, which is always beneficial to the patient. Are her eyes dilating?'

'Oh yes,' replied Ray.

Victoria's eyes had dimmed to the colour of a shaded pond in summer. Her mouth was slightly open and she languidly licked her lips. She was halfway to subspace already.

'It is so satisfying to bring a patient that level of relief without the use of drugs. Do you agree?'

'I do,' said Ray, nodding for emphasis. 'But I worry. What about her heart?'

'Not to worry. It will stop when it stops. In the meantime she should have everything she wants, don't you think?'

'I want the paddle,' mumbled Victoria before Ray could reply.

Veruschka smiled for the first time, a wider smile than Ray would have imagined. 'What do you say?' she growled at Victoria.

'Please, nurse, please smack my ass with the paddle.'

'That's more like it!' Veruschka drew her right arm back and whacked Victoria's ass, hard, with the flat surface.

Victoria shrieked, a noise that did nothing to deter the onslaught of blows that proceeded to play a resounding melody on her ass.

Ray's cock rapidly went rigid. He resisted the impulse to lean forwards for a better glimpse of Victoria's ass as it took the beating, because that way he wouldn't be able to see her face, or Veruschka's determined grimace, as she delivered ten, twelve, eighteen uniformly ferocious blows. Ray exhaled when Veruschka dropped the paddle, only then realising he'd been holding his breath.

Victoria's face was streaked with tears.

'Good girl,' said Veruschka. 'Come see, if you like,' she said to Ray.

He went to stand beside her. The paddling had left both cheeks flaming scarlet.

'Nice,' he said, 'but no ridges.' Ray picked up the crop Victoria had laid out on the bed the day before. 'Now this would leave ridges. If you think she can take it.'

Veruschka took the crop from his hand, pursing her lips. 'It's unorthodox,' she mused, 'but perhaps...' She tapped Victoria's thigh with the tip of the crop. Victoria trembled. 'Do you want it?' asked Veruschka.

'Please, nurse, may I have the crop?'

'Hmm.' Veruschka whisked the crop through the air a couple of times, always stopping far short of the target. Each time, to Ray's sympathetic amusement, Victoria's ass clenched in anticipation of a blow that failed to fall.

'It's OK. baby,' he murmured. His heart went out to Victoria – would she stop at nothing to attract him? Why? And what if she were doing this for his benefit only? What if she didn't really like it?

As if sensing his concern, Victoria turned her head to look at him. Her eyes were deep pools of green; her pupils pinpricks. Her mouth seemed loose, as if on the verge of falling open to drool on the bedclothes. Obviously, the thought of the crop marking her already beaten ass was making her delirious with pleasure.

The crop sang through the air to deliver its first stinging blow. Veruschka seemed pleased with its performance and delivered another couple of sharp blows in rapid succession.

Ray was so turned on the head of his cock was in danger of being exposed above the waistband of his pants. He discreetly rearranged himself. He didn't need to be reminded, yet again, that Veruschka was a real nurse. Somehow, this 'fact', however absurd, helped heighten what was already an intensely erotic experience. He wasn't one to be dommed, but he found obeying Veruschka's demand for respect gave him a thrill.

The crop whistled again and again. He found himself wincing with each blow. Victoria trembled as if she might collapse but held her position, taking all of the half-dozen bruising slices that were delivered. It wasn't until Veruschka grunted, 'Enough,' and laid down the crop that Victoria's taut pose relaxed and she sobbed out loud.

Together, Ray and Veruschka examined Veruschka's handiwork. Each cheek was decorated with ribbons of purple that were puffing up even as they watched.

'Touch,' encouraged Veruschka. She took his fingertip and licked it, then set it on one of the puffy little ridges.

Ray traced the skinny livid line with his finger and Victoria moaned.

'She is a pain zlut,' said Veruschka.

Ray nodded, dipping his finger into Victoria to find that she was, just as he'd thought, wet inside, as hot to the touch as a furnace in the middle of winter.

'Goodbye,' whispered Veruschka, bending down to kiss Victoria's flushed cheek.

Victoria raised her hand to stroke Veruschka's face, then let it drop. She was so full of endorphins she was more liquid than solid – a melted, shapely molten mass. 'You're my favourite nursie ever, Veruschka,' she whispered. She tilted her head and Veruschka leant forwards so that they could kiss again, succulent lips to succulent lips. 'Do you have to go?'

Veruschka put her hand to Victoria's head and pushed gently on it in answer. Victoria collapsed under her touch, her face buried in soft pillows. She stretched languidly.

Roy's cock ached to plunge into her before the blush faded from her cheeks. His fingertips tingled with anticipation; he wanted to touch those bruised ridges of raised flesh again; he wanted to squeeze her crimson ass as he entered her and make her cry. He wanted the mark of his hand to leave an imprint of its own, the subject of this work of art, illuminated by the livid background Veruschka had already painted.

'I'm already late for my next appointment. If I may use the washroom?' Veruschka was already disappearing into the room as she spoke.

Ray started at her words. He glanced guiltily at his watch, and then began pulling on his shoes. Victoria lay face down on the bed, too blissed to notice.

'It hurts, Ray,' she mumbled into the bedclothes.

'You were a very brave girl,' he said. He allowed himself another moment to stroke the ribbons of purple that were streaked across her scarlet cheeks.

'It makes all my other pain go away,' muttered Victoria. She seemed on the verge of sleep, and that was, Ray decided, exactly what she needed.

Veruschka emerged from the bathroom. She pulled on her trenchcoat and belted it tightly. 'I'm on my way then,' she said.

'Darling,' whispered Victoria in a voice that managed to be husky and girlish at the same time, 'will you see Veruschka out and then come back to bed, please?'

'Sure. That is –' Ray followed Veruschka to the door '– I'm more than happy to see your nurse out, Victoria, but I'm afraid something rather important has come up. I have to go.'

'What?' Victoria struggled to a sitting position. 'You're going? Where?'

'I – uh – I promised a friend, that is, some friends, that I'd – uh – do a little sightseeing with them today. Well, really it's more of a – a working tour of the city. Yeah. You know how it is.'

'You can't be serious! Ray, what about my marks? They'll fade!'

'I won't be gone long, I promise. But right now I've got to run.' Ray pushed Veruschka out the door ahead of him and closed it before the astonished look on Victoria's face distorted to anger or, worse, dissolved in a flood of tears.

11

A grey limousine cruised close to where she stood at the corner of Regent Street and Oxford Street, then abruptly came to a stop. The passenger door opened. Ray pulled her into the air-conditioned interior. She gasped 'Cheater!' as she fell into his lap.

Lonnie wore a denim mini-skirt belted with a piece of leather almost as wide as it was long. Burnt-sienna leather cowboy boots matched the belt but her top was a filmy bit of turquoise satin and tulle. Her handbag, like her belt buckle, was so big it threatened to weigh her down. She squirmed and he wrapped his arms around her to make her stay put. The nerve of the man!

'All your bling is making you heavy,' Ray mock-complained.

'It's not bling.'

'No? Why not?'

Lonnie wriggled in his lap some more. Something big stirred inside his khakis. She tried to shake off his arms but he just rearranged them so that she was still held fast, though now her arms were free. 'Bling is when it is shiny! This is just leather and – whatever belt buckles are made of –'

'Silver?'

'No! More like pewter, maybe? Or steel? I don't know but I know it is not bling.' She squirmed, trying to find the sweet spot in his lap. 'I wanted you to join me and my friends on the bus tour!'

'For what I have in mind the bus won't do.' Ray

grinned at her and squeezed her waist. 'Not even upstairs in a double-decker.'

'Phooey.' Lonnie made a moue. 'What's the big deal? Public sex is fun.'

The glass divider between the passengers and the driver was already in place. Now, Ray pressed a button that caused an opaque divider to rise, covering the glass and affording them complete privacy. He cuddled her close and started kissing her bare shoulder. 'What is it with you and exhibitionism, anyway?'

'I don't know.' Lonnie shrugged. The kisses felt nice on her shoulder and the limo *did* have a sunroof. She started to relax. 'Do you know why you like the things you like, sexually?' Ray pondered this until, belatedly, Lonnie thought to ask, 'What *do* you like sexually?' She batted her mink lashes at him.

Lonnie twisted until she was straddling Ray. She ground against his khaki-covered groin, riding him to an erection. A terrified thrill ran through her lithe little body – he was just as big as she remembered.

Ray slipped his hand in to unzip his fly but she put her butterfly-delicate fingers to his wrist. 'Wait.'

'I hope,' he whispered intently, 'you aren't a common cocktease. Are you?'

'No.'

'Promise.'

'I promise.'

He withdrew his hand. 'What do you want?'

'Look! Buckingham Palace!'

Ray obliged Lonnie by looking out the window at the palace. 'Quite a fine example of the monarchy's insatiable appetite for excess.'

'I know! Isn't it fabulous?'

Ray laughed and ran his hands through her ink-black mane.

'I tell you what I want, OK?' Lonnie grinned at him;

her excitement made her dark-brown eyes sparkle impishly. 'Tell your driver to loop back and drive as slowly as he can past the Palace again, and I will try to suck you.'

'Try?'

Lonnie's cheeks reddened. 'My mouth is not so big . . .'

'Are you afraid of my cock? Is that it?'

'Little bit afraid.'

'How much is a little bit?'

Lonnie raised her hands until there was a space between them about eight and a half inches long. 'This much.'

Ray let out a laugh that was so deep and full of mirth Lonnie couldn't help but join in. Her merry giggles were the melody to his booming bass line. When he could speak he pressed a button on the console and said, 'Driver, do whatever the lady wants.' He nodded at Lonnie.

'Please go back and pass the Palace again, slowly,' she said.

The car sedately obeyed. Lonnie pushed on Ray's chest and he settled back into the upholstered comfort of the limousine seat, gesturing with his hands to indicate surrender.

'Since you have seen fit to secure this sinfully expensive and luxurious limo in order to seduce me,' she said, 'we should make full use of it. Champagne?'

'Capital idea,' replied Ray in his best upper-crust English accent, which wasn't really very good.

Victoria located the cell phone in the pocket of Ray's robe, hanging on the hook in the bathroom, just as it stopped ringing. That was just as well as it saved her from having to decide whether or not to answer it. At least now she had something of his that he might come back for.

He was horrible. Only a horrible, horrid man would leave her with a molten-hot bum, fresh from Veruschka's ministrations. She needed to keep the endorphins flowing like lava until they culminated in a mind-blowing volcano of an orgasm. Didn't Ray realise that? Of course he did! Victoria wasn't sure if she wanted to kiss Ray or kill him, but she'd like the choice!

She buried her face in the folds of Ray's terry robe and inhaled. No man ever smelt exactly like any other one and Ray was no exception. He was part soap and water and part light cologne and all uniquely Ray. She exhaled. She'd just have to wait a little longer. Victoria glanced at the mirror and saw her pitiful reflection, pressed against an empty robe. It was doubly embarrassing to be embarrassed by her behaviour when she was alone. Damn him! This weekend was the end of her obsession, one way or another. Either he joined her on the trip or this relationship was over forever.

Victoria rubbed her cheek against the soft terry. For now, she would believe his thin excuse for leaving her. She chose to accept that the action he was taking now was – in some way she didn't quite understand yet – for a greater cause. She would do her part by being patient and waiting for her man. She inhaled once more and stepped away from the robe. Victoria balanced his leather-cased cell phone in her hand. He'd be back. Till then, she'd just have to amuse herself.

Penny was uneasy, standing in full view of the public in the lobby of the Plaza. She hovered in front of the elevator doors, tapping her foot impatiently. As her luck would have it, a large group of conventioneers began pouring in the doors of the hotel. Any moment one or more of them was sure to recognise her and then there'd be autographs and poker tips and all that good stuff. Penny wasn't exactly shy about her growing celebrity, just a little uncomfortable with it. After all, it wasn't as if she were royalty or even a talented performer. More and more, she and others of her ilk were considered 'athletes' in the sport of gambling, and she had a hard time seeing it that way. Still, better it be considered a sport than an addiction. At any rate, poker certainly paid the bills and, if notoriety came with the territory, Penny would simply have to show that famous English stiff upper lip or, as the folks across the pond would say in their slightly coarse colloquial manner, 'suck it up'. Penny inhaled, sucking in her tummy and straightening her stance. The elevator doors opened.

Before the people inside the elevator could disembark, the unruly conventioneers descended, jostling and pushing their way into the car.

'For heaven's sake!' protested Penny, suddenly feeling much more invisible than famous. An elbow poked her breast and she teetered back in her heels, blushing, suddenly furious. 'Bloody hell!'

A capable hand closed around her elbow and she was gently steered into the protective shadow of a tall black gentleman. He wore an intricately embroidered red Dashiki and a small embroidered hat on his head. She looked up into his kind brown eyes. 'We'll take the next one,' he said in a rich melodic baritone. He stepped aside, taking her with him, to let the elevator leave without them. Whether he recognised her or not, Penny certainly recognised him. A knight in shining armour had come to rescue the beautiful maiden, not from a dragon but from something as terrible as any fire-breathing monster – the making of a huge mistake.

Penny had known from the moment she hadn't been able to locate Ray that what had started out as a lark had taken a darker turn. Now that he wasn't where he was supposed to be, Penny *had* to know where he was. Perhaps he was hiding out in his hotel room, alone or with someone, not answering his phone. Penny knew she was treading the delicate ground between 'ex-lover with a lovely surprise' and 'stalker', and now, just in the nick of time, a handsome man had stepped into play. Not a knight after all, but a king.

'The Fire of London,' he said. 'I am Chief Nobatu.' He inclined his head to indicate that she should precede him into the elevator that had just arrived.

'Chief?'

'Don't worry, it is an elected position.' His smile was at once sensuous and friendly. He was obviously delighted to have run into her. 'Are you staying in the hotel?'

Penny stepped into the elevator and he followed her. 'No,' she replied but added nothing more. He looked her over appreciatively but without leering, the way a man might look at a Grecian urn that pleased him. As Penny had not pressed a button yet, he pressed the 20th-floor button and, after a moment, the doors closed.

'I hope you are not uncomfortable, alone with me. I assure you, nothing untoward will happen.'

'What a pity,' replied Penny. She gazed up at Chief Nobatu. Talk about exotic! Every cell in her body called out to him. She was grateful and excited at the same time, a heady combination that had propelled her into the elevator and now caused the provocative words to escape her mouth.

'Oh?' His laughter was loud and appreciative, open but not common, like his glance. The doors closed on their smiling faces.

Ray glanced to his left and right, taking in the view. From his position, feet wide apart on the upholstered leather bench-seat and his chest and head emerging from the open sunroof, he had a grandstand view of London on a sunny day. If he looked straight down the view wasn't bad, either – Lonnie delicately lapping at his manhood like it was a Popsicle in danger of melting.

He wasn't in danger of melting at all, nor was he in danger of exploding. He felt he could endure this forever. Not that her ministrations weren't pleasurable. They were – excruciatingly so. It was just that everything was so terrific he was determined to do all he could to make it last.

There had been that moment – after she'd arranged him the way she wanted him and then unzipped him – when he'd realised with a simultaneous gladdening of the heart and disappointment of the mind that she was very talented at oral sex. Happily, Ray no longer took any notice of the dampening of his spirits that threatened to come with the reptilian understanding that she'd done this many times before. He chose to resolutely focus on the joy a man knows when he can tell from the confidence of the girl's seeking tongue and the gentle way she uses her lips to protect him from her teeth that he is in the hands – or mouth – of an expert.

She was doing that little 'play me like a flute' thing she'd done with her toes in the restaurant, only this time she was using her fingers so it was even more delicate and delightful. He felt a warming spasm in his gut and focused on the Palace again.

She was clever, this Bai Lon from Hong Kong. Somehow she'd guessed that he'd find the trappings of royalty a perfect juxtaposition to fellatio in a limousine. On such a beautiful day it was great to be in his shoes, the wind in his hair and his pants to his knees, enjoying Lonnie's touch and lips, as satiny smooth and flitting as the wings of a butterfly. Life couldn't get much better, and Ray was enough of a sensualist and self-disciplinarian to strive to make the moment last.

Interesting, the way once he'd actually emerged through the opening in the roof he found it more liberating than embarrassing. It was true, just as Lonnie had promised, that he felt safe and anonymous in a 'look at me I'm a tourist' sort of way. He was ignored for the most part, probably assumed to be drunk by anyone who bothered to assume anything. The limo was going fast enough for him to feel anonymous and slow enough to feel safe and there was the added bonus of seeing the landmarks of London at a more accelerated pace than a bus tour could possibly provide. He'd never actually bothered to tour London before.

Ray sighed as Lonnie stroked him with both hands. She'd lubed him with a cool, sweet-smelling lotion from a bottle that she'd pulled from that trunklike bag of hers. He made a mental note never to tease a woman about the size of her bag again.

They were passing near the Palace gates now. Ray saw crowds waving at the guardsmen. He wondered how many people waved at them every day, what it was like to stand there without acknowledging them, realising that guys like Ray were getting fantastic blow jobs while they were left behind, eating limo dust.

Ray shuddered as Lonnie stroked him for a dozen slow 'along-the-top-and-over-the-head-and-down-the-underside-of-the-shaft-and-then-back-again' strokes. Fantastic. She was so good at everything so far that he felt like he was falling in love.

Ray looked down at her. The whole 'you're too big for delicate little me' gambit was oddly moving, given that there was very little chance it was true. She gazed up at him, her eyes wide and her lips pursed in a classic porn face. He might have to marry this girl if this kept up. 'Suck me,' he whispered.

Lonnie licked her lips and opened her mouth wide, in a perfect circle. Ray was sure he could fit in there. When she put her lips around him it was like being taken into a tunnel sheathed in wet red velvet. Her tongue was alive, tasting his maleness, teasing it like a tiny dancing cave courtesan. Ray tilted his hips, slipping an inch further into her mouth. They moaned in unison and he tried to turn his attention back to the scenery.

They were past the Palace now, but he couldn't concentrate on the view. Her mouth was luscious and her lips and tongue so soft against his rigidity. He felt his balls tighten. It would be so easy to let her carry him along in the stream of her passion. He remembered the little orgasm she'd elicited from him using only her feet. What would this one be like if he went with it, too, the way he'd gone with her foot play?

She moaned softly. The sound waves made his skin tingle. He was so sensitive to her every move it was if he were two men, one watching and one experiencing what the other watched.

Ray focused on a stand of trees. He tried to remember what they were called. Plane trees? It was no use. Lonnie was holding him in her mouth now, laving the head of his cock with her lips and tongue.

He experimented, tilting his hips again to introduce another inch into her mouth. He didn't want to make her gag, not by any means, but he did want to see how much of him she could take, and it seemed she could take more than enough.

A kite was successfully launched in a nearby park and, as the speck of bright red rose into the sky, Ray allowed himself to relax. He quit tensing and let Lonnie's talented mouth envelop and release him while her fingers stroked him towards the coming climax.

She kept him afloat until the current of her passion carried him over the edge. He chose to look straight up, at the dazzling blue sky dotted with a few uncharacteristically fluffy white clouds and one tiny soaring red kite.

'God!' he bellowed as the first spasm rocked him. He

slapped his hands down on the roof of the limo to steady himself. She was sucking him dry, the bitch!

He wanted to tell the driver to go back so he could announce himself to the Palace as 'King Fuck!' but he didn't. Instead, he pointed at the sky and yelled, 'Fantastic!' so anyone looking at him, and people *were* looking at him, would think he was remarking on the blue sky or the red kite and not on the orgasm that was bolting through him in a rocking rhythmical way that threatened to make him pass out.

He didn't, of course. When the spasms stopped, he slid out of her mouth and down from the sunroof and on to the seat. He stretched out on it, zipping himself up. 'You are so good, it's just – it's almost too much,' he moaned.

'It's fun, isn't it, to have people look at you when you come?'

'It was a thrill, I admit it.' He grinned at her. She kissed him on the mouth, letting his tongue part her lips and find hers. Their first kiss. It burnt his mouth like candy cinnamon hearts.

'My turn,' said Lonnie.

'What is my tell?' demanded a naked Nobatu. Naked, that is, but for his square hat, which she had learnt was made in the kitenge kofia style, as was his four-piece outfit. Whatever the style, she'd taken the shirt off his back and now she'd claim that hat, in what was obviously their last hand of strip Texas Hold 'Em.

'If I tell you, you won't believe me,' replied Penny, grinning at him across the round table in his palatial suite.

'I find it most unsettling,' he allowed.

Nobatu frowned greatly at his cards. Penny glanced at her hand, her poker face firmly in place. She, of course, was only down one pair of frilly white panties, and that had been a sacrifice to keep Nobatu from losing heart before she'd enjoyed making him lose his pants. He had a terrific body, at least as far as she'd been able to see. While not being coy in the least, he had managed to manoeuvre himself so that his private parts were hidden behind a point of the square tablecloth. She saw that his skin was uniformly ink black. She'd been with a black man in the past but that man's skin had been paler in the places where the sun never reached it. But Nobatu was a deep rich chocolate colour all over. How had he managed that? He must have ample opportunity to be nude, she surmised. At any rate, he was truly a lovely man to behold.

When they first arrived at his room, they'd been greeted by a gaggle of officials. Nobatu was part of the same symposium Ray had been attending. He'd remained behind, with a number of colleagues from other countries, to enjoy an all-expenses-paid few days in England's capital city. This appeared to be equal parts schmoozing, sightseeing and serious business making. Before he'd been able to shoo away his employees, Nobatu had had to sign documents, assign tasks and juggle his appointment book. Once they were alone, his attention had focused as completely on her as if he had all the time in the world.

Naturally, it had been his idea to play poker and her idea to play strip poker instead of poker for money. Much as he tried to disguise it, Nobatu had an air of superiority that Penny had decided to tackle. She'd deduced – perhaps incorrectly, given how easily he was enduring his nudity – that strip poker would accomplish her goal more easily than playing for mere money. He'd been wearing more garments than had at first appeared to be the case. There had been four of the richly embroidered red brocade outer garments, not two, as well as briefs, shoes, a number of medallions and, of course, the hat. Penny had only her Olympus-inspired toga dress, French-cut panties and high heels, which might have made Nobatu assume that the game was stacked in his favour. If that had been the case, he was dead wrong.

'I see that I am going to lose my hat,' he grumbled as he set down his cards, a pair of Jacks his only combination.

'Unless they changed the rules of the game while I was sleeping last night, I guess you're right,' said Penny, displaying her winning hand royal flush side up.

'You are astonishing,' he crowed.

'Thank you.' She flashed him a dazzling smile.

'I could play poker with you all day and well into the night. But I wonder if it would make a better player of me.'

'Probably.'

'You must have something like a knack or a talent with numbers, is it? Or the ability to judge people or read their minds, perhaps?'

'Yes, that must be it. I have ESP.'

'No, no, not to belittle your talent, pretty Penny. I am just having a very hard time learning poker. It is not like learning to speak another language or even learning how to be politic. More like learning an art, it seems to me, than a craft. But you cannot learn art and you can learn poker, or so I am told.'

'I think it's just a game, Nobatu. A complicated numbers game, yes, but, still, just a game. One that has captured the popular imagination recently, probably because of the large sums of money involved.'

'And now, with the Internet, everyone can play.'

'Sometimes I feel bad about that. There's an addictive component that makes Internet access to poker dangerous. It's like offering an alcoholic access to booze twenty-four/seven.'

'Yes, they say the brain patterns of the gambler actually mimic those of the drunk or drugged.'

'Really?' Penny regarded her host with some surprise. 'When do you have time to learn these things?'

'I have done a study of addiction, for personal reasons – not that I am an addict, but members of my family have been addicted to some things, from time to time. One of my friends has decided recently that he is a sex addict.'

'But not you?'

'No, not me.' Nobatu smiled gently at her. 'And I do not think you should feel complicit in the problems of the gambling addict any more than I should feel that I am contributing to the demise of the drunk every time I enjoy a glass of wine, or feeding the sickness of a sex addict when I make love.'

'I see your point.' Somehow Penny had expected that they would be interrupted again long before their poker game ended but here they were, alone, making conversation while one of them remained fully clothed and the other lounged behind a bit of tablecloth.

'You are curious,' he observed.

Damn. He'd seen where her gaze had wandered. Penny's cheeks reddened, even though it was maddening to the extreme to be the one who blushed in such a situation. 'I suppose I am.'

Nobatu rose, raised his hands to his head and ceremoniously removed his square hat, then placed it on the table. 'I admit I'm curious, too,' he said.

Penny looked him up and down. He was beautiful. His balls were two dark crinkled sacs, big and tight against the base of his midnight-coloured cock. She stood too. Two steps and she was close enough to inhale the musky smell of him, almost touching the tightly curled hair on his chest. 'How about all or nothing?'

'If I win, you will take everything off?'

Penny nodded. 'And if I win –'

Nobatu laughed. 'If you win, what? I am already entirely disrobed. It would seem that I have nothing to lose.'

'If I win, you perform a sexual favour for me.'

'I see.' Nobatu pondered this. His thick brows knit above his expressive brown eyes. 'Things have progressed quickly between us.'

'Yes,' agreed Penny, glancing appreciatively at his half-erection.

Nobatu let his right hand drop to caress his manhood. 'I can't imagine why I'm so sure that this hand will be to my advantage. Yet I am.'

'So, another hand?'

'Deal the cards! If you lose, you will disrobe and, if I lose, I will tend to your every whim. But I warn you, I am feeling extremely lucky.'

Penny dealt the cards. The first community card was quite decent, the King of diamonds. Her cards were good too, the Queen of diamonds and a nine in the same suit. She didn't bother to send Nobatu a tell, real or fake. He hadn't caught on to any of her signals, poor guy.

Nobatu glanced at his cards and then carefully stroked his eyebrows. Penny smiled inwardly. He fancied he had a good hand then, for the eyebrow stroke was his tell. She was going to have to play well to win and, whether he knew it or not, the stakes were high. There was something she'd always wanted to experience but had never had enough courage to request, not even from the adventurous Ray. If she won she would ask Chief Nobatu to service her in a way that she didn't dare even think about, not yet, lest she lose her concentration.

Penny banished her indecent thoughts and focused on the game at hand.

* * *

Victoria kept her gaze riveted on the television as she grabbed one of the brass posts at the end of the canopied king-size bed and hung on tight. She was naked. Her left hand was thrust between her legs, two fingers buried inside her while her thumb worked her joy button. She was close, so close. Embarking on this solo journey had been madness but she'd persisted until she'd tumbled past the halfway point. If she could keep her mind on the task at hand, she'd soon be lost in the foggy other-worldliness of orgasm. Yet, and perhaps this was the height of her perversity, the closer she brought herself to the brink, the more her thoughts swirled around her head, forming questions that pulled her in another direction entirely – towards sober contemplation of events.

'Bastard!' yelled the brassy blonde big-bosomed 'actress' in the porn she'd selected from the many X-rated titles available on her hotel TV. The woman had got herself into a few scrapes until finally she'd arrived at the place advertised in the story description – bound to a bed and helpless at the hands of her tormentor, a buff white male no more than 25 years old.

'Bastard,' muttered Victoria.

'You love it,' growled the man on screen.

'Prove it!' challenged the woman. She writhed on the bed, humping her torso up at regular intervals as if already engaged in the explicit sex that had yet to begin. He worked his way quickly between her legs and reached under her, grabbing her ass with both hands.

Victoria knew how much that would hurt her, right now, fresh from a good cropping. Veruschka hadn't spared the rod, that was for sure. The stripes were so tender they still felt as if they glowed, though she knew from a glance in the mirror on the wall opposite the bed that they did not. There were still thin livid lines criss-crossing her bumcheeks, and the cheeks themselves still blushed. It really would hurt if someone were to grab her flesh.

She gripped the post harder and rubbed herself faster. That was the beauty of this adventure into autoeroticism – the only things that would be done to her were precisely the things she chose to do and could do. She might take a few clues from the action on the screen, though, and now the man was humping the woman with a ferocity that made the woman writhe and moan.

Victoria moaned. In her mind's eye, she selected images from a repertoire that included dreams and literature and movies and life to add to what she saw on the screen. 'I'm going to come,' she murmured.

In the movie, the man pulled out of the woman and crawled up the bed to her face. He began smacking her face with the head of his cock. Victoria was shocked. What would that feel like, not to take an offered cock in the mouth but to be slapped, even lightly, with it?

'You want it, you know you do,' he said.

The woman turned her face and he smacked the other cheek with his cock. For a moment the hand between Victoria's legs faltered as she watched the screen. She couldn't climax to images of coercion, no matter how fake they might be, and these scenes skirted the edge.

The woman turned her face to his cock and started licking and sucking it wildly, obviously driven mad with desire by his dastardly behaviour.

Victoria closed her eyes, and began to pick up speed again. She had what she needed to take herself all the way. She imagined the heavy rubbery head of a hard cock smacking her across the cheek. Not like a hand might feel, not at all. Or would it feel similar?

'Mmm...' If she let go of the bedpost she'd be able to concentrate more fully on her orgasm but the tension in her arm was exciting, as if she were tied to the bed; as if Ray, after spanking her hard, had tied her to the post and then had the audacity to smack her face with his cock.

The woman on the TV screen moaned and Victoria pretended she wasn't alone, that Ray was there and with him another woman, a woman who was coming as she watched Ray use his cock to bring a flush to Victoria's face.

This time, when she sensed she was reaching the point of no return, Victoria reran the scene again, filling in a few more details to make it last. The fingers between her thighs moved quickly, elegantly, steadily towards climax.

Ray moved from the ass he'd freshly spanked to hover by Victoria's head. Victoria was bound to the bed; at least one arm was bound to the footpost of the bed so that she couldn't escape. She slid down the bedpost a little, so she'd really be in position for what she pretended was really happening.

Ray hovered by her face. From the corner of her eye she could see the blonde's eyes grow wide with shock. As if the spanking hadn't been harsh and sexy enough, now he smacked Victoria's face with his cock. It was incredibly humiliating! Victoria's moan was louder than the other woman's gasp. He did it again, smacking the other cheek, lightly but not so lightly that she couldn't feel it. He did it again, and she turned her face quickly in the hopes of catching the head of his cock with her mouth but he gently said, 'No.'

Once, when they'd been making love, she opened her eyes to see Ray above her, watching her face. He pulled out and, when she asked if something was wrong, he just shook his head. He slid up beside her head and started stroking himself, still watching her face. She'd been puzzled but said nothing, just watched as he brought himself to the brink of orgasm. 'Close your eyes, baby,' he said, 'it stings.' She did as she was told so she didn't see him when he came but she felt the warm spurts hit her forehead and cheeks.

She didn't know what to think. It felt good to please him and she knew from the gentle way he mopped her face and the warmth of his kiss that she had. He asked, 'Do you know why I wanted to come on your face?' and she replied exactly what she was thinking, not in a confused or upset tone, just in a very matter-of-fact way, 'Because it amuses you to humiliate me?'

From the catch in his voice as he replied, she knew her answer had surprised him. 'No, that's not it at all,' he said. 'It's because you're so beautiful.'

Victoria loosened her grip on the bedpost as the memory and the pornography and the way she was stroking herself and above all his voice, declaring her beauty as he claimed it in an unorthodox but powerful way, carried her over the edge and into orgasm.

'Jesus,' she groaned. She fell forwards on to the bed, capturing her hand between her body and the mattress and humping at it. Even the memory of him made her so hot she couldn't help herself; she had to ride through the first orgasm and on into another. 'Jesus,' she moaned again as another paroxysm gripped her. She kept her fingers moving, greedy for everything she knew her body could deliver. She stuffed her other hand between her legs and hurriedly stuck two more fingers deep inside. 'Yes!' she cried out, drowning out the noise of the TV with her victorious whoop. The last contraction rippled through her, leaving her spent.

Victoria groped among the bedcovers until she found the remote. She aimed it at the TV and pressed 'Off'. She didn't need to see the end of the video. She didn't need anything except Ray. And he'd promised to return.

'What is it?' asked Nobatu.

Penny was kneeling up on an armchair, her arms

crossed across the top of the back of the chair, the hem of her flimsy dress pulled up and tucked into her belt. If she'd stripped she'd have lost control of the situation but she needed her bottom to be bare for her fantasy to be acted out.

Nobatu's voice was muffled as he was behind her, his lips at the base of her spine. 'What is my tell?'

'It's not fair if I tell you.'

'Not fair to whom?'

'To your opponents, of course.' Penny shuddered as he laved her tailbone with the flat of his tongue. 'Plus it wasn't part of the deal.'

'You are complaining?'

'No,' she said. Penny sighed with delight.

'Good,' he said. 'I like you to be happy.'

'I am,' cooed Penny as Nobatu parted her cheeks with his hands.

'Tell me what you want.'

'I *did* tell you!' Penny had managed to stammer her request once. She really didn't want to have to repeat herself.

'Be specific, please, pretty Penny.'

'OK.' She felt his smooth face burrowing between her cheeks and then the delicate precise touch of the tip of his tongue against her sphincter. 'First, I want you to rim me. I want the tip of your tongue to run circles round and round and round until I can't stand it any more.' As she spoke, he complied, which sent shivers up her spine and made speaking all the more difficult. 'Then slowly spiral in. Can you do that?'

London on a sunny day became a blur of colour. The limousine was moving faster now, at Lonnie's request, and the breeze lifted Lonnie's heavy hair and made it stream behind her like a black silk scarf. They were on the way to the Tower of London.

To her disappointment, she'd discovered that, when she stood on the bench-seat as Ray had done, her head barely cleared the opening in the roof. Ray had fixed that by lifting her and settling her on his shoulders with his face nestled between her thighs. Her perch wasn't exactly precarious but it wasn't all that stable, either. For some, the awkwardness might have been detrimental to pleasure but for Lonnie it only added to it.

'Trust me,' Ray had said as he pulled her into position. He was strong and his big hands were very capable, so Lonnie did as she was told. His hands supported her by cupping her bottom, and his lips and tongue were inches from the bare flesh of her pussy. The way her legs were spread made even Lonnie feel exposed – which was just the way she liked it best.

Ray was running his tongue along her slit, just barely parting the lips, and he'd been doing just that for a few minutes now. It seemed from the languid way he was lapping at her that he was perfectly comfortable with her perch and in no hurry.

Lonnie waved to the pedestrians on the street, then hastily put both her hands back on the roof of the limo, for balance. The roof was warm to her touch and the sun was hot on her face, but the greatest heat was right at the sweet spot where Ray now lingered. He circled the dainty little bud with his tongue and then sucked it into his mouth.

For a moment Lonnie simply felt relief. At last, he was focusing on her clit. But almost instantly his steady attention to it became unbearably intense.

Lonnie wriggled a little, trying to escape the direct assault on her pleasure centre. Ray relented. Instead, he entered her with his tongue. It was a much more subtle feeling, allowing Lonnie to focus for a moment on what was going on around her, rather than what was being done to her.

There was a lady walking an obese dog, and a couple kissing at the top of the steps down to the Underground. There was a man staring at her, and another man who was too busy flirting with yet another man to pay her any mind. All around, people got on with their lives while she, in the centre, had a man at her centre making her crazy with lust.

He was back at her bud now, his tongue and mouth insisting on this exquisite torture.

'Ray,' she called down to him, 'I will come in seconds if you . . .'

Her words were lost to the wind and it didn't matter because she was already speeding past the point of no return. The first orgasm was always this way for Lonnie, quick and intense, and so as the contractions started to shudder through her she abandoned her protest and welcomed the pleasure. It soared through her body and she threw back her head, opened her mouth and let it sing.

Just as well because when she opened her eyes Lonnie saw that they were approaching the Tower of London.

Ray put his hands under her arms and lifted her off his shoulders and down. She wrapped her arms around him and curled up small in his lap.

'You come big for such a little thing,' he teased.

'I come many times over, too,' she said.

'I can't wait for that,' he said, as his hand wormed up her short skirt.

'Ray, I want to see the Tower. My friends are here and my minder is expecting me. Also I want to fuck in the Tower of London.'

'I don't know if we can do that. It's bound to be packed with tourists.'

'But that's what I want. I want us to fuck in the middle of a bunch of tourists. Right under the watchful eye of Lo Song. When you touch me it is the most exquisite torture, Ray, and it would be perfect to feel that way in the Tower. Because that is where people were tortured, once, right? You make me feel like a queen but I would just love to feel like a queen in a place where a queen was once imprisoned. Does that make sense?' Lonnie looked up at him, her glance hopeful, yes, but also challenging. She wondered if he were man enough to do as she requested.

'I don't think it's a good idea. Why don't we go back to the hotel?'

Lonnie's eyes became little dark disappointed slits in her face and her mouth turned down at the corners.

Ray began to hedge. 'Maybe it won't be too busy,' he said. 'If we could find a spot where we aren't likely to be arrested, maybe we could pet a little. There are some very steep spiral staircases. You could go up ahead of me and I'd get a delightful view up your skirt or maybe "cop a feel". Wouldn't you like that?'

'Oh fine then. Let's go,' she muttered. She slid off his lap and began pulling on her thong. 'Driver,' she called. The partitions between them were still up and Lonnie poked and pushed at the console like an errant child until both partitions were lowered. She could feel Ray's irritation at her display of pique and it fuelled her own irritation. Why couldn't he just play along? 'Driver, pull over please.'

When the limousine had stopped, she waited until Ray's door was open and he was standing on the pavement waiting to help her out. She slammed and locked it.

'Take me to the Plaza,' she barked, and the driver, obeying Ray's instructions to do as the lady wanted, pulled away.

Lonnie waved a cheery farewell to Ray as the car sped off without him.

Penny's head fell forwards on to her crossed arms. Her hands opened and closed, trying to clutch the tight fabric covering the back of the chair. 'Oh, Nobatu,' she groaned, as unself-consciously as if he'd been her lover forever instead of only for a few minutes. He was kneeling on a cushion, his face between her cheeks. His tongue was squirming its way into her, exploring her darkest tightest entrance. She pushed back a little, shamelessly trying to take him deeper inside.

He grunted his approval and for a moment they stayed still, connected to the fullest. He withdrew until he was almost free of her, then stabbed, his tongue stiff and insistent. He stabbed again, and again, taking her in a perverted miniature version of sex.

Penny's forehead was slick against the backs of her arms. As the weather had so suddenly become unseasonably warm and almost unpatriotically bright, Penny imagined the heat in the room might be set too high. But that was unlikely to be the cause of her sweat. The taut exertion of restraining herself from moving under the onslaught of sensations he was creating had set her temperature rising in a way that did credit to her nickname. 'Nobatu,' she moaned again. She wasn't interested in articulation. She might mutter 'It's too much' or 'I can't take any more' or even 'We shouldn't . . .' and she didn't want to give voice to what were little more than random thoughts. It *wasn't* too much and she *could* take more. Penny could hardly believe a stranger was orally sodomising her. It was so wildly exciting it seemed impossible, but part of the excitement came from the fact that she had made it happen. First, she'd let him pick her up in the hotel, then she'd beat him at strip poker and then – what thrilled her the most – she'd asked for something she'd always wanted!

Penny wasn't big on anal sex. It was just too overwhelming. Besides, she was never with anyone long enough, any more, to allow herself to be put in such a powerless position. A woman could get hurt! But this ... she'd always longed for this ...

Oh, it felt good to focus her formidable powers of concentration on his target and what he was doing to it with his tongue. So delicate. It was incredibly thrilling for what was, really, a very dainty sensation. Every little lick made the pit of her belly glow. She felt dominant, as if, because he was using his tongue and not something hard, he was the submissive and she was the one in charge.

This was the sort of shocking behaviour that she'd often imagined but never indulged in. Sure, she was 'The Fire of London' and she'd been a Montreal showgirl for a while during the wildest days of her youth, but the truth about Penny was that she considered herself a pretty good girl. She could count all her lovers on one hand – well, two hands at the most.

Nobatu's breath came in quick pants, hot against the sensitive skin of her inner cheeks. His tongue plunged into her again, then withdrew entirely. He rested his damp forehead against her hip. 'I want to take your ass,' he said.

Before she could respond, his hand was between her legs and his fingers had found her clit. The finger he slipped inside her pussy received a warm wet welcome. Penny moaned as her muscles involuntarily clenched, as if her body wanted to cling to the slim digit that had entered her.

'I will give you an orgasm you will take with you forever, pretty Penny. I promise. And I will never speak of this, to anyone. It will be our secret, forever, pretty Penny.'

His words were gently spoken, and she knew they were truly the words of a gentleman. His hands were superb, not so busy as to force her to come but obviously talented enough to take her there in time. The glow in her belly had become a fire.

Penny tilted her head so that she could see him over her shoulder. She wanted to say she didn't like sex that way but suddenly she wasn't so sure. His tongue had opened her up so that she could take more and, if a tongue had felt good inside her, wouldn't his cock feel fantastic? She licked her lips and opened her mouth to speak but no words came out. For a moment they listened to the sound of their panting breath while he fingered her.

'I would wear a condom and I would not hurt you.'

'It's not possible to do it without hurting me,' she protested.

'Of course it is. I simply take my time. So? May I?' He began kissing her tailbone.

Perhaps it was Nobatu's hand and lips that convinced her, or perhaps it was the promise he made, or maybe just the way he sweetly asked permission, but suddenly she knew it was exactly what she wanted. The word tripped off her tongue. 'Yes,' she whispered.

'You stay as you are,' he instructed.

For a moment Penny was alone in the room. She kept her face buried in her arms, as if to protect herself from what was imminent. She shuddered when she heard him return. In another moment she could feel him inches from her skin. Then he was entering her.

She gasped as he began to push his way inside. His mouth had made her wet and his tongue had opened her a little, but receiving his cock was a terrible thrilling shock. She gasped again, then bit her lip. If she spoke she would certainly protest that it was too much but it wasn't. She knew that. She could take it and she *would* take it.

'Am I hurting you?' he asked and she shook her head.

As soon as he could reach around her to finger her pussy, he did. Pain was transmuted by the instant pleasure his hand created as he rubbed and stroked her. It helped her stay brave until he was entirely inside. His fingers danced lightly on her clit, as his cock stayed still where it was buried inside her. It was a deep heavy sensation.

'So warm,' he murmured in her ear. He licked the beads of sweat from her temple as he withdrew slightly and quickly thrust inside her again, so deeply that she felt his pubic hair press against her cheeks. 'Is it hurting?' His pubes ground against her tailbone.

'I'm OK,' she said. She strained her head round to reach his and their lips met in a feathery light kiss before her head collapsed on her arms again.

Nobatu began thrusting rhythmically, but very, very slowly. In no time he'd smoothed the way for his entry, but that didn't make him pick up the pace at all. It must be agony for him, she thought. It certainly was sweet agony for her.

'Tell me,' he said, 'how you want my fingers.'

'Fingers are fabulous,' she moaned.

'Faster?' He rubbed her faster.

'Faster fingers are fabulous,' she moaned.

'Maybe harder?' He pressed his fingers harder against her slick clit.

'Oh baby, oh yeah . . .' She groaned. The lower half of her body was being pierced and stroked at the same time. She pressed her breasts against the back of the leather chair. Her nipples were so hard they indented the sleek fabric.

She was an arrow in his bow and suddenly she was soaring through the air.

'Ow, ow, ow,' she yelled. She raised her head from her arms and tilted her chin back, jabbing her nipples into the chair, and began to howl. The orgasm wasn't painful but the contraction that gripped her was so great she felt sure it must hurt. 'Owwwwwwwwww!' she howled as her body began to jerk at the mercy of her climax.

'Good!' Nobatu pressed himself against her, one leg bent at the knee on the cushion of the armchair and the other foot on the floor. He took her in short thrusts. Her spasms squeezed him, hard in the centre of her, and he groaned.

Penny dropped her head. The culmination of orgasm left her as limp as a marionette whose strings had suddenly been cut.

Nobatu slowed the pace of his fingers, though he kept one finger swiping slowly across her clit until her shuddering ceased. Then he gripped her hipbones with his hands and unleashed the full fury of his orgasm. He thrust into her three times, fast, then abruptly stopped pumping and pressed hard against her in a triumphant climax.

Penny stayed absolutely still, taking everything he had to give. He seemed to be coming in waves of bliss, judging from the deep moan he was emitting and the way he remained pressed against her. They were so tightly connected she could feel him begin to lose rigidity as he came.

'Good ...' she murmured. It was, too. She'd opened up to him so that what had seemed impossible became simple. After the fury of her orgasm it was marvellous to be the one who could make him moan like that. When she was young, she'd sometimes felt validated by the greatness of the man she was with but that had meant less to her in recent years. She was a woman now and women validated themselves. As it became obvious she was never going to need to rely on anyone but herself to get by, she'd been set free in more ways than financially. She no longer listed 'big' or 'powerful' in her mental list of traits a man needed to display in order to attract her. Perhaps, though, she still wanted him to be as 'good' as he was 'bad'. Anyway, Nobatu fit the bill and that included big and powerful and good and, certainly, bad.

When it seemed as if he were done, she shook her fiery mane to free the damp tendrils that were sticking to her cheeks. 'Nobatu,' she whispered one more time. He groaned and she felt him jerk inside her, one more time, before he slid free of her body and they were separate once again.

Victoria stood on the balcony of her hotel suite to watch the sunset. The sky was just beginning to turn pink, but it was already obvious that it was going to be spectacular, for London, anyway. Victoria felt blessed. It was as if the sunset had been arranged just for her last evening here, but at the same time its natural beauty made her feel utterly insignificant. Victoria, always one to enjoy a paradox, revelled in the contradictory feelings.

It was a pity she was alone, of course. No question about that. She'd napped and eaten and bathed and °dressed and still no Ray. The sunset champagne was well chilled in the bucket she'd brought out to the balcony table, along with champagne glasses and a bowl of strawberries.

She left the railing of the balcony and strolled over to the table to help herself to a berry. The champagne could wait another few minutes but then she'd have to drink it by herself or it wouldn't be sunset champagne any more.

The satin dress she wore clung to her every curve as

she took her strawberry back to the railing with her. She knew the bustier top of the dress accentuated her cleavage and made her waist even tinier than usual, which in turn accentuated the curve of her hips. She knew the blush colour suited her hair and skin. Her eyelids were dusted with emerald shadow, with gold shimmer slicked just below her brow. Her lips were painted with a darker stain than usual, a creamy dark-red wine colour, precisely applied using a lipstick that was so expensive it smelt good.

There'd been no need for underwear and her bum was too sore for it anyway. But she'd slipped on a pair of simple pale-pink leather sandals by Verna of Venice that had sexy little kitten heels. They were for Cuba, as was her dress, both a delicate rosy hue that matched the colour of the sky. The London weather had been so surprisingly unseasonable that she'd decided on impulse to debut them early. It was the first impulsive thing she'd done since she'd decided, some months ago, to lure Ray to her hotel room and convince him to join her on the trip. Victoria delicately bit into the strawberry. It felt good to enjoy the taste of the fruit and the sunset and the feel of satin against her skin and forget about Ray for a few minutes.

She'd called his room a half-hour ago and there'd been no answer. Since he'd left his cell phone in the suite when he'd gone running out some hours ago, she obviously couldn't contact him that way. What would she say, anyway? Goodbye?

In the grand scheme of things, her situation was enviable. If Ray didn't come back tonight, she'd leave for Cuba in the morning and never speak to him again. She'd promised herself all along that if he didn't choose to accompany her to Cuba it would be his definitive answer to her declaration of devotion, whether he admitted it or not.

There were plenty of other men, anyway. Perhaps Cuba had gigolos. She had money. Perhaps she would find a man, maybe a Cuban, maybe a tourist, but some man she could keep as her sex slave. While he pleased her, that's what she'd do; when he bored her, she'd dismiss him.

Or perhaps not. It's not as if she needed to pay a man to spend time with her. She didn't want to keep one, anyway, not with her money. Maybe she'd just flirt with men for the rest of her life. Maybe she'd make a game of it, seeing how much in love with her she could get them before she dropped them without a second thought.

That might not be much fun, though. She wasn't a sadist, at heart.

'Men,' muttered Victoria. She popped the rest of the strawberry into her mouth and sashayed back to the table to uncork the champagne, which was, of course, a man's job.

Penny turned the handle of the door to Ray's suite. Naturally, it was locked but, luckily, in the old-fashioned key-in-the-door manner not electronically. She knocked again but there was no answer. She glanced to her left and right to make sure she was alone in the hallway and then, using the ace of spades from the deck of cards she carried in her purse, she 'loided it open.

She'd tidied up and left Nobatu's room shortly after he'd paid his poker debt in the decadent manner she'd requested. He was expected at a state dinner and Penny'd been belatedly stricken by a bout of conscience. She *had* to find Ray.

He wasn't in his hotel room; she now knew that much for a fact. His clothes and shaving kit were still here, though, which meant he definitely intended to return.

Penny considered staying put until he arrived – that would really be a surprise! But it was likely he'd be spooked to find an old girlfriend lounging in his room, and that wasn't what she wanted at all.

A daybook lay open on his desk. It hadn't been written in since he'd scrawled the name of a trendy Italian restaurant and a time, eight p.m., on the page for Saturday. That didn't explain why he wasn't around on Sunday. Or did it?

There was an incongruous pink envelope lying amidst the masculine junk on top of his bureau. Penny pounced on it immediately. 'Victoria Ashe,' she read aloud.

The telephone rang. Penny hesitated for a moment, then picked up. 'Hello?'

'Hello,' said a soft surprised feminine voice.

'Victoria?' said Penny, still looking at the envelope.

'Yes.'

'Ray's not here.'

Three sharp knocks sounded on Ray's door. Penny's heart leapt up into her throat, its beat pounding in her ears. Sometimes, as in her present situation, she behaved like a bad person but in truth she really was a good girl. The proof of that was in how frightened she became whenever it looked like she might get caught doing something bad. She quickly cradled the telephone.

Silence. Penny thought she heard a muffled laugh. She waited another moment but whoever was at the door apparently didn't have a key or a way with a playing card, because the door remained shut.

Penny tucked the pink envelope into her bag and hurried across the room. She couldn't wait any longer. She had to get out. Carefully, Penny began to ease the door open.

* * *

Bai Lon was dog-tired. She leant against the door of her suite with her giant handbag on one upraised knee, rooting through it for her room key. After twenty straight hours of fun and going without sleep for a good ten hours before that, she was out of fuel. What she needed was a flashlight to plumb the depths of this bag! One of those miner's helmets with the attached light would be even better, so she could excavate the contents of this ridiculous (but so adorable) bag.

Lonnie was very surprised when the door to Ray's suite slowly began to open. She'd been sure that she would get back to the hotel long before he did. That's the only reason she'd knocked on his door in the first place, purely for the evil amusement she knew she'd get from discovering he wasn't there. She'd arranged to meet the Posse at the entrance to the Tower, which meant they'd have spotted Ray and descended on him. He'd been a favourite conference speaker among her gang and all the women knew he was single. They'd insist that he join them for a tour of the Tower or, at least, for a round of photos.

Lonnie would've giggled at the idea of her polite eager pals offering their camaraderie to a frustrated Ray Torrington if she hadn't been so weary. She was disappointed, too. Ray was probably stuck in the Tower right now, feeling very sorry that he hadn't agreed to her proposition. Serves him right. Since she was leaving Monday it was now pretty unlikely that she'd get to have sex in the Tower of London on this trip. By now Ray should've been willing to have sex on the buffet at his grandma's eightieth birthday party if it meant having it with the Hong Kong Bombshell.

Lonnie finally located her key and hastily slipped it into the lock. The last thing she needed was a tedious confrontation, so, in case whoever it was that was inching Ray's door open was actually Ray, she wanted to be ready. Lonnie reached in for the 'Do Not Disturb' sign on the inside doorknob of her room, ready to switch it to the outer one. Before she could, to her further surprise, a woman slipped out of Ray's room.

She was a tall attractive redhead, all dolled up for a night at the Forum, with a very guilty look on her face. Lonnie looked her up and down. Ray had good taste in women, but she already knew that.

'Hi,' she said. 'Ray is touring the Tower of London.'

'Oh,' said the redhead. 'That's right!' She snapped her fingers. 'I remember now! We were going to meet up for a bit but then our signals got scrambled and I couldn't remember if we were meeting here or – or there.'

A grin played across Lonnie's lips but she suppressed it. The obviously guilty woman should never have opened her pretty mouth but, now that she had, she couldn't seem to close it again. Lonnie let her bag slide down her shoulder to the floor; she might be here for a while yet.

'Is that a Balenciaga bag?'

'Yes,' said Lonnie, her voice warm with pride of ownership. 'It's the city arena motorcycle bag in sea foam.'

'Gosh. That must've cost a fortune.'

'I live in Hong Kong. I get everything for much less cost than you.'

'Really? Hong Kong. How fascinating. Anyway, I have to go.'

'Maybe I will see Ray later. Do you want me to mention you dropped in?'

'Oh, no – that's OK. It's no big deal. He's – we're – we're distant cousins, actually, very distant, he might not even remember me.'

'I think anyone would remember *you*.' To Lonnie's amusement, the redhead actually blushed. 'Why don't you come in my room and wait for him. We could have tea.'

'I – I have to go. Thanks anyway.' With some effort, the redhead closed her mouth firmly but still seemed rooted to the spot. It was only when the doors to the elevator opened that she seemed able to move. 'Nice meeting you. Bye!'

With that, she fled towards the entrance to the stairwell as fast as her strappy gold sandals would allow.

Lonnie laughed out loud. For someone supposedly hoping to visit her *cousin* Ray, the redhead had certainly vamoosed fast enough when the possibility of actually bumping into him presented itself! Lonnie zipped into her room and shoved the door shut. It was just as well the other woman had turned down her impulsive invitation to tea, as she really had no interest in talking to anyone at the moment.

Lonnie threw herself down on her bed and almost instantly fell into a deep well-deserved dreamless sleep.

Ray exited the elevator and stormed down the hall to Lonnie's room. Her behaviour was absolutely unacceptable. He'd come to the conclusion, in the cab over to the Plaza, that she was a brat looking for a spanking and Ray Torrington was just the man to give it to her. His palm itched to teach her a lesson.

'Do Not Disturb,' he read aloud. The bitch! He raised his fist to pound on her door but didn't. He was too damned angry to confront her at the moment. It was, suddenly, all too obvious what to do.

In his room, Ray quickly washed up. He packed his personal belongings into a valise and zipped his daybook and work-related papers into his briefcase. He was done with Bai Lon and the Housing Symposium and the Plaza hotel. For the first time, he allowed the pangs of conscience that he'd kept suppressed all day to surface. Victoria.

He'd been a fool to toy with her emotions for the sake

of a little nouveau pussy. Victoria knew who she was dealing with. She knew damn well he could be pushed too hard and too far and when that happened he could and would take a walk.

He remembered, now, that it *was* him who had dumped Victoria, and not the other way around, though he'd suffered the loss of her keenly. There had been someone else, before Cuba, he remembered that now, too. He'd shown Victoria that he would only take so much foolishness from any woman. Ray had taught Victoria not to mess with him and she'd learnt her lesson. Why on earth had he chosen to chase after a woman who needed to be taught the same tedious lesson when he already had Victoria waiting for him? Ray cursed his own machismo.

He glanced once around the room to be sure he hadn't forgotten anything and then departed. He was a man on a mission and there was no time to lose.

12

Victoria opened the door to her suite and stared. 'Do I know you?' she asked.

'Very funny. May I come in?'

Ray looked one part remorseful, one part weary and one part something Victoria didn't often see – angry. His valise and briefcase were evidence that he was here to stay. Victoria stepped aside to let him enter.

'You're just in time,' she said. 'I was about to cancel the evening's festivities.'

Ray set his stuff down inside the suite and grabbed her around the waist. When he kissed her, his mouth tasted like toothpaste.

'How was the sightseeing?' Victoria couldn't be blamed if a hint of sarcasm slipped into her tone. 'Did you like the Tower of London?'

'I did. My new friends have sent a photo to my cell phone – have you seen it, by the way?'

'It's right there.' Victoria had left his phone on the coffee table so he'd have to enter the suite to get it. Now, as he crossed the room to pick it up, she wondered if it were the only thing he'd come back for. But, if that were the case, surely he'd have left his luggage in the taxi.

Naturally, being Ray, he checked his messages first. Victoria watched, cool on the outside but waging a battle of emotions internally. She *must* be a masochist to stand by, in her own suite, and wait to see if anyone more interesting had been trying to reach him. She tried to make herself turn her back, and failed. 'The photo?' she said instead.

'Coming, dear,' he replied. If it irritated him to be prodded for proof, he was wise enough not to let her know. 'Here we go.' He handed her the phone.

She had to smile at the picture of big Ray surrounded by a lot of little Asians. 'Darling, it's delightful! Who are they?'

'They are some of my very young and very committed comrades in the movement to house humanity.'

'I'm so proud of you, Ray.' Victoria covered his face with kisses. 'I don't tell you because I think you must know, but I'm telling you now – I'm proud of you and what you do.'

'It's nice to be appreciated,' murmured Ray. He caught her jaw in his hand, stopping her from dispensing any more little kisses, and gave her one long slow kiss that left her breathless.

'Come to the balcony, Ray. You can still see the sunset over Green Park and the sky is blushing pink.' Victoria tugged on his hand. 'We have sunset champagne.'

'What's that?' Ray asked, following Victoria through the open French doors to the balcony.

'It's pink champagne. To match the sky. See?' Victoria picked up her glass from the balcony's edge. A pained look crossed Ray's face. 'What is it?'

'I shouldn't have left you the way I did. Here you are on your last night in London, drinking alone.'

'Silly.' Victoria was light-headed, and not only from the glass and a half of champagne she'd consumed. It was marvellous to know that Ray had been telling the truth. She'd been foolish to think that he'd been with another woman; as long as she'd known him he'd always been a workaholic. His politics may have driven them apart, once, but his willingness to abandon his own wants to serve the needs of a greater cause hadn't helped. Last time they'd been lovers she'd been immature enough to think that a hard-working man of conscience was a poor choice in a mate. Ten years later and she'd almost made that mistake again. Victoria was giddy with relief. 'You're here now and that's all that matters.'

'The colour of the champagne matches your dress.'

'Do you like it?' Victoria vamped for him. The skirt of her dress was mid-calf, fairly tight but with a slit up the left side. She dragged it up her thigh and the shimmering satin fell in folds to each side, exposing a white length of leg and the swell of her bottom.

'Show me,' he said.

'There's not much left to show, now,' she replied.

'I bet there is. Nursie gave you a wicked whipping.'

'She's very good,' murmured Victoria, tugging her skirt a little higher, until the welts on her left cheek were exposed.

Ray smiled. 'Beautiful, baby.'

'Thank you.' She pulled the skirt up until her left cheek was entirely showing.

'You were very brave.'

'Thank you.' Victoria leant on the railing, letting her skirt fall to one side so that her bare bruised bum was fully displayed to him.

Ray cupped her behind with his hands. 'Not even warm,' he moaned. 'I'm sorry.' He knelt to kiss her cheeks, first one and then the other. He traced the raised edges of the welts with his tongue.

'Mmmmm.' Victoria's pleasure rumbled from her throat like the purr of a cat. 'I like that sooooo much.'

'I can never get enough of you. My craving for Victoria is insatiable.' He nibbled the fleshy part of one cheek and Victoria shuddered.

'Maybe you should start a twelve-step programme for Victoria addicts,' she said.

'The rooms would overflow.' Ray stood up.

Victoria's dress fell back into place. 'I don't think so,' she said.

'I do. But I would always be the president of the club because my addiction would always be the worst.' Ray wrapped his arms around her and cuddled her from behind.

Victoria leant back against him. She rested one hand on top of his arm and raised her glass with the other. 'I don't think twelve-step programmes have presidents. They're run by the proletariat.'

'Oh. Well, good for them. This is perfect, isn't it?'

'Mmmmm.' Victoria sipped her drink again, and then offered the glass to Ray.

'No thanks,' he said. 'I had some earlier.'

'Oh?' Victoria frowned. 'I didn't know you could get champagne on tour buses.'

'I wasn't on a bus.' Ray's voice took on the sharp edge it always did when he felt that she was prying into his business.

'Still, champagne?' Victoria's voice had an accusatory tone.

'Kids these days. When they're not working for the world they're dancing and when they're not dancing they're drinking. It's impossible to keep up.'

'I bet. I wonder what they do when they're not working or dancing or drinking.'

'I wonder...' Ray loosened his grip. 'I enjoyed the show today, with Veruschka, but I would have enjoyed it a lot more if the three of us had ended up in bed.'

'I see. So, if she hadn't been a real nurse, you would have happily entered into a threesome?'

'Yup.'

'What about your champagne sightseeing tour?'

'I wouldn't have left for anything, not even sightseeing.'

'Then I guess it's my turn to apologise. I'm sorry.'

'I forgive you,' said Ray. 'I just think you should know that there are some things I haven't done in my life, and I intend to do them before it's too late. That's one of the reasons I'm hesitant about this trip to Cuba.'

'You don't think there are women in Cuba who would want to play with us?'

'I don't think you'd do it, Victoria.'

'Why? You think I'm a prude?'

'I think you're possessive. I don't want to be someone's possession.'

Victoria laughed shortly. 'I could never own you. I know that. I just want to be with you and, for some reason, that makes me unattractive to you.'

'I've never called you unattractive. You know how beautiful you are in my eyes.'

'But only when you're looking at me, Ray! You forget me the moment I'm out of your sight.'

'It's not that simple! Dammit, Victoria, I'm too tired for this.'

'I'm getting kind of tired of it myself.' There. She'd said it. Let him leave, if that's what he wanted to do.

Their eyes met. His were dark and hard. 'I've checked out of the Plaza. I was planning on spending the night here. Do you still want me?'

'I always want you, Ray. Maybe the one who needs the twelve-step programme is me, not you.'

'I think that would be one very lonely meeting.' He was poised for flight.

'I'm used to being alone.' Victoria sipped her drink. The bubbles in the glass had gone flat and the sun had set. She shivered. Being with Ray was like riding a roller coaster, and she'd never liked the cheap thrills that came from amusement-park rides. Then again, once she'd climbed on board she wasn't one to abandon the ride before it was done. Victoria had always been impulsive but she was wise enough to know that, much as she wanted to see him to the door and out of her life, she'd regret it forever if she did. So, though it cost her pride to do it, her next words were spoken in a gentle conciliatory tone. 'I don't know what we're arguing about. Do you?'

'Not really.'

'Why don't we rest? Darling, let's go to bed.'

13

Ray lay on the bed while Victoria fussed about, making him comfortable. After the tension on the balcony, she seemed to have come to her senses and once again she was as sweet as sugar. Maybe it was just as well they'd talked about her trip. He'd successfully dealt with the Cuban crisis, at least for tonight, and that was helping him relax. He'd been too damn busy for too damn many hours these last few days.

Victoria tenderly stripped him of his clothes and tucked him in between clean white sheets.

'Join me,' he cajoled.

'OK, but I'm not getting undressed. I'm not sleepy and this is the outfit I'm wearing for tonight's dinner.' She curled up on top of the sheets with her head on his shoulder. 'Besides, if I get in, we'll have sex again.'

'You think so?' He tousled her silky hair. 'Would that be so bad?'

'Rest, darling. Here, wear the blindfold. It'll keep the light out.'

'Silly,' he said.

'Please.' Victoria slipped the black leather blindfold over his eyes and the room was instantly pitch black. 'Doesn't it feel good?'

'You know, it does at that.' He wasn't kidding. The leather was soft against his eyelids and he began to drift off. He heard a shuffling sound and his hand shot out to grab her before she could get away, but she was right there. 'Did you hear that?'

'I didn't hear anything.'

'Don't you go anywhere,' he grumbled.

'I'll stay right here beside you. I promise.'

'I have plans for you, miss,' he muttered.

'Me too, darling,' she whispered. She may have spoken again but if she did he didn't hear her; he was already fast asleep.

Something wasn't right about the sky. 'Am I dreaming?' he said. He looked at his hands. His fingers were long, not wide like they should be, and there were eight per hand. He *was* dreaming.

Ray was a lucid dreamer, which simply meant he was sometimes aware that he was dreaming while he was asleep. He'd always been a lucid dreamer, but as he'd grown older he'd started to wonder about it. He didn't believe in soul travel or communing with spirits, but sometimes, reflecting upon his dreams, he'd wondered if he should. So, when he'd first found a name for this weird state of mind he'd been relieved. It turned out the dream state called 'lucidity' was much sought after by Buddhist monks and New Agers alike.

The difference between Eastern and Western approaches to lucid dreaming was fundamental. Buddhism treated it as a state of 'witnessing'. The dreamer watched the dream unfold without exercising his power to immediately change it into something more to his liking. That way he could explore his own unconscious mind. A Westerner, like him, was much more likely to engage in one of three dream activities once he realised he was dreaming: flying, chatting with the dead or, Ray's personal favourite, having sex.

Now that he'd come to awareness about his dream state, the situation was laughably unreal. What was wrong with the sky? It was pure pink, probably because, while the one sun was setting, two moons were on the rise. He was in coliseum-like ruins, alone. He might change that, shortly, but, then again, he might not. He'd had plenty of sex in the last while and when he woke up there'd be more. It was one thing to conjure up a movie goddess or a four-breasted sex slave from Venus or even his best buddy's pretty wife when he was alone. It didn't seem quite right to cop a quick wet dream in the company of a woman. There was a good possibility Victoria, sensitive as she was, would take it as an insult. And Ray knew Victoria was there. He could feel her body, right beside him like a good girl. If he really wanted to, he could reach out and touch her satin dress or satiny skin, but that would bring him back to consciousness.

Ray had no interest in 'talking to the dead'. He'd tried chatting with Lenin and it was fun but he knew he was really only chatting with his own impression of Lenin so it wasn't like he learnt anything new. Once was enough.

No, the thing to do with his present state of lucidity was to fly! Nothing was more liberating than lifting off into the air, like Superman without the cape, and either zipping straight up, towards those heavenly bodies, or skimming the surface of the terrain, feeling the brush of blades of grass on his face or the wet of a raging river inches below his horizontal speeding body.

In a split-second, Ray was hovering above the ruins, a solitary figure in an endless dream-pink sky. He tilted his head up to catch the sun's rays on his face. Bliss. He began to glide above the intricate but battered buildings below. A mistral of calm blew across him.

But he was being called from below. 'Ray,' whispered a woman's voice in his left ear. He mumbled a reply. A soft breath warmed his balls. 'Ray,' she whispered again.

He wasn't flying any more. Now he was lying face up on a big bed in the midst of one of the ruins. The rapid descent made his head spin.

'Oh, baby, oh yeah . . .' she whispered. He felt his cock stir with recognition though his mind was a blank. And how, if she was whispering in his ear, was she blowing on and now flicking her tongue at his dick?

'Am I dreaming?' He spoke with difficulty, the words as thick as oatmeal in his mouth. He raised his hands to look at them but he couldn't see an inch in front of his face.

The lips that circled the head of his cock had to be Victoria's. Her hand tickled his balls, making them tighten in their sac. Another hand steadied his shaft so that the mouth – Victoria's mouth – could begin a steady descent.

Feathers tickled his ear, a sensation that was oddly familiar. No, not feathers – a tongue – it was the tip of a tongue that was exploring the rim of his ear, just the way he liked it. She giggled, a light little sound, not throaty, like Victoria. Wet fingers circled his left nipple, then his right. Another hand slid between his ass and the mattress, against the flat of his left buttock. Impossible.

He opened his eyes. Black. He felt her – Victoria – gently coaxing him to erection with her mouth. Then he heard her – *not* Victoria – whisper in his ear again and he knew he was awake.

'Who are you?' he whispered. He raised his hand to his blindfold but she caught his wrist, holding it lightly in fingers that were longer than Victoria's.

'Don't you remember me, Ray?'

Damn! He almost blurted out Lonnie's name but stopped himself in time. It couldn't possibly be her, anyway. He wasn't thinking straight, and no wonder, with four hands and two mouths teasing him.

He knew he wasn't but just in case he said, 'Am I dreaming?' The words came out easily this time.

'Silly!' Victoria cupped his balls with two hands, one

in each palm. 'You're wide awake now!' She ran her tongue up the underside of his rigid shaft.

'Veruschka?' Ray knew the accent was all wrong but it was the only possibility that made any sense. Both women laughed.

'I'll give you a big hint – I'm "The Fire of London".'

'That's a *huge* hint!' protested Victoria. But when she saw that it meant nothing to him she gave him another clue. 'Your old flame The Fire of London has come to shed her lovely light on us, Ray. Are you pleased?'

'Very,' he replied. He let the sensations ripple over him, revelling in the fact that this was no figment of his imagination. Somehow, Victoria had arranged to make his dream come true.

'Only if you say my name, though,' the other woman said sternly.

She had an English accent. Old flame? What was it he'd felt in his ear when he'd first become aware of her presence? Feathers?

'The showgirl! From Montreal!'

'Good, but not good enough.'

'How –'

'Not how. *Who*.'

He tugged his hand free of hers but didn't raise the blindfold. He didn't need to see her; he could remember her now, the feathers, the red hair, the way she'd rimmed his ear and – of course! The words she said when she came: 'Oh, baby, oh yeah'; that breathy little sigh that made him want to go into real estate or public service or something, anything so he could buy her a house and keep her in it forever.

'Penny!' he shouted, tearing the blindfold from his eyes.

'In the flesh!' she crowed.

Her face was inches from his. She was wearing something filmy and white that showed off her slender body and made the most of her cleavage. He remembered rubbery nipples that blushed from pink to scarlet when she got excited, and a fragrant flame-coloured bush. 'How –?' he began.

Penny nodded towards Victoria, who, kneeling between his legs, clapped her hands with glee. 'Everything's gone exactly as I'd planned!' Victoria cried, her voice exultant.

'But –' he stammered.

'Questions later. Kiss me first!' Penny cried.

Ray put his arm around her shoulders and pulled her close. Their lips met for the first time in too many years. The kiss was sweet, pleasantly familiar, then more intense, something altogether new.

Victoria's tongue tasted his shaft again. She wormed her way to the head and took it in her mouth. For the first time in his life, Ray kissed one pair of lips while a second pair of lips pleasured him. It was even better than he'd dared to dream it would be.

He broke the kiss and wriggled to a sitting position, freeing himself from Victoria's mouth in the process. 'What the hell is going on?' he demanded.

14

They'd anticipated this. Penny let Victoria lead, since this whole thing had been Victoria's idea in the first place. She poured the champagne while Victoria sat back on her heels and filled him in.

'Penny and I met shortly after I arrived in London, about four months ago,' she began. 'I was still living on the estate in Hampshire, settling Gordon's affairs. One of our charities – I mean one of the charities that Gordon and I contributed heavily to – invited me to a charity poker event. I went and over the course of the evening Penny and I got to talking and somehow or another –'

'We talked about Canada.'

'That's right, I told you I was Canadian and you told me you'd been a showgirl in Montreal!' recalled Victoria.

'I certainly did not!' Penny said in a flustered voice. She took a sip of the glass of champagne she was serving Victoria before handing it over.

'No, you certainly did not. But you did say you'd lived in Montreal a lifetime ago.'

Ray took the glass Penny offered him and gulped, saying nothing. His eyes said it all, as he glanced from one woman to the other.

Penny knew she looked good. After her liaison with Nobatu, she'd freshened up in his palatial bathroom before speeding over from the Plaza in a taxi. There'd been nothing for it, she and Victoria decided, but to wait for Ray. She stretched her legs. It had been cramped in the wardrobe but the look on his face made the whole thing worthwhile.

Victoria couldn't stop smiling. She seemed awfully sure that Ray was going to relax. 'We started talking about naiveté,' she continued, 'you know, innocence lost? And your name came up.'

Ray sputtered. 'So you said, "Do you know Ray Torrington?" and you said, "Yes"?' He nodded from one woman to the other.

'Basically,' Penny agreed. 'Victoria said the first time her heart was broken was when a man she'd loved *intimately* abandoned her to go to Cuba and I said, "Fancy that, me too!" And *then* she said, "Do you know Ray Torrington?" and I said, "Yes."'

'I knew it. So now you two are going to exact some kind of terrible revenge on me?'

'Nothing of the sort, darling,' Victoria said in a soothing voice. 'We kept in touch by email until I read about the Symposium on Housing and I thought, I bet Ray is coming to town. And I was right! So we got together.'

'*That's* when Victoria suggested we surprise you, first with her and then with me. Surprise and double surprise!' Penny gently bit into a big red strawberry. She leant across Ray's left leg with the berry between her teeth, offering the exposed half to Victoria. Victoria delicately nibbled the berry until it was gone and her lips were on Penny's. The kiss was sweet and girly gentle.

Both women sat back again, Victoria between Ray's legs and Penny by his side on the bed. When they saw the excited worried look on Ray's face, they both suppressed giggles.

'That's all there is to it then? A fun-filled night with Ray?' He still sounded leery.

'Not all,' Victoria reminded him. 'There's the trip to Cuba, too.'

'That's right.' Penny nodded in agreement. 'But you don't have to decide about that just yet. All we want right now is for you to tell us what you want.'

'Anything?'

'Uh-huh.' Victoria answered first. She drained her glass and handed it back to Penny. Victoria slowly elaborately licked her crimson lips.

Penny giggled and then copied her.

'Well, I think you know what I want, right? I mean, I want – what do I want?' Ray rubbed his face with his hand. He glanced from one woman to the other. 'I want to watch you pleasure each other. Can you do that?'

'Of course, darling. We've been practising!' cooed Victoria.

They had, too. From the first, Victoria had been astonishingly frank. She'd been a terrible poker player so she hadn't lasted long in the tournament, but during the dinner portion of the event they'd been seated at the same table. While the men rambled on about poker, Penny and Victoria had struck up a conversation that had quickly become more intense than Penny would ever have thought possible. At the time she'd supposed that Victoria's recent widowhood had forced her emotions to the forefront but she'd since learnt that that was the way Victoria always was – intense. Not in an energy-sucking way, though. Victoria had invited Penny inside her intensity, so that she too could experience life as clearer and bigger and more important than she'd imagined. That included friendship. Though they'd known each other less than a year, Victoria was the first real girlfriend that painfully shy Penny had ever had.

It was quite possible that even if they hadn't had Ray in common they might still have ended up exploring their mutual bisexual curiosity. But it wasn't until they'd known he was coming to town that they'd met for their first night of fun and frolic. It hadn't been hard at all.

Penny giggled out loud. That was exactly the thing that was so appealing about being with another woman. Everything was soft and sweet and pretty, even parts that she'd have thought would be too weirdly similar to her own parts to be alluring. All it took was a sip of champagne and a giggling kiss and before either of them had known it they'd been all over each other. The fact that they'd never done such a thing before made them giddy. (Well, Penny had spent a weekend with a lesbian once, back when she'd been in her experimental phase, but that had been different. She'd been passive, letting her more experienced partner guide her. And afterwards there'd been some nonsense about love and such that had left her feeling guilty, so she preferred not to think of it at all.) With Victoria, it had been a totally different experience – both women were equally active participants. Victoria had been as eager as she was and even more committed to the plan. Penny knew that this time she'd have no regrets.

They kissed, both pairs of lips eagerly parting. Penny yielded to Victoria's tongue as it wiggled between her teeth and into her mouth. Victoria's sweet taste was intoxicating. The knowledge that an obviously entranced man was watching them made shivers run up and down Penny's spine. God, it was fantastic! She eagerly met Victoria's tongue with hers and they twined their tongues together, neither woman withdrawing until they were both gasping for breath.

Ray blinked. It was possibly the first time he'd blinked since he'd discovered Penny in the bed. He still seemed a bit dazed but the tense way he'd held his body was beginning to loosen. For the first time, a smile played across his lips.

'For me? You did all this for me?' His voice was incredulous, but pleased, nonetheless.

'Uh-huh,' said Penny.

'I'm impressed.' Ray nodded at Victoria. 'Well done, Beauty Puss.' She preened under his approving glance.

Penny fought off a tinge of envy; she was here for reasons that were much less acute than Victoria's. This was something new and exciting to do, yet much safer than an encounter with strangers or, at least, so she'd thought until this morning. She knew the relationship Ray had had with Victoria had been longer and more all encompassing than the brief time she and Ray had enjoyed together. If anyone was going to suffer the pangs of jealousy, it might be Victoria or maybe even Ray, but Penny immediately determined that it was not going to be her.

'It was Penny that hid in the closet, not me,' Victoria said magnanimously. Ray stroked Penny's ear, then followed the line of her cheekbone to her jaw with his finger.

'My shiny new Penny,' he said. She felt the warmth of his approval bathe her in a delightful glow. 'Hiding in the closet just to surprise old Ray.'

She'd done plenty more than that but she saw no reason to let him know she'd 'loided the lock to his hotel room and rifled through his belongings. Penny was adept at dismissing discomforting thoughts and she dismissed this one post-haste.

'I got here a few minutes before you did and Victoria and I decided you'd be weary after – after sightseeing, so I just slipped into the wardrobe and waited for you to fall asleep.'

'I stayed right beside you, Ray, just like you told me to,' continued Victoria, 'and once you were asleep Penny tiptoed across the room and joined us on the bed.'

'We didn't even giggle, not out loud,' said Penny. Both women giggled at this, the laughter they'd stifled earlier erupting to the surface now that it was safe.

'You're both clever and beautiful and delightful and desirable and – and very, very good,' said Ray. 'Please, continue. Show me how you play.'

Penny closed her eyes as Victoria's hand went to her chiffon-covered breast. It was still odd to feel long nails and fingers more slender than her own touch her in such an intimate place. Penny slid the metallic strap at her left shoulder down her arm, baring her breast. The tongue that delicately flicked her nipple and the gentle lips that sucked it until it tingled were entirely female, but the pleasure they elicited was as great as any a man had ever drawn from her.

Penny arched her back. She and Victoria had practised poses, too, and this was one of them. The idea of creating a tableau of their passion had always been forefront in their minds – at least, once they'd concluded that they were very capable of being truly passionate with one another. She stole a glance at Ray.

Ray punched a pillow behind his head and stretched his legs out on either side of Victoria. His face had such an incredulous expression on it that in another context it might have seemed comical, but in this context it was entirely appropriate.

Things were unfolding exactly as planned. And why not? After all, she and Victoria knew Ray just as well as he knew them, and now they knew each other, too. The relief of getting past the planning stage and finally into the event itself was profound. Penny could have melted into a puddle of pleasure just at that, but this – the woman at her breast who was now nudging aside the chiffon that covered her other breast and claiming it, too, with her mouth, and the observing man, his pleasure equally evident in his eyes and the hardening of his manhood, *this* was bliss.

The golden crown of Victoria's head bobbed from side to side as she teased one nipple and then the other. Penny ran the nails of one hand up the back of Victoria's neck and grasped a handful of hair. 'Mmm...' she moaned. She closed her eyes, sinking further into the sensation, then immediately opened them again. The situation was too exotic to shut out, even for a moment.

'Your mouth is so sweet,' she cooed. They'd determined to keep the patter going between them because Ray was such a fan of pillow talk. Victoria glanced up and Penny saw gratitude in her eyes. It made her heart melt. She stroked Victoria's cheek with her other hand. 'Your skin is so soft, Victoria,' she murmured.

Victoria was on all fours, her knees between Ray's but her hands on either side of Penny. Ray reached down to tug the skirt of her satin dress up until her bum was exposed. 'It's not all that smooth here, at the moment,' he said. 'See, Penny.'

Penny's dark-blue eyes widened at the sight of Victoria's bruised behind. This was something she hadn't been warned about. 'Ray, you brute,' she exclaimed. The marks were truly shocking.

'I didn't do it, Nursie did. Do you know Nursie?'

'I've heard about her but we've never met.' Penny knew Victoria liked it rough, sometimes, but she hadn't realised until now exactly what that meant.

'Later, I'll spank you so your bum matches hers,' said Ray, rubbing the marks that crisscrossed Victoria's exposed flesh, eliciting a moan.

Victoria shot Penny a pleading glance. 'Thank you, Ray,' murmured Penny. They'd discussed Ray's dominant nature but only in general terms, and now Penny saw why. Sure, Ray had given her bum a few smacks from time to time when they'd known each other in Montreal, but, perhaps because he'd been nursing a broken heart, he hadn't taken it any further. Obviously, his taste for the rough stuff, like Victoria's, ran a lot deeper than she'd thought.

This was going to be even more of a challenge than Penny had imagined, especially since she'd already entertained a back-door visitor earlier in the day. She shuddered. For the first time since she'd greeted Ray, she wondered if she were up to the challenge.

The only way to dispel her sudden reticence was to delve deeper into the experience. Penny grabbed Victoria's shoulders and dragged the other woman up to her mouth. Again, they kissed passionately. This time Penny refused to release Victoria when they relinquished each other's mouth. Instead, she fell back on the bed, taking Victoria with her.

Victoria stretched out on top of Penny. Her movements were delightfully feminine. Ray moved too, probably turning on to his left side so he could observe them more closely, but Penny didn't so much as glance at him. How often, after all, does the performer look directly at the audience? She needed to keep her focus and for that she needed Victoria's satin-sheathed breasts pressed against hers and Victoria's delicate scent filling her nostrils. She needed to hump up and feel nothing harder than satin rubbing chiffon and, beneath that, skin rubbing skin. It was astonishing how sexy the absence of a cock could be.

Victoria slid down Penny's body, using her hands to drag the chiffon dress down with her. As Penny's bright bush emerged from beneath the delicate material, all three of them moaned. In another moment, Penny was naked except for her heels. She arched her back and bent her legs at the knee so that now Victoria was kneeling between them, gazing with as much admiration at the pink split lips as she'd shown earlier at the sight of Ray's cock. Penny didn't need to look at Ray to know he, too, was delighted with the sight. Either the champagne they were drinking had been laced with spirits or she was getting drunk on approval. She tilted her pelvis as an invitation to Victoria to continue admiring her from a closer point of view.

Victoria dipped a fingertip into Penny and raised it to her lips. 'You're wet,' she said, licking her finger.

'Give me some,' said Ray.

Victoria dipped her finger again, lingering between Penny's labia, coating her finger with the juices that were beginning to pool there. Then she leant across Penny to proffer the slick finger to Ray.

The sight of her décolleté inches from Penny's nose inspired Penny to lean up on one elbow so that her face was buried between Victoria's breasts. Victoria held her position as Ray sucked her finger and Penny lapped at her cleavage.

Soft. So soft, these breasts, each one easily twice the size of Penny's. Someone, probably Ray, unzipped the top of Victoria's dress so that the bustier-type bodice loosened and Penny could burrow deeper between the mounds of white flesh. Her lips sought Victoria's nubby pink nipples. If her breasts were twice the size of Penny's, her two nipples together couldn't match one of Penny's for size. Penny already knew this but it always came as a bit of a shock to her. Or perhaps the source of the shock still lay in the contact of her tongue on another woman's nipple. It was tiny, like the buzz from static electricity, subtle but still surprising.

The tip of her tongue slithered over the areola of Victoria's right breast and flicked against the nipple. Penny's mouth and nose were sealed by satiny breast flesh for a second. She heard the sound of a zipper again and the bodice of Victoria's dress fell open. The soft breast flesh caressed Penny's cheeks.

When she glanced up, she saw that the pupils of Victoria's dreamy green eyes were dilated. She was enjoying this every bit as much as Penny was. Penny grabbed one of Victoria's breasts with each hand and squeezed them. If Victoria liked the rough stuff, maybe she could oblige. Victoria moaned.

Satin glided down Penny's leg as Victoria's dress was tugged off her body. The only material between them now was a thin layer of chiffon, though, like Penny, Victoria still had her heels on.

She could hear Ray slurping at Victoria's finger. He was obscene. They both were. Penny determined she wasn't going to be left behind in that department. She humped up, capturing Victoria's thigh between her legs. This was what girls did, they'd discovered, to bring each other off. They found a hard place somewhere on each other and rubbed against it, clit against bone-covered flesh. It felt damn good.

She was wet all right; she could tell from the way the chiffon trapped between them started clinging wetly to her. God, it was like nothing else! She tossed her head, her lips grazing one of Victoria's pendulous breasts and then the other.

Victoria hastily snatched her finger from Ray's mouth so she could balance herself above Penny. She slid down a bit, so that Penny was now humping one of her hipbones. Even better. Penny grunted with approval and humped up harder. It was good, so good, to finally have something, anything, hard against her. She rubbed Victoria's nipples with her thumbs so that her partner, too, might feel something hard against her flesh.

They were both panting now. The sound filled her ears. For another moment they humped wildly but then Victoria pulled free. 'Wait!' cried Penny. She'd wanted to keep going, faster, harder, until her clit was as hard as a little prick and it would be hard flesh against hard flesh, surely to be followed by release.

'Slow down,' crooned Victoria. To Penny's disappointment, Victoria dismounted. She knew Victoria was right, though. Nothing need be rushed. She needed to savour the moment like a bride must, at her wedding reception, when the hard part is over and the rest of the evening stretches before her as one long well-organised night of pleasure.

Penny saw that Ray's big thick cock was rigid, though it hadn't been touched since the two women had begun to frolic. He had both hands around his champagne glass, probably to make sure he didn't touch either himself or them. Obviously, though he was excited, Ray was in no hurry, either.

Victoria stripped Penny of her chiffon garment so that both women were naked except for their heels. It had been Victoria's idea to strip, because Ray was a nudist, but leave their heels on, because Ray was a perv.

It was true, Victoria knew him much better than Penny ever had. Penny had Victoria's assurance that there'd be no jealousy in her green eyes if Ray enjoyed Penny as much as they anticipated. Still, it must be difficult for Victoria, who'd spent a lot more time weeping into her pillow over the man than Penny ever had.

As if in need of courage, Victoria paused to sip her champagne. Penny caught and held her glance. She didn't want to give voice to her concern by asking out loud if Victoria was OK. At the same time, she had promised herself that if it got weird she'd get out.

The answer in Victoria's eyes was clear. She smiled an odd little closed-lip smile, but the reason for that became evident a moment later when Victoria straddled Penny's face in the sixty-nine position and Penny felt the effervescent tingle of champagne filling her. Another surprise! One that guaranteed Penny her partner was more than fine; she was *loving* it.

Penny extended her tongue so that the tip grazed Victoria's blonde bush. It was different from Penny's, the hair so fine and pale, but beneath it her tongue found pink lips and a tiny pink button that were similar to her own. Of course, she'd only tasted her own juices where they'd lingered in the mouth of a man, so Victoria's intimate flavour had been a new one to her tongue the first time they'd enjoyed this position. She'd discovered she liked the subtlety in taste and texture, so unlike a man's ejaculate. She'd also discovered she could use her mouth to make those juices flow, and she liked that, too.

Liquid dribbled into Penny's mouth and she realised Ray must be pouring champagne down the curve of Victoria's bum so that she, too, could drink from Victoria while Victoria drank from her. Victoria was slurping greedily at the pool of champagne she'd squirted into Penny, and Penny likewise obliged.

Of course, she'd sixty-nined with a man before, but, this time, though she was the one on the bottom, she had no fear of being gagged by a cock thrust too deeply into her throat. She found she wanted to be engulfed by the intricate shell-pink flesh that still hovered an inch or so above her mouth. Penny grabbed Victoria's ass cheeks, eliciting a squeal from the other woman, and pulled her closer. Now she could stab her tongue into Victoria and feel the soft walls surround it. Astonishing that this tight canal could open to accommodate a cock, especially one as big as Ray's. But it would, as would hers, now splayed obscenely open to welcome Victoria's mouth.

'God,' breathed Ray. That might have been funny, because she and Victoria had talked about how Ray the atheist liked to say 'God!' when he came and here he was saying it when he wasn't even close to orgasm. Unless, that is, Ray could come without being touched, which she doubted.

But Penny was far from the giggly girl she'd been when Ray had first discovered her in the bed. The sound of his voice was a reminder, as if she needed it, that she and Victoria were on display as they pleasured each other.

Penny groaned. Her clit was a pinprick of heat, the coal at the heart of the fire that was starting to flicker outwards, spreading warmth. Victoria's clit had swollen and become hard, like a little seed. That and the wetness that flooded Penny's mouth even though Ray was no longer pouring champagne told Penny that her ministrations were having the same effect on Victoria that Victoria's were having on her.

Though they'd both expected Ray to take his time, they'd anticipated that he'd be so overtaken by lust at this point that he'd intervene, but that was not the case. It didn't matter, though. Penny knew if she and Victoria kept this up much longer she, at least, would climax. She tried to tear her attention away from the immense heat that was building in her groin so she could focus on the tongue fucking she was giving Victoria. She gripped Victoria's ass harder with her hands, getting fistfuls of tender flesh. She felt the ridges on each cheek with her fingertips. Mmm. Warm pussy juice was leaking out the corners of her mouth. She tilted her head, enough of an action to take her lips from the centre of Victoria's slit to the top, where her clit seemed to positively pulse with need. She sucked it into her mouth and Victoria stopped grinding. Penny held Victoria captive but then Victoria dipped her head again and now held Penny captive in exactly the same manner.

The fire in Penny's groin shot white hot flames through her belly and higher, into her breasts and her lips and out through her tongue. It was going to happen, she knew that now. She wanted to take Victoria along but, either way, it was going to happen in another moment. On either side of her head, Victoria's thighs tensed and a sense of triumph rushed through Penny. She wiggled her face deeper into Victoria's pink centre, so deep she could feel the silky skin of the inner lips surround her mouth. Divine!

She'd known she was close but the moment had been suspended – like a long string of pearly sex juice – for so long that when it broke it came as a shock. Penny groaned into Victoria, the sound amplified in her ears so that all she could hear was her own desperate acquiescence to pleasure.

The first spasm rocked up her so that her cunt bumped against Victoria's teeth. Dimly, she was aware of Victoria's hands gripping her thighs, and then she heard the soprano trilling of Victoria's voice competing with her own sustained groan. The wet flesh pressed against her face contracted as if it would capture her mouth in its grip. For a moment they formed a continuous current, from mouth to cunt to mouth to cunt, and it held them for so long it was almost unendurable. Then Penny was jerking beneath Victoria and Victoria was grinding down hard on Penny's face. They groaned into each other, like obscene throat singers trying to draw music from each other's cunts instead of their mouths.

Sparks ignited. Penny was riding a rocket aimed straight up but every few seconds the rocket stopped, shuddered, jerked like it was out of gas and then reignited and sped higher, ever higher. Her mouth moved automatically now, sucking the clitoris it held fast. The sky burst into view, studded with stars.

Penny's voice rose to a muffled scream as her last spasm, as intense as the first, left her floating on a cloud.

Victoria writhed above her and Penny caught and held Victoria's engorged clitoris with her lips, working the tip of it with the tip of her tongue. 'Come on, girl,' she silently encouraged the shuddering blonde above her.

'You're such a hot little slut, Victoria.' Ray's words sounded harsh but the admiration in his tone made it clear they were meant to help, not hinder. 'Show me what a bitch you are, baby. Let your bitch lover bring you off.'

Victoria moaned. Suddenly, Penny's busy mouth filled with liquid but this time it wasn't champagne. She was so surprised she almost turned her face away but just in time she realised what was happening. Victoria was squirting! It tasted like jasmine-infused water and there was so much of it Penny found she had to swallow, and then swallow again. Jesus! This had never happened when they'd rehearsed. Penny felt she had no choice in the matter. To turn away would be to reject the other woman's offering and that would upset any woman, never mind one as sensitive as Victoria was. Besides, it wasn't so bad; it wasn't as if she were drinking pee. In fact, it was damned exciting! She must be awfully good at cunnilingus to make her lover squirt! Penny squirmed with excitement and pussy juices streamed from the sides of her mouth. 'Mmm...' she moaned, letting Victoria know everything was OK. She kept doing what she was doing, alternately swallowing and licking until Victoria stopped grinding and madly squirting and groaning above her.

15

Through the haze of euphoria that enveloped Victoria she dimly became aware of two things. One – Penny was gasping for air beneath her. Two – Ray was on the move.

She rolled off Penny and landed on the bed between them.

He pushed the damp tendrils of hair from her cheek. 'Beautiful, baby,' he pronounced. He kissed her full on the mouth, his lips and tongue eager for the taste of – of her? Or of Penny? Sure enough, after allowing her to bathe in his approval for all of five seconds, he was clambering over her to get to 'The Fire of London'. Of course, in kissing Penny's mouth he would taste her intimate juices, too. Either way, she won.

Ray stopped kissing Penny's mouth and started working his way down her body. Victoria realised Penny was looking at her. The two women were face to face for the first time in a while. Victoria blushed. 'I squirted,' she whispered.

'I noticed,' Penny replied with a grin. 'You taste like sugar water, because you're so sweet.' Incredibly, Penny blushed as well.

For a moment, the two women were connected with an intensity far beyond the sixty-nine connection they'd just experienced. Penny groped for Victoria's hand and held it as Ray buried his face between Penny's thighs.

Victoria gripped Penny's hand as Penny began to moan. She had engineered all of this with the precision of a clockmaker, carefully setting every cog and wheel in place so that now the three of them were together in a king-size bed with champagne and strawberries and linen sheets and, most incredibly, each other. It was no surprise to Victoria that the first woman Ray truly tasted once the ménage had begun was Penny. After all, he'd already tasted Victoria plenty over the last 24 hours. Still, she hadn't squirted with *him*! Shouldn't he want to taste her sugar water himself?

Victoria almost laughed – she was too twisted for her own good. She should be thrilled – she *was* thrilled – that Ray was responding as she'd hoped. The next few hours would be mind-blowing, at least as wild as what had just taken place. Maybe she'd squirt again, though she didn't think she had that much liquid left inside. Of course, she wouldn't have thought she'd had that much in the first place. She wished she could have seen the rivulets of juice that had streamed out the sides of Penny's mouth once it was full to the brim. Where did it come from? Was there more? Could she and Ray make Penny do it too?

'Have you ever –?' Victoria began, but Penny's attention was elsewhere.

Victoria leant up on her elbow, though she continued to clutch Penny's right hand with her left. That way, the three of them were connected, even if, for the moment, the action didn't include her. Ray sure seemed focused on Penny. Victoria should be glad, too, as she needed a moment after her orgasm and she imagined Penny might, too, although, from the sounds the other woman was making, perhaps not.

Somehow when she'd been planning this she hadn't expected to have a moment to think and she hadn't ever imagined that she might start thinking about Ray, fresh from the end of his love affair with her, finding solace so quickly with this Titian-haired beauty. Victoria had buried herself in her studies and received her Masters degree that spring, but so what? After all, she hadn't done much with it, while Ray and Penny, with much less schooling, had both accomplished plenty.

Ray was licking and kissing his way from Penny's wild patch of bright-red pubic hair up the pale skin of her belly. 'I remember you,' he announced, obviously addressing Penny. He tickled and licked her belly button with the same eagerness he'd shown when tonguing her pussy.

How was it that Victoria had not considered, during the careful planning stage, that arranging a threesome with another woman who Ray already knew might hurt? Victoria used her free hand to grab a glass of champagne from the bedside table. She'd arranged for six bottles of Dom Perignon to be chilled in the fridge. She sipped the expensive liquor. The bubbles burst in her mouth. Only the best.

'I remember this belly button and these –' he grabbed Penny's little breasts in his big hands and started working the nipples with his thumbs '– these fabulous nipples!'

Victoria preened. They *were* fabulous. The sudden warmth that suffused her was as welcome as it was new. After all, they weren't *her* breasts he was admiring, not her nipples that were trapped between his fingers now. It was almost masculine, the sense of ownership that infused her. She knew now, first hand, how a man like Ray felt when he said, 'I'm so proud of you,' as he was taking her. It was more intoxicating than the champagne.

It was Victoria who had made it happen, and now she determined to let this new sense of proprietorship guide her. She would not, not for another second, allow herself to *suffer* because her plan had succeeded so perfectly.

Victoria drained her glass. She bent over Penny's

chest and sucked one of her big, now scarlet-stained nipples into her mouth. She batted her lashes at Ray, giving him the same 'whore face' she used when she was sucking his cock. Only this time her lips were pursed in a tiny O to accommodate the delicacy of the nipple. This time, he could join her in the feast and he did, taking Penny's other nipple into his mouth and sucking it while his eyes locked with hers.

Penny writhed between them. Only a moment ago Victoria would have identified with her but now she was on the other side, with Ray, intent on using Penny's body to slake her own desires, whatever they might be.

Ray's wet mouth moved over to join Victoria sucking Penny's other breast. Together they lapped at Penny's nipple until it was a little lava-red volcano and Penny was mewling for mercy. They abandoned the breast, then, and their lips found each other's in a quick sloppy kiss. Then Ray moved from her mouth to Penny's.

He was above Penny, his weight on his hands, kissing her ferociously and the slut was kissing him back with equal abandon. Victoria managed to slither her tongue into their mouths for a moment. Two frantic tongues, darting and licking each other, left little room for hers but the sensation was delicious.

She slid down the bed. Ray was rigid. Victoria lashed her tongue out, first tasting Ray's precome and then tasting, again, Penny's musky flavour. She grasped him in her hand and guided his tip to Penny's opening.

'Good,' he grunted.

Encouraged, Victoria wiggled his cock a little, working it just inside Penny. Again, Victoria felt a masculine thrill, almost as if it were her cock she was introducing to the soft yielding flesh. It must be great to own such a magnificent specimen, and to know you had the prowess to make a woman beg for it.

'Beg for it,' she said immediately.

'Good,' grunted Ray again.

Penny moaned. She'd told Victoria she wasn't nearly as naturally submissive as Victoria was, nor did she have any experience in rough sex beyond that which she'd experienced with Ray, and it had been half-hearted.

Remembering the long conversations that had led to confessions that had led to embraces that had led – once she'd come up with 'The Plan' – to sexual experimentation reminded Victoria that Ray was not the only one who'd known Penny before she'd arrived tonight. She knew her, too. Intimately. Victoria determined to use her understanding of Penny as fully as she'd always intended to use her understanding of Ray to make this event a roaring success.

'You're "The Fire of London",' she cooed. 'We know that, Penny. Now beg like a whore.' She continued swirling the tip of Ray's cock just between Penny's lips. She could feel the thickness of him swell in her grip. He wanted to plunge into Penny but he was allowing Victoria to control his manhood. What was the sensation that surged through her body? Power? She felt like a goddess, one that had as much ability to destroy as to create. It was a heady feeling, but not swooning, as a girl might feel. There was a harder edge to it, making her grip his cock a little more firmly and dip it another tantalising fraction deeper inside the other woman. 'Do it.'

'Please ... please, Ray ... and Victoria ... please let me have it.'

'Nice,' muttered Victoria. 'What is it, though, and where?'

'Your cock – his cock,' Penny babbled, 'I want it inside me.'

'Where do you want it?' asked Ray. He shifted his weight a little. It must have been getting difficult to support himself on his hands but, if it was, he wasn't complaining. Victoria loved that he was holding his position, as she had held hers for him so many times in the past. They were a team, working over one very willing victim.

'I want it in my –' Penny faltered, but managed to say, 'In my cunt. Please.'

'Beautiful,' murmured Ray.

Victoria had to agree. She released her grip on him so that he could completely enter Penny. He did so instantly, driving his impressive shaft so deep into Penny that her groan, from Victoria's angle, anyway, was not as loud as the sound his balls made as they slapped against Penny's perineum.

Victoria sat back. 'Give it to her, Ray!'

He gave her a look that let her know she'd taken her new Alpha-Male attitude too far. 'Lie down!' he barked. He grabbed a handful of her hair and pushed her backwards on to the mattress, her face inches from Penny's.

She'd moved from dominant to submissive so quickly it made her head spin. Ray was in charge again. Letting go of control was as heady as holding it for a few brief moments had been.

'Kiss!' he commanded, and the two women obeyed. At the same time, Ray jerked free of Penny and scrambled impatiently across her right leg and Victoria's left. In an instant, his big cock penetrated Victoria.

Once again, she and Penny played the part of throat-singers, moaning, this time into each other's mouth, as Ray proceeded to take each of them in turn.

How could he stand it? Victoria surged with pride at Ray's ability to stall his climax as he moved from one woman to the other, sometimes gracing her with more than one stroke, sometimes Penny, but always making sure that neither woman did without for more than a few moments.

'Fucking fantastic!' he exclaimed, then, 'Fucking out of this world!'

It was. Fucking fantastic and fucking out of this world. Her body floated from post-orgasmic release to pre-orgasmic tension. Jesus, she was going to come again. If only she could have his cock for more than a couple of strokes.

Penny's sustained groan let her know that, like her, Penny was on her way up into the stratosphere. Dear God, they had to take Ray with them, this time, or he'd have them coming again, and again, while he held off his own release. He was a beast that way – a big man beast that made her feel like a needy princess or a common prostitute or a lascivious whore, any kind of female, the kind that needed taking and fucking and screwing . . .

'Jesus Christ, Ray!' She tore her mouth from Penny's to roar the words. He was inside her again and she was coming again. Her legs wrapped around him, desperate for him to stay deep inside her to give her inner walls something hard – no, not just something hard but a cock, and not just any cock but this cock, *his* cock, now!

Victoria groaned as he ground his pubes against hers, making contact with her clit and allowing her to ride to the crest of her orgasm. Three hard fast contractions rocked her body. Her legs slid down his hips and he shook them off his backside like a horse shaking off two flimsy pieces of straw.

Through the dim haze of post-coital bliss, Victoria could hear Penny panting in her ear again. She turned on her side, exhausted but eager to help Penny, and especially Ray, along. But before she could so much as tweak Penny's nipple Penny was howling and, even better, so was Ray.

She'd never seen all of Ray orgasm before so she took the opportunity to watch. She saw the way his body shuddered and his cock jerked and his face scrunched up and his hands formed fists, all at the same time, as he pounded into Penny.

'You bitch!' he yelled.

Victoria didn't wonder which of them he was addressing; she was pretty sure it was both. A couple of fine bitches. She grinned to herself. It was just as great to be a bitch as it was to be a goddess, she realised, but it was brilliant to be both.

Victoria slid her hand between the two heaving bellies, the tip of one finger managing to find Penny's bud. She exerted gentle pressure until it was flattened against Penny's pubic bone. As she'd learnt over their experimentation in the last few months, this little move helped Penny come. She had only to exert pressure a little more on one side and Penny's clit slid down one side of the bone and made Penny yelp. Now she let the pressure pass over the middle of Penny's clit and down the other side of the pubic bone and Penny started yelping and didn't stop.

'God!' roared Ray, as he pumped into Penny. Each stroke ended with his pelvis bumping Victoria's finger, which then pressed harder against Penny, making Penny's body spasm.

'God!' he roared again, trembling all over as he came.

'King Fuck!' yelled Victoria, as much to add her voice to the mix as for any other reason.

'God!' yelled Ray again.

'Please . . .' groaned Penny.

Ray tumbled free of Penny. He stretched out at the bottom of the bed, still moaning. 'I saw fireworks. I did! Just like in the movies,' he muttered.

Penny lay still, eyes closed, though a little smile let Victoria know she'd heard him.

Victoria relaxed against the pillows and closed her eyes too.

The sound of three people panting was all that could be heard. The air seemed thick, as if, should she open her eyes, she'd be able to see her breath, and Penny's and Ray's, too. As if their bed were a big sled and the three of them had just managed to make it to the finish line of a long fabulous winter's ride before losing their grip on gravity and tumbling off the sled in a tangle of arms and legs.

Penny shifted but didn't get up. Ray stayed where he was, at the foot of the bed, groaning every once in a while as aftershocks gripped his gut.

Peaceful – that's what it was. Somehow, their sex romp had taken them all the way to bliss and on into peace, as if the three of them had been meditating, even praying, together.

She would have giggled if she hadn't been so utterly content. Ray had yelled 'God!' not once or twice, but three times, and she'd been calling out to Christ, herself. It did seem as if all her prayers had been answered.

'Hey,' said Ray, 'I'm hungry.'

16

Penny was happy to lounge beside Ray while Victoria relayed their meal orders to room service. Ray had decided that they were two Pussycats and he was the Owl, and no one was to leave the pea-green boat. So far, she and Victoria had complied but soon Penny would have to brave the sea of carpet between her and the bathroom. She could only hope there were no sharks circling just below the surface.

'I've had too much to drink,' she moaned. 'I'm not making sense.'

'Sure you are,' mumbled Ray.

'Not in my head I'm not.'

'What – you're thinking? My mind is mush,' he replied.

'Good point. I think I might have to get off the boat, though. I have to go to the bathroom.'

'Proceed with caution,' he said.

Penny took the opportunity to wash up and try to run a comb through her hair. It was starting to curl, of course, from the dampness generated by three gyrating bodies. She grinned at herself in the mirror. Sex could even turn a bad hairdo into a personal triumph.

They'd been fantastic, the three of them, and both of her orgasms had been humdingers! Thank God, Ray's stomach had called a halt, however temporarily, to the fun and games. She didn't know if her heart could take any more. She glanced at Victoria's pill bottle on the shelf, idly wondering if one would do her any good. Probably not, she decided. She still felt woozy and, obviously, her thoughts were still silly, but at least she smelt fresh. She slipped into one of the terry robes hanging on a hook on the bathroom door.

As she left the bathroom, she paused in the doorway to look at her partners in crime. Victoria had finished ordering their food and now filled Ray in on what they'd be having for dinner, as if he hadn't first helped put together the menu and then lay there while Victoria relayed the order. He was listening, though, a look of utter contentment on his face. They made a pretty picture. The only thing that would make their picture prettier, in fact, was if she rejoined them on the bed. She let her robe slide to the floor.

'Hey, get over here!' called Ray.

'Watch out for crocodiles!' said Victoria, giggling.

'Eeeeek!' shrieked Penny. She skedaddled to the bed as if a big croc was snapping at her heels.

'Don't get off the boat!' they sang out in unison when she was safely aboard once more. Maybe they were all a little tipsy, or maybe none of them was and they were just giddy with the success of their threesome but, either way, they all three shook with the force of their laughter.

'Cut it out,' sputtered Penny when she could speak. 'Don't be funny. I'm drunk or something.'

'Or something?' Victoria tried to pour champagne into a glass but the bottle was empty. 'Doesn't matter, I've got five more bottles!' she cried gaily.

'Don't get off the boat,' mumbled Penny but Victoria was already on her way to the fridge. It seemed they were magically back to three in a bed, which was magical enough in itself.

'The room-service guy will be here soon. I think I'd better greet him at the door so he doesn't see you two lying in my bed like – like a lion and his pick of the pride,' said Victoria.

'I pick you too!' said Ray. Penny was glad he did. She'd wondered if Victoria would feel any jealousy once the three of them were together. After all, Victoria had done all the work and it was she, not Penny, who'd first managed to get Ray to the room in the first place. All Penny had to do was wait her turn and Ray had been served up to her on a platter.

Penny laughed. 'I hid in the wardrobe.'

Ray laughed, too. 'You're a nut. You could have greeted me at the door with Victoria and I'd have been thrilled and surprised.'

'Not *as* surprised, though,' said Penny. Especially, she thought to herself, if he'd found her in the wardrobe of his suite, not Victoria's. But he hadn't, and it seemed from his behaviour that he hadn't talked to that gorgeous Chinese girl with the Balenciaga bag yet, either. She wondered if she should confess to having been in his room earlier that day, but she instantly decided against it. She wasn't that drunk. Besides, then she'd probably end up confessing to her liaison with Nobatu and that would lead to Bryce Stafford, Junior and none of that, she was quite sure, was anybody's business but her own.

When Victoria handed her a full glass of fresh champagne she took it, even though she knew she should wait until the food arrived before having anything more to drink. Still, the food would be here soon and she had an idea for another perfect moment, one that wouldn't require any exertion from any of them. 'Mind if I smoke?' she asked. Ray instantly shook his head but Victoria took a moment to consider this before replying, 'No, I don't mind at all. In fact, I might join you.'

'Hold on,' said Ray. 'What about your heart?'

'One cigarette won't kill me,' replied Victoria.

Penny jumped off the bed and skipped over to the wardrobe she'd hidden in earlier. Her bag must still be inside it. She rooted around on the floor of the wardrobe, deliberately keeping her legs straight and bending at her hips.

'That view is going to give me a hard-on,' Ray warned her from the bed.

Penny quickly stood, bag in hand. His words sent a thrill running through her. He'd said he wanted to beat her with the crop, earlier. Obviously, he hadn't forgotten his threat, even if she had. She glanced at Victoria, who was leafing through a drawer, tossing flimsy bits of satin and lace around as she looked for another outfit. The woman's ass was pink with blotches of purple. Some of the marks, Penny realised, would be black before they would disappear.

Victoria wiggled her bum. 'I'll have these marks for a week,' she said. 'That means I'll have to be careful, in Cuba, to make sure my bikini bottom covers them up.'

'That's right,' said Ray easily, although he probably wasn't happy to hear the subject of Cuba come up. 'All the guys will be after you if they see your bruised bum.'

'Why don't you come along as my bodyguard?' she said to Ray. Victoria abandoned her search through the drawer and walked, naked, towards the bathroom. She picked up the robe Penny had dropped by the bathroom and took it with her to the bed. 'Please, Ray.'

'Why don't you take Penny with you? She's a lot of fun.'

'There's a thought!' Victoria said brightly.

'I'm going to Cuba too, Ray,' said Penny. She grabbed her cigarettes and let her bag drop. She scurried to the bed. 'Surprise,' she said brightly.

'Is that so?' Ray was obviously taken aback.

Penny slipped a cigarette between her lips and lit it. She inhaled deeply, letting her nicotine-deprived lungs relish the first blast of relief. 'Yup. Still smoke?'

'Of course not. *No one* still smokes.'

'I do,' said Penny. She drew on the cigarette again,

without inhaling, then let the smoke escape her mouth, drawing it upwards by inhaling through her nose – French plumes, she thought smoking fetishists called it.

Ray laughed. 'Give me one,' he said.

'Me, too,' said Victoria. She drew a cigarette from Penny's pack and lit up. Penny lit another for Ray and handed it to him.

'I love smoking,' she said.

'It's sinfully bad for you,' said Ray.

'Lots of things are,' said Victoria. 'But it doesn't mean you can't love them.'

Her words hung in the air, heavy as the smoke, for a moment. 'Oh hell,' said Penny, 'let's not talk about love.'

'That's something I've always liked about you, Penny,' Ray said. 'You don't ruin the moment with an unquenchable thirst for more.'

'Love isn't –' began Victoria.

Penny felt powerless to stop Victoria from making a big mistake. Happily, at that moment a knock at the door interrupted Victoria before she could finish her sentence.

'Coming!' she called. She shrugged into the terry robe and hurried to the door.

Penny and Ray smoked in companionable silence while Victoria handled the room-service man, firmly turning down his offer to wheel the cart all the way into the room.

'That's what I *love* about you, in fact,' said Ray, glancing at Penny as he took another drag on his cigarette.

Penny came to a decision. 'I always wished you'd said goodbye,' she informed him. It was the truth and he might as well know it. She didn't want Ray to play favourites. For their night of pleasure to be a complete success, they had to all be of the same mind. Three on a boat, as it were.

17

Ray groaned. Women! He took a last drag on his smoke and stubbed it out, using the empty strawberry bowl as an ashtray. It almost made him wish he were somewhere else. He wondered what Bai Lon was doing behind that 'Do Not Disturb' sign. 'I sent a postcard,' he said.

'It was indecipherable!' Penny protested.

Victoria wheeled a cart laden with food to the bed. Ray grabbed his plate. 'It said "Goodbye",' he muttered.

Happily, that made Penny laugh. He'd thought it would but you could never be sure. She was a good sport, a much better sport than Victoria, but still ... Ray dug into his eggplant sandwich with gusto.

Victoria had chosen a clubhouse, and Penny, he noticed, seemed positively thrilled at the sight of her deluxe hamburger. She noticed him watching her.

'That's right,' she said, taking a big bite. 'I'm not a vegetarian any more. In my line of work, I need the protein meat provides.'

'I'm not going to argue,' he replied. 'What is your line of work, anyway? Who is "The Fire of London"? You're not still a showgirl, are you?'

'No, I've gone all respectable on you. Now I play poker for a living.'

Penny and Ray shared a laugh but Victoria didn't join in. She said earnestly, 'Penny's practically a celebrity, Ray.'

'Maybe I should get your autograph then,' he said.

'So you can sell it on e-Bay?' asked Penny.

'Yes,' he replied and they laughed again. 'Although the money –'

'Let me guess,' said Penny. She adopted the mannerism of a psychic, hand pressed to her forehead as if reading his mind. 'The money would go to a good cause.'

'That's right!'

Penny had polished off her hamburger and was now digging into her fries. 'You haven't changed a bit,' she said.

'But you sure have,' said Ray. 'You don't eat your food in alphabetical order any more.' Ray grabbed Victoria's hand and kissed it. It wouldn't do to leave her out of the conversation for long, even if he and Penny did have a lot of catching up to do. Victoria was a complicated creature who could easily turn cold. 'Penny used to eat each thing in alphabetical order,' he explained. 'But, if that were still the case, she'd have eaten her French fries first.'

'Maybe you are counting it as a burger and fries?' offered Victoria. 'Or even a burger and chips?'

Penny shook her head. 'That would be cheating. Besides, there's also the missing pickle to consider.' She gestured to her plate where, indeed, the pickle was missing. The other two considered this lack of evidence. 'But I haven't really changed all that much,' she confessed. 'Somewhere along the way I realised it was odd to eat my food alphabetically,' she explained, 'so I decided to break the habit by eating it backwards, starting at "Z" and working my way towards "A". And it stuck.'

Victoria and Ray considered Penny's almost empty plate. 'Pickle, hamburger, French fries,' mumbled Ray. 'It works!' He polished off the rest of his sandwich.

Victoria looked from him to Penny and back again.

'What?' said Penny.

'I hadn't realised you were so weird,' said Victoria. She took a bite of her sandwich and thoughtfully chewed it. 'It's almost scary,' she pronounced.

'I'm not the one with the black and blue bum!' cried Penny.

'That's true,' acknowledged Victoria. She grinned wickedly at Penny as she stole one of her French fries.

'Hey!' Penny pretended to try to take her fry back. The women giggled like innocent girls.

The food was good and the champagne was great, but it was the sight of two tousled women in his bed that elevated this experience far above any other in Ray's life. He gazed fondly from one to the other, embedding the delightful image in his mind where he could call upon it, from now on, whenever he needed cheering up – although he'd already accumulated so many images from today it had become a mental slideshow, which was all to the good. 'I love it,' he announced without thinking.

'*It*, yes,' muttered Victoria.

'I love you, Beauty Puss,' he said, stroking her head. 'How many times do I have to tell you?'

'No more times, Ray.'

'And you, The Fire of London, the truth is that I love you too.'

'You don't have to say that,' said Penny.

'I know. But it's true.'

'I love you too, Penny,' said Victoria.

'Well, I love you too, Beauty Puss and King Fuck,' said Penny solemnly. They all laughed.

'That calls for a round of drinks,' announced Ray.

'The thing is . . .' mused Victoria.

Ray almost groaned. Victoria could always be counted on to dig deep into banter, thus destroying it. He poured the drinks anyway.

'What does it mean, to love someone? I think it means something very different to me than it does to you, Ray. Probably to Penny, too.'

'To me,' said Penny, taking her glass from Ray, 'it means telling the truth to the other person, caring about the other person, and, at least as far as the present company is concerned, desiring the other person.'

'I'll drink to that,' said Ray. He and Penny touched their wineglasses together, then drank.

'That's it?' asked Victoria. 'That's great, for tonight, but, if that's all there is to it, why wouldn't we stay together?'

'They say love conquers all but I think it's the other way around,' Penny ventured. 'I think all conquers love. Probably, in order to keep loving someone, you have to get away from him. Or her.'

'That's the part I don't understand. It makes no sense to me at all,' said Victoria.

'Victoria,' said Ray in a gentle tone. 'You don't understand that, for me, just knowing you are in the world makes me happy.'

'But you forgot all about Penny.'

'Never!'

'Oh you did, Ray,' argued Victoria. 'You said you didn't even remember having another relationship after me and before you went to Cuba.'

'I did?' He hated that Victoria was putting him on the spot like this. Maybe he had forgotten Penny's name, or even, once reunited with Victoria, he'd temporarily forgotten the time he'd spent with Penny. But why bring that up now?

'It's OK,' said Penny, though she looked hurt. 'I just wanted to see you again because – because I thought it would be fun. And I wanted to know what the postcard said.'

'Goodbye,' said Victoria. 'Did you at least sign it "Love, Ray"?'

He wanted to say yes but he knew the answer was no, and she probably did, too. 'I signed it as I signed everything in those days,' he replied, '"In solidarity, Ray."'

'God,' groaned Penny, 'I'm glad I didn't know what it said, I might have cried over you for two days instead of just one.' She drained her glass.

Ray was touched. 'You cried when I left?'

Penny nodded.

Ray rubbed her cheek with his thumb. 'Now that I've seen you again I promise never to forget you,' he vowed.

'It would be easier if you came with us, to Cuba, to never forget her,' said Victoria. She stared at him over the rim of her glass.

'We'll see,' he said, setting down his empty glass beside his plate on the tray. 'I'll think about it.'

Ray sat up and swung his legs to the floor. 'What time is it?' he asked. It didn't matter but he wanted to remind Penny and Victoria that he'd made no commitment, yet, not to either of them. He'd told Victoria that he'd planned to spend the night but plans could change.

The room was littered with abandoned shoes, clothes and accessories. He almost tripped over Penny's bag, so he picked it up. It hung open and Ray saw a pink envelope. His blood ran cold.

'What the hell is this?' he asked, as he fished the envelope out of the bag and held it up.

'Don't read my mail!' yelled Penny, but it was too late.

'It's addressed to me!' He stormed over to the bed. 'This is the note Victoria left for me at the Plaza. How did it end up in your purse?'

'I'm sorry, Ray,' said Penny. 'It was – I went – I went

to your room to see where you were. But you weren't in so I –'

'You let yourself into my room.' He finished the sentence for her.

'You taught me how to do it, remember? From *The Anarchist's Handbook*? I always remembered that trick and, of course, these days, I'm always carrying a pack of cards, so –'

'I don't like it.'

'Well, that's why I didn't mention it,' said Penny miserably.

'I don't like it one little bit.' He observed both women coolly. If he wanted out he'd just been handed the perfect excuse. But that wasn't what he wanted, not yet. His glance fell to the crop, caught among the bedclothes in a heap at the end of the bed.

'I'm sorry, Ray,' said Penny.

'I'm afraid you'll have to be punished, Penny,' he said.

18

His words made Penny shiver with fear. Her mouth moved as she tried to protest, but nothing came out. She stared at the bag in his hand, willing it to be closed, with the damning letter tucked safely inside. How had she been so careless? She remembered – she'd been in a hurry to have a cigarette. It was true, she decided. Cigarettes really were bad for you.

'I'm sorry,' was all she could manage to sputter. She glanced at Victoria for help but Victoria seemed just as much at a loss for words as she was. No wonder. Victoria hadn't even known she'd taken the envelope. She didn't even know why she had; it wasn't like she hadn't known where Victoria was staying. She recalled that there'd been a knock at his door and she'd panicked.

'A girl –' she began. She wet her lips and tried again. 'A girl knocked at your door and I put the envelope in my bag and I left.'

'What girl?' Ray dropped the bag and approached the bed. But instead of climbing in he stopped at the end and picked up the crop.

'She had a Balenciaga bag,' said Penny, but that seemed to mean nothing to Ray. 'A Chinese girl with a Balenciaga bag.' She was afraid she was going to start babbling if he didn't stop glancing from the crop to her and back again.

'Who is that, Ray?' asked Victoria.

'Someone from the tour, I suppose,' he said irritably. 'A colleague from the symposium. I don't know, I didn't see her.'

'Her room was close to yours,' offered Penny.

'We're not talking about her, Penny; we're talking about *you.*'

'I shouldn't have taken the envelope but I was so scared when she knocked on the door I just dropped it into my handbag and left.'

'It's not the taking of the envelope that concerns me, it's the fact that you let yourself into my room.'

'I said I was sorry.'

'Not good enough.' He flicked the crop and it snapped the air. 'Not near good enough.'

'Please don't. I never have.'

'I spanked you myself, silly girl.'

'That was ages ago and you only used your hand. Please, Ray, I'm serious –' Penny didn't dare look at Victoria. She knew the other woman would be sending her silent begging messages that said, 'You promised you'd do anything,' which she had, but she hadn't expected this.

'You have two choices. Either you must submit to a good whipping or I'm leaving.'

'No!' cried Victoria. She turned to Penny, her eyes already brimming with tears. 'Please, Penny!'

Damn the woman. Penny really did love Victoria and she knew just how much Victoria wanted Ray on their trip. She also suspected that, while she felt willing to bid adieu to him without a backwards glance after two weeks in Cuba, Victoria hoped he'd stay with her. Not that Victoria had ever said as much but Penny could tell, now that she'd seen the two of them together. Victoria was mad for Ray.

'I'll do it,' she said. 'But I won't like it!'

'I think you will,' said Ray. He swished the crop through the air, grinning. 'I bet you're a pain slut at heart.'

'How much do you bet? 'Cause I bet double or nothing I am *not* a pain slut!'

'A wager it is!' announced Ray. He snapped his wrist again and the tip of the hateful crop cracked the air. 'I bet you twelve strokes of the crop that you're a pain slut! If I win, you'll welcome my cock up your ass and, if you win, you may give me a taste of the lash!'

'Ray!' Victoria was clearly shocked.

'You're on!' Penny shouted the words before she'd truly considered their meaning. She never lost a bet – well, almost never. She wondered if a fake tell would be of any use to her in the game she'd suddenly found herself playing.

'Arrange Penny so she'll be comfortable while I beat her ass,' Ray instructed Victoria.

'Yes, Master,' whispered Victoria.

Penny saw the way submissive language made Victoria blush. The words lingered in the air, like smoke. Victoria's statement should have sounded silly, like she was aping a sitcom genie, but it didn't. It sounded sexy.

Penny's limbs felt heavy as she allowed Victoria to manipulate them into position. It was as if she were no more than a doll with moveable joints. She was just as frightened as she'd been in Ray's room when she thought she was about to be discovered. On the verge of panic. How on earth did such a good girl manage to get herself into these perilous situations?

She and Victoria had talked about Ray's taste for rough sex, but she hadn't expected him to be packing a crop in his briefcase. She glanced suspiciously at Victoria who gave her a guilty look.

'*You* brought the crop!' accused Penny.

'I like it, honey, and so will you. You'll see. Trust me.'

Penny almost laughed. For three people who liked to tell the truth, she suspected not one of them was in the least bit trustworthy. Still, she allowed Victoria to arrange her naked body so she was on all fours, a stack of king-size pillows between her and the head of the bed.

'If you need to, you can collapse on the pillows later, or grab this,' said Victoria, tapping the bronze rail of the headboard with her fingernails.

'Great,' muttered Penny. She refused to meet Victoria's eyes with her own.

Victoria grabbed a handful of Penny's hair, twisting her face towards her own. She pressed her succulent mouth against Penny's lips. Penny yielded.

Victoria's tongue found Penny's and flicked it, as if to remind her that they'd already performed plenty of perverted tricks with and to each other. What, after all, was one more? Penny closed her eyes. She'd felt fear when Nobatu had wanted to take her from behind, but it had soon turned to pleasure. She'd been afraid, a little, the first time she and Victoria had played together. And that had been delightful. Still – she couldn't stand the idea! The kiss ended much too soon for Penny.

'You'll see,' Victoria whispered. 'It's like nothing else, a combination of pain and pleasure that –'

'Quiet!' ordered Ray. Victoria stopped talking. 'You –' he pointed the crop at Victoria '– you may count the blows. You,' he said, tapping Penny's bottom with the leather triangle at the tip of the crop, 'you are expected to take at least twelve from the crop, and as many as I wish to dole out with my hand.'

'Yes, Master,' said Victoria. She left the bed to stand beside Ray. Penny could see both of them in the mirror opposite the bed, but she didn't want to watch so she closed her eyes.

'Yes, Master,' Penny said. She tingled all over. How easily she'd acquiesced in a language she'd never before spoken. Maybe this wouldn't be so bad.

It wasn't at first. Ray spanked her half a dozen times with the palm of his hand. Penny felt heat, first on the surface of her skin and then, incredibly, beneath it. His firm smacks were making her glow inside! Victoria stayed close, running her hands down Penny's back, smoothing her hair and generally offering a great deal of encouragement. Penny felt like a special guest at a kinky celebration.

Ray paused. Penny tensed her muscles, even though Victoria whispered, 'Relax.' As if!

The crop whistled through the air and then the first stinging blow landed on her poor bare bum. 'Ow!' she protested, twisting sideways. Her eyelids flew open and she yelped. 'It hurts!' She twisted to glare at the two of them.

'It's supposed to hurt. Hold still!' barked Ray. His pale-blue eyes were so sharply focused she couldn't bear to look into them. He was enjoying it, all right.

'That's one, Master,' Victoria dutifully counted, but bit her lip and dropped her glance when she saw Penny glaring at her. The bitch blushed!

Penny shook her head at her own reflection. Idiot! She faced front and squeezed her eyes shut. She didn't like it at all! She didn't like the second blow, or the third, either. But the fourth felt different. Not lighter, or softer, just – deeper, somehow. As if the pain were seeping into her skin, or being drawn into her body by her sexual organs.

'That's four, Master,' reported Victoria, and then, 'That's five.'

Thankfully, Ray paused at this point. He ran his hand gently over her behind. God, she was glowing, inside and out. 'Nice,' he said. His voice was proud, though she didn't know if it was pride in her, for enduring the pain, or in himself, for the prowess he'd displayed in laying on the crop.

'Thank you, Master,' she mumbled, just to be on the safe side.

She *was* safe, she realised. Safe in the hands of a sadist and his slavish assistant. Crazy, maybe, but true. The situation was so bizarre, the sensations so perversely erotic, she felt light-headed. Another crack of the crop across her backside failed to yank her back to earth; in fact, it pushed her deeper into a misty muddled state.

'Six, Sir,' said Victoria. 'She's feeling it.'

'Have you ever had your nipples clipped? They're begging for it, you know,' said Ray.

'No, never,' said Penny. She wished he'd get on with the whipping. The warmth was starting to subside and that made the centre of her need – that little throbbing greedy seed – twinge.

'I'd take care of that oversight right now if I had a couple of nipple clips. Or even a couple of clothes pegs. I know!' Ray snapped his fingers. 'Victoria, you will be my nipple clamps. Get up on the bed.'

Victoria rushed to do as she was told. She knelt on Penny's right side. First, she petted Penny's head as if she were a pony, then pushed down a little on the small of her back so Penny's bum tilted up more steeply. Finally, she reached under Penny and took a rubbery scarlet nipple in each hand. 'Now?' she asked.

'Now,' said Ray.

Penny shrieked as Victoria crushed her nipples, then shrieked again as the crop rained down on her and the heat radiated inwards again, like a missile seeking a source of ignition. Victoria tightened her grip.

'Stay still!' barked Ray.

'Seven, eight, nine, Master!' cried Victoria, once for each crack of the crop.

Penny bit her lip to keep from begging him to stop. She couldn't even remember their wager now, but she was determined to take her twelve strokes. It had become a source of pride for her and, anyway, with Victoria's fingers twisting her nipples, she now had three heat-seeking missiles set to blast her into outer space if she could just, somehow, survive another two blows.

'Ten!'

Either Ray wasn't hitting her as hard now, which was unlikely, given the way the crop sang as it streaked through the air, or she wasn't feeling the blows in the same way any more. The pain was close, now, to reaching its goal.

'Beg for it, bitch,' said Ray.

'I want two more!' she cried, then added, just in time, 'Please!'

'You love it, don't you?' said Ray. 'Look at me and tell me you love it!'

Penny opened her eyes. She glanced down at her little breasts, covered with Victoria's delicate hands. Her nipples poked between Victoria's fingers, engorged and purple. She looked in the mirror and saw Ray with his arm raised, the instrument of her deliverance high above her scarlet-striped backside. She twisted to look Ray in the eyes but Victoria didn't move with her. The sensation in her breasts intensified.

'I love it, Master,' she said. The words sounded far away, almost as if someone else were saying them. He seemed bathed in golden light.

'Her pupils are dilated, Master,' reported Victoria.

'That's my girl!' The pride was evident in his voice and his face and the way he lifted his arm a fraction higher so that the second-to-last blow would sting a little more.

Penny watched the crop descend. The blow drove the sensation deeper inside, almost reaching her core.

'Eleven, Master!' shouted Penny, speaking in unison with Victoria.

She closed her eyes and steadied herself for the final

blow. The force of it rocked her but Victoria's hands, clamped on her breasts, kept her in position.

'Twelve, Master!' cried Victoria, as she released Penny's nipples.

Fire from both pulsing points burnt deep into Penny's breasts, so deep it connected somewhere in her groin to the feeling the beating had caused. It was as if she'd become nothing more than a transmitter for pain.

Hands were touching her, soft on her breasts and her face, rougher between her legs. Thank God in Heaven for the hand that groped among the wetness to find her clit and press it, like a finger on the ignition button of a bomb.

There was a short terrible silent countdown and then all points connected and it was all systems go and Penny shuddered and shrieked as she blasted off into outer fucking space.

'What happened?'

A cool cloth was pressed to her forehead. There was something cold on her chest and when she put her hands there she felt a cold cloth covering each of her breasts. Her nipples ached.

'Thank God, you're OK. I thought it might have been too much for you.' It was Victoria, her dear friend Victoria, hovering solicitously by her head.

Penny glanced around, familiarising herself with her whereabouts. Right. Hotel room and Victoria and ... 'Where is that sadistic bastard?'

'Right here, cupcake.' Ray exited the bathroom, holding a couple of bottles of pills and a glass of water. 'Take this,' he said, handing her one of the pill bottles.

'What is it?'

'I found something that might help reduce the swelling.'

'I'm OK,' she protested. She twisted to bare her backside to the mirror and moaned at the pattern of stripes that was tattooed on her red-hot ass. 'I think.'

Ray grinned at her. 'I'm glad it's not you who has the bad heart. You looked like you'd died and gone to heaven.' He gave her a knowing glance. 'Here's your pills,' he said to Victoria, handing her the other pill bottle. 'You're to take two a day. We don't want Nursie getting mad at us, do we?'

'Nope.' Victoria opened the pill bottle and took her pill.

'I want to see,' said Penny, as she sat up. 'Ouch!' She stood hastily, relieving the pressure on her behind, and found she was unsteady on her feet.

Close up, what she saw shocked her. Her ass was scarlet, crisscrossed with livid purple marks.

'Jesus, Ray,' she moaned. 'I'll have these for ages.'

'Not at all. They'll be gone in less than a week.'

'Promise?'

'Yes. I can also promise you that by the time they're gone you'll miss them.'

'Oh, God,' she moaned. What if he were wrong? Or right? 'Now what? I'm a masochist?'

'Well, you're a pain slut, sweetie. This much we know.' Ray chuckled. 'But don't worry, it'll be our little secret.'

Victoria joined her at the mirror. 'You were brilliant, Penny. You came in seconds and you were, like, howling and then you fainted dead away. You just loved it.'

'What if I don't want to love it?' wailed Penny.

Victoria turned her back to the mirror so they stood side by side. 'Silly. It's another piece of the puzzle that is Penny. It's good. And they really will fade, honey. Look how bright yours are compared to mine, and I got mine just this morning.'

It was true. Victoria's marks seemed settled into place, while Penny's looked as if they were still swelling, like delicate puff pastries glazed with pink frosting.

'I'm still tender,' said Victoria. 'But not like you, I bet.' She wet her finger in her mouth and traced one of the marks across Penny's backside.

'Ouch,' Penny mumbled. The marks were tender to the touch.

Ray came to stand between the two of them. He faced the mirror while they remained with their backs, and backsides, reflected. He tilted his head to the right and then to the left as he compared his handiwork to Veruschka's.

'This is a sight to remember,' he said. 'I will never forget this and I will never, ever forget what you did for me.' He kissed them, first Victoria and then Penny. The kiss was gentle. It was, Penny realised, the kiss of a grateful man. She dropped her glance and almost groaned. A *horny*, grateful man.

'Come back to bed,' he said, hooking his arms through theirs. 'I've won the wager, Penny,' he reminded her, speaking in his phoney English accent. 'It's time for me to fuck your arse.'

19

Victoria's eyes opened. The room was so dark for a moment she thought she must still have the blindfold on. She didn't for a moment fear that she was alone in the bed. Ray was beside her, lying on his back with his arms spread wide and snorting with every fourth breath. On his other side, lying on his right arm just as Victoria was lying on his left, lay Penny.

What would it be like all of them together in Cuba? She'd booked three rooms, of course, so they'd each have their own space. Would he end up moving from bed to bed? Or would they stay like this, for two weeks, always cuddled and curled up together?

Victoria rolled on to her side, towards Ray.

Soon. Soon they'd rise and have breakfast and shower and head for the airport. She was almost sure Ray was going to join them, though he hadn't yet actually committed to it in words. But actions spoke louder than words, especially where he was concerned. He'd been insatiable. So dominant in his demands. Rock hard. He'd taken Penny from behind and then her, each time feasting on the breasts of the woman he wasn't penetrating. He'd flipped her and Penny around like they were inflatable toys, lightweight and designed only to satisfy him. Now that Victoria considered it, she realised Ray had pretty much enjoyed all of the orifices available to him, if only for a moment or two, before he'd ejaculated. For a thrilling instant Victoria couldn't remember where he'd actually come. It was the most decadent moment of her life.

Neither woman had been in need of another orgasm; they were both well taken care of by the time the three of them headed back to the bed. She and Penny had been delighted to serve him and he'd been more than happy to indulge himself wholeheartedly. They hadn't actually been back at it for all that long when he climaxed while she and Penny pleasured him with their mouths. They'd sucked him dry. King Fuck was sated at last.

Poor Penny. Maybe Victoria should have been clearer about Ray's penchant for punishment. But Penny had known Ray, too. She said she was confident she could take whatever Ray had to dole out, and Victoria had left it at that. If Penny thought of a spanking as a few smacks of a hand on the bum and Victoria knew better, so be it. They both understood perfectly, now. Penny had enjoyed it, too. That was what mattered – not necessarily that one imagined one might like it, but that one did when the moment arrived. She and Ray had expanded Penny's horizons and all three were pleased with the result.

Victoria snuck her hand under the covers and gently cupped Ray with it. He groaned and shifted free. Perfectly sated.

She got up and padded to the bathroom. He was hers now, or hers and Penny's. Perhaps more accurately, she and Penny were *his*. No matter. What mattered was that she'd proven to him that love sweetens the pot, not sours it.

She used the toilet and washed her hands, then briefly considered freshening up and diving into the bed for another romp before deciding against it. Better to catch a few more hours of rest before it was time to depart.

Her eyes had adjusted to the dark by the time she got back to the bed so she could see Ray and Penny sleeping soundly. She felt a rush of affection for both of them. It was all very exciting and a lot of fun but, beyond that, they'd formed a bond with their bodies that lingered after the last climax.

She stroked Penny's cheek. No matter what happened, she'd make sure there was always room for Penny in her and Ray's life. Perhaps they could visit her, or meet her while she was on a poker tour, or she could come to them for a holiday. Once a year, at the very least, they'd welcome Penny to their bed with open arms.

Penny's eyelids fluttered open. 'Is it time to go?' she mumbled.

'Not yet. Back to dreamland with you.'

'OK.' Penny nodded off again.

Victoria was only a couple of years older than Penny but she felt oddly maternal towards the other woman. Penny's hand was trapped beneath her warm cheek and it made her appear vulnerable. Victoria kissed the other woman's head. The room was silent except for the soft sound of three lovers breathing.

A new sound hummed to life. It was coming from Ray's cell phone, which was recharging on the bedside table. He'd left the phone on.

'What's that?' mumbled Penny. 'Please, no vibrator.'

'It's Ray's cell phone,' hissed Victoria. She picked it up and the sleek leather-clad instrument vibrated in her hand. Victoria glared at the screen as a text message scrolled across it. Victoria read it aloud. 'Ray, come fuck me in the Jacuzzi.'

Penny squinted at Victoria. 'Who's it from?'

'Someone named Lonnie.'

'What should we do?'

'I don't know yet.' Victoria's sense of wellbeing was absolutely shattered. He *had* been sneaking off to spend time with another woman while Victoria had patiently waited and made excuses for him. This magical evening she'd arranged was nothing more than another notch on his belt. Probably not even that, given that he'd already screwed Penny and Victoria separately when the three of them were younger.

Fear and anger battled for dominance in the pit of her stomach. 'Goddamn you, Ray,' she snarled. Victoria tried to find the power switch to the phone but couldn't see it in the dark room. She reached for the charger, intent on yanking it from the wall, but before she could do so the cell phone rang. Victoria froze.

Ray stirred as the phone rang a second time. 'Is that mine?' he mumbled.

Victoria sprang into action. She dropped the phone and grabbed the handcuff at the head of the bed. 'Get him!' she yelled at Penny.

Victoria slapped the cuff around Ray's right wrist. 'Gotcha!' she cried. She clambered across his chest to imprison his left hand with another cuff before his eyes were open. Her heart was pounding a mile a minute.

'What the hell?' Ray was awake.

Penny watched, wide-eyed, as Victoria latched on to Ray's left foot with both hands.

'Help me, Penny!' yelled Victoria. 'We can't let him get away!'

Penny scrambled across Ray. She and Victoria managed to cuff Ray's left leg to the bed while he was still struggling to sit up.

'What's going on?' Ray looked from his left cuffed wrist to his right.

'Nothing,' said Victoria, panting. She and Penny latched on to his right leg, as he kicked out, realising at last that the cuffs Victoria had attached to the brass bedposts – the cuffs that had been abandoned and forgotten during their threesome – were now being put to good use. By then it was too late.

Ray lay, spread-eagled, naked, bound and helpless. The look on his face was terrible to behold.

Victoria searched among the bedclothes for the still-ringing cell phone. 'Who is Lonnie?' She was gasping for air. She felt a chair bump the back of her knees and sank into it. She cast Penny a grateful look, then focused on Ray.

'She's a business associate. She was one of the women on the sightseeing tour. That's all.' His voice was cold.

'That's it?' Victoria glared at him but he didn't answer. 'Ray?'

'Untie me and let me answer the phone.'

'I think I know why she's calling. She wants to know if you got her text message.'

'That's right, Ray,' said Penny. She held out a glass of water to Victoria but when Victoria tried to take it her hand shook so badly that Penny tipped the glass to Victoria's lips instead. 'Steady, girl,' whispered Penny.

Ray groaned. He struggled briefly against his bonds, then lay still. 'Obviously I didn't.'

'Well, I did. It said, "Ray, come fuck me in the Jacuzzi."'

'That sounds like her all right,' Ray replied. 'Penny, release me from these cuffs and I won't charge you with being an accessory to forcible confinement.'

Penny looked from Ray to Victoria to the still-ringing phone in Victoria's hand.

'How could you, Ray?' Victoria asked.

'I couldn't help myself. That's the truth. If you could see her, you'd understand what I mean.'

'That's a good idea,' said Victoria. She pressed a button on the phone and it abruptly stopped ringing. She held the phone to Ray's ear. 'Say hello to Lonnie, honey,' she said.

20

Ray's voice sounded different, but at first Lonnie attrib-
uted that to the pre-dawn hour. 'Ray!' She was excited
so she spoke quickly into her cell phone. 'The hotel is
going to let us into the recreation centre early. My
friends are already in the pool. Come, quick, we can fuck
in the Jacuzzi. Won't that be fun?' She listened to his
voice on the other end of the phone. 'Huh? You mean all
tied up, like, busy?' She listened to him again. 'Ohhhh.
Like kinky?' She pulled her cell phone a little distance
from her ear as his voice rose. 'I see. Let me talk to one
of them.'

Lonnie sat on the edge of her bed, dressed only in a
black bikini. 'Hello. Who are you? Ray says you have
him all tied up?'

She listened as Ray's predicament was spelt out to
her. 'Send me your picture,' she ordered, when the
woman on the other end of the line had stopped speaking. 'OK, send me her picture too and I'll send mine.'

The next few minutes were spent transferring pictures back and forth. 'Oh, I know this one!' murmured
Lonnie when she saw Penny's picture. 'You are very
pretty girls,' she said when the picture exchange was
complete. 'Let me speak to Ray again.' When he was
back on the line, she said, 'Oh, Ray, you are a very bad
boy to sleep with your cousin!' She laughed into the
phone. 'You forgive me for stealing your limousine?
Promise? OK, I am coming. Don't move!'

Lonnie disconnected and then started punching numbers on the phone. She'd have to make arrangements

with the Posse to have her luggage transported to the airport and she'd have to check out now, plus clear her appointment book for the morning and check in with Lo Song. And she wouldn't be making an appearance at the recreation centre after all. No time for mere fun. The Hong Kong Bombshell to the rescue!

21

Ray watched Penny and Victoria dash around the hotel room, primping and straightening up in anticipation of their guest. He was astonished by their girlish glee. They should be trembling in fear at the thought of what he would do to them once he was free again. They had their reputations to consider! Of course, so did he . . .

He glowered at Victoria but she just planted a kiss on his forehead as she flitted by. 'You're going to love this, darling,' she promised.

He'd had to stop protesting out loud because Victoria had threatened to gag him if he didn't. It was bad enough to be powerless, but the idea of a gag made him shudder. So he'd promised to 'behave', which meant to lie still and stop making verbal threats that he couldn't possibly, at least for the moment, make good on.

Oh, he'd underestimated Victoria, that was obvious. He never should have come to her room in the first place; he'd known in his heart of hearts that nothing good could come of it. He'd *known* when Penny appeared out of thin air that it was all too good to be true. No one would be looking for him, not at the Plaza, or at either airport, Heathrow in London or Pearson in Toronto.

Penny ran from the wardrobe to the mirror, half-naked, then back to the wardrobe again, tearing her clothes off with both hands as she went and wailing about being in the throes of a fashion crisis. No, she wasn't about to listen to reason, either. It had appeared for a moment that he might be able to convince her of the folly inherent in this 'kidnapping', but then Victoria had threatened him with the gag and he'd been forced to shut up. Since then, Penny seemed happy enough to follow Victoria's direction.

'How do I look?' Penny stood on her tiptoes in her latest outfit turning her attention from the mirror to Ray, and back to the mirror again.

'You look beautiful,' he replied. There seemed to be no talking sense into Penny or Victoria. He'd just have to wait for Lonnie and hope he could talk sense into the three of them. Victoria and Penny had popped a fresh bottle of champagne and had toasted each other more than once since Lonnie had agreed to come to Victoria's room.

'It's my only Armani,' said Victoria, fussing with the ties at the back of Penny's skimpy black dress.

'Does it really fit?' Penny twisted and turned in front of the mirror. She hadn't wanted to put her chiffon dress back on and, Ray gathered, her luggage was already at the airport, so she'd had to make do with the contents of Victoria's wardrobe. Naturally, as Victoria was not as tall as Penny, and more curvaceous, most of her clothes wouldn't fit, but they'd managed to find a couple of items with which she might make do.

'Which do you prefer, Ray?' Victoria held a purple tube in front of the dress Penny had on.

'I like them both,' he said.

'And what do you think of my outfit?' Victoria grabbed the hem of her green halter-top dress and lifted it on both sides. It fanned into a plethora of British Racing Green crinkled pleats. 'Silk,' she said, as if he'd asked.

She'd lifted the dress so high he could see the tops of her stockings and a thin strip of delectable white flesh above each of them. He felt the stirring of desire start in the pit of his stomach. 'Lovely,' he said, focusing on her treacherous face. 'I can hardly wait to tear it off you with my teeth.'

'That's the spirit!' If Victoria heard the threat in his voice, she wasn't responding to it. She bustled about for a few minutes, adjusting the many lamps and lights in the room until everything was bathed in forgiving muted light, almost as soft as candlelight. In this light, his situation didn't seem nearly so unusual.

'Almost ready, Penny?'

'Are you wearing heels? I'm going barefoot.'

'You go barefoot; I'm wearing heels. I'm taking the foil off the top of the champagne bottle so we can pop it as soon as she gets here! So, are you ready?'

'One more coat of mascara and I'm good to go!' replied Penny.

'Good. Ray, open up. I want you to eat a breath mint.' Victoria literally skipped across the room in her high heels. She leant across his chest to make sure he couldn't grab any part of her as she held her hand to his mouth. 'We want your breath to be nice and fresh for your friend.'

Ray nibbled the mint from her fingertips without protest. Victoria might know everything about him, and he'd thought he did about her, but it seemed she still had a few new tricks up her sleeve. He barely recognised this determinedly cheerful hostess who made the macabre seem acceptable.

Ray gritted his teeth to keep from straining against his bonds. He'd *known* the damn handcuffs were still on the bed! It hadn't even occurred to him that she might use them to imprison him. She'd have to be brave to do such a thing and the Victoria he knew was meek. He wanted to gnash his teeth thinking of what a sucker he'd been, falling asleep with a woman on each arm and not a care in the world. Victoria had appealed to everything about him that was male and he'd fallen for it hook, line and sinker. Dammit it, she knew him too well. Right down to the goddam vegetarian hero sandwich.

In his heart of hearts, Ray knew that he would have abandoned Victoria and Penny for one last chance to nail Bai Lon. She'd managed to worm her way into his psyche day by day, first at the symposium and then at dinner and in the limousine. Ray felt like Pavlov's dog, with Lonnie ringing the bell. Damn them all! Damn Lonnie for knowing he'd jump into a pair of trunks and wade into a Jacuzzi full of his peers if it meant a chance to slide right into her. Damn Victoria for knowing it, too. And damn Penny for her helplessness in the face of Victoria's persuasive charm.

There was a knock at the door. Penny and Victoria shrieked as if they'd seen a murderer or a mouse, then doubled over with laughter.

'You get it!' gasped Penny, still trying to add a third or fourth layer of mascara to her lashes. 'I'm going to blind myself if I don't pay attention!'

'You get it!' Victoria whispered. She twisted her hair up into a messy chignon and stuffed a clip into it. 'I haven't done my hair!'

'Don't even talk about hair!' Penny's hair was a bright aureole of curls that framed her face.

'Your hair is to die for,' said Victoria, 'and you know it.'

The knock sounded again and, again, both girls shrieked with exuberant alarm.

'Why don't you both get it?' suggested Ray.

'Coming!' called Victoria. She said to Penny, 'I know, we'll both get it.'

Penny capped her mascara wand decisively. She and Victoria hurried to the door. Penny tickled Ray's foot in passing. 'Ray, it's going to be OK,' said Penny. 'You're going to love it.'

'Wanna bet?' asked Ray.

His only hope was that Lonnie would talk some sense into the other two women. The door opened and Ray heard a whoop of girlish exclamations. Lonnie swept into view. Her thick black hair was coiled up on top of her head, making her face seem even more delicate than usual. She wore black heels and a tight white lace dress with a wide black velvet band below the bodice. The cups of the bodice were overlaid with black netting and Victoria and Penny were making a big deal out of it.

'It's so adorable. And you, Lonnie, you're beautiful!' cooed Victoria.

'You two, too!' purred Lonnie.

'I'm so excited!' shrieked Penny.

All three women erupted into yet another prolonged course of giggling.

'Lonnie!' shouted Ray.

'Oooh,' said Lonnie. She waltzed to the foot of the bed, with Victoria and Penny hanging like sorority sisters off her arms. 'I've never had a man in captivity!'

Ray groaned.

22

Even for a girl as sexually sophisticated as Lonnie, the scene in Victoria's hotel suite was breathtakingly new. Here was Ray, spread out like the centrefold in a woman's magazine come to life, accompanied by two beautiful, and beautifully dressed, women. It would be a terrible pity to rescue Ray prematurely, she very quickly decided.

'Do you know I can make him come with my feet?' she asked her new friends. 'I did it last night.'

'With your feet?' The redhead, the one who'd claimed to be Ray's cousin when they'd met in the hallway at the Plaza, was named Penny, and it was Penny who now echoed her words.

'I knew it. When he got back here, all he wanted to do was cuddle. He said he was all tired out.' Victoria, the curvy blonde, paused in the process of pouring champagne.

'I thought to myself, Why is Ray not so sure I can do it? Maybe he already had a big orgasm today?'

'I don't like to be talked about as if I'm not in the room,' said Ray.

All the women laughed. It was so like him to try to wrest control of a situation that was so completely out of his hands!

'Ray is right,' said Lonnie. She perched on the edge of the bed. 'We must be considerate of his needs.' She let her hand drop to his belly and rested it there. 'You are very handsome when you are naked, Ray,' she said, batting her mink lashes at him.

'Please, Lonnie, I have not agreed to be bound. It's wrong. You know it. You all three know it!'

'It is so difficult, sometimes, to know what is right and what is wrong,' mused Lonnie. She ran her fingertip around and around his bellybutton. 'Maybe it is wrong to go from one woman to the other on the same day, never admitting it?'

'Maybe it's wrong to use housing humanity as an excuse for fooling around,' said Victoria. She held a glass of champagne in each hand and she delivered one to Lonnie and the other to Penny, who was perched at the foot of the bed. She fetched herself a glass and sat back down in the chair Penny had pulled up for her earlier.

'Or maybe it's wrong to use the crop on a girl who doesn't want it,' said Penny.

Lonnie's eyes opened wide. 'Ray likes to crop girls?'

'Ray *loves* to crop girls,' said Victoria. 'Show her, Penny.'

Penny rose from the bed and yanked the back of her dress up. Lonnie gasped at what she saw. Penny's bum was covered in red marks.

'I think that must be wrong,' she murmured.

'She loved it,' said Ray.

'Is that true?' asked Lonnie.

Penny nodded. 'In the end I thought it was absolutely great. The orgasm I had was out of this world –'

'She even fainted,' said Victoria.

'Fainted?' Lonnie couldn't remember ever having an orgasm that intense. 'So in the end what he did was maybe not so wrong at all.'

'That's true. And maybe what we've done here, chaining Ray to the bed, maybe it isn't so wrong either,' Penny said.

'Maybe it's the *right* thing to do,' said Victoria.

Lonnie nodded and raised her glass. 'To doing the right thing,' she said.

'Cheers!' said Victoria.

The delightful bubbles tickled Lonnie's nose as she sipped her drink. 'I am not so used to being with other women,' she said, 'so it will be new and fun for me, but maybe a little scary.'

'We'll start with kissing, Lonnie, and see where it goes,' said Victoria.

'I do not want to be cropped. Also, I need someone to watch,' Lonnie stated frankly. 'Being watched is important to me.'

'That's fine,' said Victoria. 'I'll watch. I'd like to rest up a bit anyway. Bad heart.' She tapped her chest.

'I don't want anything up my arse,' Penny announced. 'I've had enough of that for one day, thank you.'

'Ray likes to put things up there?' asked Lonnie.

'He loves it,' said Victoria and Penny nodded vigorously.

'Hmm.' Lonnie carefully filled Ray's bellybutton with champagne. 'You are so bad, Ray. Much worse than I was thinking.' She smiled at him and bent her little head to his belly. Using the tip of her tongue, she delicately lapped up the liquid. It was going to be exquisite to make him hard under these circumstances.

Lonnie heard the rustling of Victoria's pleated silk dress and the scent of perfume filled her nostrils. The tip of a tongue tickled her bare earlobe, so delicately. She lifted her head from Ray's belly and her lips met Victoria's. No man, no matter how lush his mouth, had ever tantalised hers with a kiss so sweet, so delicate. It was as gentle as a whisper.

Even as she savoured the sensations of the kiss, Lonnie could see it from Ray's perspective, and Penny's. Her tightly coiled glossy black hair framed by Victoria's loose blonde chignon, her red-painted lips pressed to Victoria's, their faces, their eyes closed, their womanly bodices almost touching. It ended too soon for Lonnie's liking.

'See?' Victoria gently traced Lonnie's hairline with a tapered red-lacquered nail. 'It's easy.'

'I want to kiss you too,' Lonnie said to Penny.

The redhead's kiss was less confident than Victoria's, which made Lonnie bolder. She was the first to open her mouth and tease Penny's tongue with hers. Again, she marvelled at the newness of it all. So similar and yet so different. Her belly tightened with desire. This kiss, too, seemed to end quickly.

'Now maybe you should kiss each other?' Lonnie didn't want to seem to be taking charge, but she wanted to see how it looked, this girl-on-girl kissing, in the flesh. She wanted to see if looking at it would stir the same feelings inside her as doing it did.

Penny and Victoria shared a lavish kiss. It did, as Lonnie had suspected, make her feel like her insides were melting and she giggled with delight. 'Oh, Ray, look how pretty your friends are together,' she cooed to their captive audience.

'I know, Lonnie,' he said. What else could he say? The situation was so erotic he'd have to be a very different man not to admit it.

Victoria cupped Penny's little breast in her hand. Instantly, Penny's nipple responded. Lonnie could see that it was big, much bigger than hers. Suddenly, she could hardly wait to see the other women naked. But she would do her best to be patient; this was a moment she wanted to make last.

Lonnie lay across Ray's chest and kissed his mouth. There it was, that roughness on the chin and broadness of the lips that made kissing him so much more familiar. She flicked her tongue and his lips parted to let her inside. He was a gorgeous kisser, generous and intuitive. It was possible to fall into kissing him in a way she hadn't, yet, been able to do with either of the women. He could hold her up on his shoulders and make her come with his mouth and hands. She knew that about Ray. She also knew he was big enough to hurt her if she wasn't careful. Not like a woman.

All four were breathing more heavily when the kissing stopped. Victoria settled back in her chair. 'Is it all right with you if I touch myself?' she asked Lonnie and Penny. They nodded. Victoria hiked her skirt up and settled her hand between her legs. The view was surprisingly demure from the bed. Lonnie couldn't see exactly where Victoria's hand was, just that it was nestled between creamy thighs surrounded by crinkled green silk.

'I might need your help,' Lonnie said to Penny. 'He's big.'

'I'll help,' said Penny. 'Why don't you take off your dress?'

'Should I, Ray? Maybe you would like to see me naked?'

'I'd love to see you naked,' he said.

'He's a nudist,' said Penny.

'A naturist,' corrected Victoria.

Lonnie stood and allowed Penny to strip her as if she were a mannequin and Penny were a window dresser. Beneath the dress she still wore her bikini, to the general mirth of all three women.

'I was going to the Jacuzzi!' she explained as she stripped off the two pieces.

'Oh my God! You have no pubic hair,' Penny said. 'Lonnie, how old are you?'

'It's OK, I'm twenty-one!' Lonnie assured her.

'She's shaved, silly!' Victoria piped up from her chair.

'Thank the Lord. I'll drink to that!' declared a much relieved Penny.

Lonnie tipped her glass to her mouth, trying to stop

giggling long enough to take a little sip. Part of the newness of the situation was the way she tumbled between laughter and eroticism. She hadn't been this close to hysterics since she was a schoolgirl. At the same time she felt determined to proceed in exploring the erotic possibilities of the situation. And Victoria promised to watch! The opportunity for exhibitionism ensured that Lonnie's girlish giddiness was transformed into feminine sexual heat.

'You're so perfect,' said Penny. She ran her hands lightly down Lonnie's body, almost as if she were tracing Lonnie's shape in the air. 'Like a living miniature. Look at your lovely breasts; they're as big as mine but your nipples are so little. Like chocolate kisses.'

'I don't even know what colour to call your skin,' said Victoria. 'In the candlelight it's the colour of sand, only in the shade, like Caribbean sand in the shade of a palm tree, on a really hot sunny day.'

'Your mouth is so sweet I could eat you,' replied Lonnie. She still wore her stayups and high heels so she tottered a bit as she struck a pose. 'I'm too little to be a model.' She pouted. 'But I know all the moves. See?' She struck another pose, and another, each a little sillier than the last. She raised her hand as if hailing a cab. 'Taxi!'

'You should have told us she was so funny!' Penny said to Ray.

Lonnie preened. She loved to be the centre of attention. It made her feel like she was glowing.

'He kept you all to himself, greedy man,' said Victoria.

'Best man is a greedy man,' commented Lonnie. She stretched out on top of Ray. Her head came to his shoulder and her tiptoes touched his calves. She knew Ray would like the sensation of her, light as a feather on top of him. It would make him feel manly. Also, she provided him with a bit of cover; she was his human fig leaf. Maybe it would help him relax. She wriggled, as if to make herself comfortable but really so she could rub against him. 'You know how much I want you, Ray? I couldn't wait for another symposium to come along. I wanted to feel you inside me before I go back to Hong Kong. Please have some pity on me,' she cooed, her face tilted up so her lips were close to his ear.

She trapped him between her thighs, loosely, so she could feel him as he began to thicken. 'I know you think I am just pretending when I say maybe you are too big for me, but maybe it is true. Will you consider it?'

He nodded and she rewarded him with a kiss.

'I will be much braver if I know you cannot hold me down and pierce me with your mighty sword. Anyway, Ray, you know I like to be watched.'

He nodded again. His pale-blue eyes, which had been so fierce when she'd first arrived, seemed to soften as she continued cooing in her most soothing voice. She interspersed her words with kisses and caresses. Always, she stayed on top of him, so tiny, so insubstantial, compared to his solid male body.

'I think we are so lucky we have these friends. Maybe Penny will help me if you are too big. Victoria will watch us and that will make me hot as a firecracker. OK?'

She parted her legs so that his tip touched her naked slit. The proof of her delicacy was there for him to feel.

'When I start to have an orgasm, Ray, it is like I cannot stop even if I wanted to, but I don't want to, so I come and come ...' she murmured against the pulse in his throat. 'Please give me permission to please myself with you.'

'OK.' Ray's verbal response was short and to the point, but it did the trick. Now she was free to use him and, perhaps even more importantly, he was free to respond.

Lonnie straddled Ray's face. It was a position that

was familiar to both of them from their scenic tour of London. She wanted to feel his tongue slither inside her again and she wanted to be really wet when she tried to mount him.

'I'll suck him till he's hard,' said Penny. Lonnie didn't look behind her; she could tell from the sounds that Penny was as good as her word.

Lonnie lowered herself to Ray's mouth. His tongue flicked between the delicate lips, seeking and finding her entrance. She clutched the brass rail at the head of the bed to keep her balance as she lowered her body a fraction more, allowing his tongue to thrust deeper inside her and pressing his lips to her slit.

'That's good, baby,' she murmured. She glanced to her right and there sat Victoria, watching avidly while languidly stroking herself.

Behind Lonnie, Victoria could hear Penny slurping at Ray's cock. 'Is he hard yet, Penny?'

'Mmmmm.' Penny didn't pause to reply with words.

'You're the best, Ray, just the best,' said Lonnie. She meant it too. Now that he'd agreed to the proceedings she was sure she could trust him to participate in their play with one hundred per cent concentration and intention. He was a player, just like her. That was something she suspected only the two of them had in common, no matter how eager Victoria and Penny were to make this scene.

'So exciting!' Lonnie bounced a little and Ray's chin hit her pubic bone. 'Ouch!'

'Careful!' warned Victoria.

Lonnie stood on the bed and carefully turned around, so that when she squatted again her feet were on each side of Ray's chest and she was facing his manhood. For a moment, she joined Victoria in watching Penny suck his cock. It was thrilling to be so passive in the midst of such an exciting event. But only for a moment. Lonnie's excitement lay in other areas. She nosed her way through his pubic hair to lick his root. Penny took the tip into her mouth.

Lonnie felt Ray's breath on her behind and then the strange sensation of a tongue slithering between her cheeks. She tensed a little when it found its target. Her bum might be unmarked but that didn't seem to make it unappealing to him in the least. She closed her eyes. For a moment Lonnie concentrated on the decadent descent of his tongue. She shuddered suddenly, so deeply that she feared she might tumble off him, so she tucked her calves under his forearms to steady herself. Even in the midst of such debauchery the lip-smacking way he was enjoying her seemed particularly obscene.

She could feel his moans with her belly before she heard them. His stomach muscles tightened and she felt that, too. At the same time, the way he was exploring a part of her that she had kept private up until now made her stomach tighten and drew a moan from deep within her, one that he could probably feel before he heard it.

With her eyes closed, Lonnie felt Penny's tongue slither into her mouth. Together they licked and lapped their way up his shaft to the tip. There they swirled their tongues, clockwise and counter-clockwise at the same time, until they coaxed it to favour them with a glistening droplet.

'He's very big,' moaned Lonnie. 'I think he will stretch me.'

'Are you serious? How tiny are you?'

Penny sat up between Ray's outstretched legs. Lonnie slid off Ray and knelt up beside his leg. Penny licked her own finger and then slipped her hand between Lonnie's thighs. Lonnie felt the wet pad of Penny's fingertip and then it was inside her.

'Hmm.' Penny played with Lonnie for a moment,

sliding her finger in and out. 'I think you can take him,' she announced. She drew her hand back and licked her finger again.

It struck Lonnie as the sexiest thing she had ever seen. This redhead, her face flushed and her lips swollen from sucking, relished licking Lonnie's taste from her finger. 'Want more?' asked Lonnie.

'All right,' replied Penny.

Lonnie lay back in the crook of Ray's left arm and spread her legs. She hooked one over his chest and the other over Penny's shoulder. Penny fluttered her eyelashes, butterfly kissing the inside of Lonnie's thighs.

'Oh, Ray, it's so good,' Lonnie murmured. She curled her right arm around his head and ran her fingers through his hair. She pressed her mouth to his temple. 'One minute it's like a truck is driving over me and the next minute so light, like a fairy is dancing on my skin.'

'Get her good and wet, Penny,' said Ray, 'and then maybe she'll be brave enough to mount old Ray.'

Penny's mouth was on Lonnie's mound so when she nodded Lonnie felt her lips brush her skin. It was tantalising. She knew Penny would find that she was plenty wet already, but if she feared the other woman wouldn't like the taste it wasn't a fear she held for long. Penny purred as she lavished Lonnie with Sapphic attention. That, in turn, made Lonnie liquefy.

'I'll come,' she groaned.

'No, don't, Lonnie, please, not yet.' It was Victoria who spoke up from the shadow of her chair. 'Stop, Penny.'

Lonnie hadn't for a moment forgotten about Victoria. How could she, when it was essential to her fulfilment that Victoria serve as witness? Now she realised that it was also essential to her that Victoria be satisfied with the tableau she presented.

Penny sat back, wiping her mouth with the back of her hand. 'How do you want her, Victoria?'

'Mount him, just as he said, Lonnie. You can do it.' Victoria's voice was warm with assurance. 'Ride him like he's your own private stallion.'

'OK,' said Lonnie. She changed position again so that she straddled Ray, facing front. 'Ready, Ray?'

'I've been ready for this for a week,' he replied.

Penny reached behind her back to tug free the bow that kept her dress on. Naked, she slid up close to Ray's left side, rested her shoulder on his and presented her right breast to his mouth. He took her scarlet nipple in his mouth and sucked.

Lonnie pushed herself up off Ray's chest with her right leg. She positioned her little body above his hard-on. 'I don't know . . .'

'Come on, baby, take it,' encouraged Victoria.

'Show me how you fuck my cock, Bai Lon,' said Ray.

'Help,' said Lonnie, looking at Penny.

Penny knelt up beside Ray and lapped at the head of his cock. Lonnie lowered herself until she could feel it bulge between her lips. Penny continued licking the shaft as it started to sink inside Lonnie, then shifted her attention to Lonnie's clit as it slowly slid down the length of him.

'Beautiful,' moaned Ray.

'It is, darling, it's beautiful,' said Victoria.

Lonnie lowered herself another inch, and then another. With Penny lubricating both Ray and Lonnie, the big cock entered her more easily than she could have imagined. Slowly she let her weight shift from her foot to her knee and finally she was straddling Ray.

'Oh my God! I'm so stuffed, I don't think I can move!'

'Of course you can. Ride him, Lonnie.' Victoria's voice oozed encouragement.

'Ride him, cowgirl!' Penny's voice joined Victoria's.

Lonnie raised herself as much as she could and felt Ray tense beneath her. When she plunged downwards, he jerked his pelvis up and the impact was bone-rattling. She shrieked as he filled her to her very centre. Penny stayed where she was, indiscriminately licking Lonnie's and Ray's flesh.

Warning signals were ringing at every one of Lonnie's pulse points. She pulled herself up, almost off him, then dropped down again, taking him to the very hilt of her. Her clit hummed as it slid along his rigid shaft.

'Goddam it, Ray,' Lonnie hissed through clenched teeth. She started riding him as hard and as fast as she could. Why not? She'd already been recreated as nothing more than a sheath for him. He entered her as smoothly as if she'd been handmade to his specifications. That didn't stop his knob from bumping up against her and making her yelp, but that didn't deter either of them from a fast hard ride; she just leant forwards slightly to better accommodate all of him.

'Good, baby, so good,' she mumbled. Her clit was a tiny ball of silver mercury that felt like it was dispersing into a myriad of tinier balls with each touch, then coalescing, then exploding. Each droplet became a shooting star and suddenly she was coming in sharp bursts so quick and bright and numerous it seemed she would surely be obliterated. She yipped like a puppy, or a real cowgirl, with every starburst.

After the last glimmer faded and the final tremor rippled through her, she was amazed to find that she had somehow managed to settle like fairy dust back into the shape of her body.

The candles were glowing when she opened her eyes. She tilted her face so she could kiss the contours of Ray's chin, then stole a glance at Victoria. She sighed with satisfaction.

Lonnie dismounted with difficulty. Her elaborate hairdo had completely come undone and her cheeks and chest were flushed pink. Her breath had not yet returned to normal. It took her a moment to realise that Ray was still rigid.

'Oh, Ray, I'm so sorry,' she said. 'I imagined you coming too!'

'That's OK, baby,' he said. 'You're a terrific fuck. So pretty when you come. Well worth the wait.'

'Thank you, Ray.'

'I'm so excited I could die!' exclaimed Penny. With that she climbed on top of Ray. Penny commenced riding him even harder and faster than Lonnie had.

Lonnie tucked herself under Ray's arm in the spot Penny had just vacated. She glanced again at Victoria, who was still languidly toying with herself within the folds of her silk dress. Victoria's gaze was locked on Ray and now Lonnie realised that Ray was staring back at Victoria with equal intensity. That left Lonnie to watch Penny pleasure herself by using Ray in exactly the way she just had.

Penny whooped exuberantly. Lonnie calmly observed. She felt pleasantly detached from her surroundings, probably since her own orgasm had only just begun to fade. It was as if she were watching a replay of the activity she had been engaged in, only this time an English actress with pale skin and auburn hair was playing her part. It was kinky to the extreme but then there was nothing about the situation that was anything else.

Penny tossed her head from side to side, her red hair flying. 'Oh, baby, oh yeah!' she howled. She froze on top of Ray, then crumpled on to his chest and lay there for a few moments until her breathing normalised. She slid free of Ray and curled up under his right arm.

Lonnie saw the obvious evidence that, like her, Penny had achieved her own orgasm before satisfying him. He was some cool customer, that Ray.

'Victoria,' he said. 'Care to climb aboard?'

'I don't mind if I do,' she replied.

23

It was the best sex of Victoria's life. Not the most romantic, but easily the best.

She was wet from watching and from playing with herself, and so was he, wet with the juices of the two women who now cuddled against him, naked and blissfully spent. It seemed right that there should be two of them, that they should be naked, that one should have a head of red curls that tumbled over his chest and one should have a heavy gleaming hank of straight black hair that lay across his arm like a pelt. She pulled the clip from her blonde hair which fell free. It brushed her shoulders as she approached the bed.

'I wondered if you would,' said Ray. He meant he wondered if she, like the others, would use him. 'So I kept some for you.' His cock was an elegant glistening pole.

Victoria smiled. She'd wondered about that, herself. Watching Lonnie and Ray in action hadn't been the same as watching Ray with Penny. She'd picked Penny to be her partner on this adventure. But Lonnie? She was the icing on the cake. Pure candy.

She reached behind her neck with both hands to loosen the strips of silk that kept up the halter-top of her dress. Her breasts bounced freely as she circled the bed. The three nude people on the bed looked wonderful from every angle.

Victoria picked up the crop. She swished it through the air and Ray's eyes widened. So did Penny's and Lonnie's. Victoria laughed. 'Sillies,' she said, dropping the crop again.

For a moment, she considered taking her dress off. Would it be best if she were naked like them? She decided against it. The crinkled green silk skirt was voluminous. She'd probably be able to cover all of them with it. The idea appealed.

She paused at the bedside table to finish her glass of champagne. She noted that the clock showed it was past five, that the candles were more than half-melted and that the champagne bottle was empty. The night that had seemed like it might never arrive was almost over. Had it been worth it?

Victoria stepped up on to the bed. She stood with her feet on either side of Ray's hips. Her dress cascaded on to his chest and over the legs of his companions. 'You must be even more handsome than I thought, to have such beautiful women in your life,' she said.

'I'm just a lucky guy,' he said.

Victoria held out her hands. 'Help me,' she said. Lonnie leant up to grab her right hand and Penny her left. Victoria lowered herself over Ray, using her knees and the support of the other two women to keep her descent slow and steady. Her skirt rustled. She didn't pause when the head of his cock bumped up against her. She just enveloped it, she *welcomed* it, inside. It had only taken two days for her pussy to become his property, moulded to fit perfectly, like a piece of the jigsaw puzzle that was him. It was just that there were so many, many pieces to the puzzle that was Ray.

Victoria settled on him, her knees at his sides. She leant forwards so she could place Penny's and Lonnie's hands on her breasts. There. Picture perfect.

Watching Lonnie with Ray had created an excitement in Victoria that she'd never felt before. Earlier, she'd experienced exultation at the way her dream had come true. There'd been many moments that had been exciting because they were new. There'd been giddiness when Lonnie had arrived. But, while the excitement from watching Ray and Lonnie and Penny play had been visceral, it had also been cerebral. It was the excitement she felt at a gallery opening when the artwork was good, or at a concert when a melody she'd never heard before was debuted. It was the way she felt when she read the latest works by her favourite author, or a piece of journalism that put together ideas she knew she'd already had to come to a conclusion she hadn't been able to give voice to. It was beauty and information, both, and that kind of excitement rocked her world.

She kept her back straight and put her hands on Ray's hips. Female fingers teased her rosebud nipples to harden. She clenched and released her internal muscles, like a fist tightening and loosening around his cock. Each contraction made her clit ache.

It would be brilliant to make him come like this. Something he'd always remember. That would have been enough, only a few hours ago, to inspire Victoria to attempt it. But now she was seeking her own release, as much as if not more than his. She wanted to ride him, just as the others had, but also make him climax, which the others had failed to do.

She put her hands on his chest and began to raise and lower her body, using his cock as her compass. She rose slowly and then slammed down hard, impaling herself on him. That was what she wanted! To be full of him, with his balls banging against her bum and his pubic bone rubbing hers, then the long slow with-drawal, and then bang! Full again!

She was panting. So was he. Penny and Lonnie had released her breasts so now they swung, pendant, above him. Each girl, Victoria noticed, had one hand between her own legs.

'Me too,' she murmured. They each slid a hand down

Ray's belly and under Victoria's skirt. Now, at the end of each hard thrust, busy fingers found and teased her clit.

'Heaven,' she said. She ground hard against his coarse pubic hair. She leant forwards, her breasts flattened to his chest, and sloppily kissed him, open panting mouth to open panting mouth.

'Beauty,' he muttered. 'Beautiful perfect puss...'

She turned her face from his to kiss Lonnie in the same messy manner. Lonnie's teeth were like little pearls, her eyes like chocolate, her lips as red and brilliant as rubies. 'Precious,' said Victoria. 'Precious Lonnie...'

She turned from Lonnie to kiss Penny, meeting her tongue with her own. The heat generated from the kiss rushed to the pit of her belly as if her throat and chest were a flume and the kiss was the oxygen needed to fan the fire that burnt there. 'Precious Penny...'

'Do it, doll.' Penny was urging her on. 'Take what you want from him. You deserve it.'

It was debatable, Victoria thought, exactly *what* she deserved. She put her hands to his shoulders and began pumping in earnest. It wasn't a matter of what she did or didn't deserve; it was a matter of what she wanted that Ray could give her. She knew precisely what that was.

'Ride him, girl,' Lonnie said, imitating the words Victoria and Penny had used to encourage her when she'd been screwing Ray.

It was almost like Victoria was screwing him, almost as if it were her cock she was pumping into him and not the other way around. She was in control, for the moment. Her clit ached so ferociously she knew she wouldn't be in control for much longer. Didn't matter. She was free, free to jerk and shriek and curse if she wanted to. Free to fuck her brains out, although for once she didn't care if she was thinking or not thinking – her thoughts were in tune with her body, fuck him, fuck him, make it happen.

'Jesus.' She moaned, as much to release the pressure that was building inside her as to articulate any particular notion. 'Fuck,' she sputtered.

She was pounding up and down now, riding the smooth wet length of him hard and fast. Her ears were buzzing, her heart pounding so hard it seemed the buzzing in her ears must be coming from her heart. 'I'm gonna die!' she groaned.

Ray pumped up from beneath her, as best he could. 'Do it,' he grunted.

Did he want her to die? Didn't matter if he did. Didn't matter if she did. She'd die a free woman.

'Free,' she grunted. She wanted him to know, just in case she really did die.

'Good,' he grunted. His belly tensed. If he came before she did she'd kill him first, she swore to herself. He'd been fucking for a long time now, but she needed him to last just a little longer.

Little fingers swiped at her clit every time she completed a frenzied stroke.

'Atta girl,' cooed Penny. 'All the way . . .'

'All the way,' chimed in Lonnie.

Victoria nodded. Beads of perspiration wet her hair and trickled down the back of her neck. It wasn't from the exertion but from the excitement, the incredible excitement of this exact moment. She hated to let it pass but she had no choice in the matter. She was hurtled into a dizzying climax.

Victoria kept moving. Her pussy grabbed at his cock with every spasm, as if to keep it trapped forever. But that wasn't what this fuck was about. This fuck was about now. And now. And now. Victoria cried out as she sailed on the bliss between the moments.

Ray grunted, his face a mask of furious need, then he grunted again and the planes of his cheekbones and forehead and chin seemed to soften as his face split into a ferocious grin. 'God!' he shouted.

'Good!' She could have sobbed with the relief her orgasm had released. Good, he was coming too. Victoria steadied herself on her knees and let him fuck up into her, fast and furious, just the way he liked it. Lonnie and Penny were moaning too, the greedy girls. 'Good,' she repeated. Little pleasure tremors were still rippling through her body. She tilted forwards a bit so her clit came in harsher contact with his cock. 'Damn!' Victoria was flying again! It didn't seem possible but there it was, one more big spasm of joy.

'Goddam it, Ray!'

'I know, baby, I know, we're so goddam good together!'

Panting and moaning and shouting and cursing filled the air. The orgasmic cacophony only ended when the last of the four had finished, which was scant seconds after the first.

Victoria lay limp across Ray's chest. She needed to straighten her knees but she didn't have the energy to do so. She thought it might be best to sleep, just for a few moments, before she tried to move.

Ray rattled his chains, disturbing her dreamy disconnected thoughts. When she didn't move, he started wriggling to wake her up.

'Mmmmm.'

'Please release me, Beauty Puss.'

Lonnie slid out of the bed and padded to the bathroom. Penny stretched and sighed and scurried to the fridge in search of refreshments. Victoria and Ray were alone.

'Hurry, honey,' said Ray. 'After all, we have a plane to catch.' He grinned at her.

'What do you mean?' Victoria stared at him.

'I'm coming with you to Cuba! You and Penny. I've decided. I wanted Lonnie, I admit it. But now I've had her. So I'm all yours for the next few weeks.'

'Is that so? Free to come to Cuba.'

Lonnie came out of the bathroom, wrapped in a white terry robe. 'What's this about Cuba?'

'Penny and I are going to Cuba this morning. We have two weeks booked at a five-star resort in Veredero.'

'Nice. I've heard about it. Good discos.'

'Good everything. I also booked a tour of the agro-industrial complex in the province of Las Tunas.'

Penny came into the room, munching an apple. She handed one each to Victoria and Lonnie. 'Cool,' she said.

Lonnie thoughtfully rolled the apple in her hand. 'I think I could convince my superiors to let me go to Cuba on an expedition funded by a – shall we say – a possible future contributor to the cause.'

'Really?' Victoria looked at Lonnie with interest. 'What do you think, Penny?'

'I think it would be great, Victoria. We'd each have our own rooms, right?'

'That's right,' said Victoria, looking at Ray. He frowned, perhaps imagining his own room in a five-star hotel in Cuba. 'We can come and go as we please, only getting together when it suits us.'

'We'll be like Charlie's Angels, without the Charlie!' crowed Lonnie.

'But what about me? I want to be Charlie,' protested Ray.

'Darling,' said Victoria, stroking his dear familiar face. 'You say Lonnie was the last but I know better. And now I understand. Truly, I do. It is the nature of the beast that is Ray.'

'No, wait a minute. I'm getting older, Victoria. I need to settle down.'

'You'll never settle down, darling. At least, not for any length of time.'

'I was thinking, after Cuba, we could go back to Canada together.'

'I'm not going back to Canada, Ray. I already told you that.'

'Victoria, wait. Think about it. You and me, together, forever. You need me to take care of you, with your bad heart and all.'

'I need something, it's true. But I no longer think it's you. I'm sorry, but my mind is made up. Lonnie, you're in.'

'Cuba here I come!' shouted Lonnie.

The alarm clock sounded.

Victoria laughed. 'Wake up, everyone! We have a plane to catch.' She glanced at Ray, shackled to the bed. 'Everyone but you that is. You can relax. You're not going anywhere.'

24

He couldn't believe his ears. 'Beauty Puss –' he began but Victoria cut him off.

'No more time to talk, Ray. I've got to get ready to go.'

'But, Victoria –'

'Hush now, darling, or I'll have to gag you.'

He shuddered. That damn gag threat again. Once again he was forced to lie there, naked and spread-eagled, and be quiet about it. He bided his time.

It was as if he weren't in the room at all, as if he were a fly on the wall of a sorority house. As far as he could tell, the three women showered together. At least, they went into the bathroom together and after a lot of squealing and splashing noises they came out together, in identical white robes and with towels piled and tucked into turbans on their heads. There was much carrying on about what to wear and what Penny had done with Mitzu, whom he gathered was Penny's cat, and whether Lonnie should call ahead to her Chinese minders or whether it would be better just to show up at the airport and surprise them with her new plans.

Victoria speedily packed the clothes she'd unpacked during her stay in the suite. Some of her luggage, he understood, was already at the airport with Penny's. She was the only one with fresh clothes at the moment but Penny and Lonnie would be able to change at the airport and they all three decided to hurry so they could get there in time to shop for cruisewear.

There was more giggling as they increased the pace

with which they prepared to depart. Ray had hoped he might get Penny alone, or Lonnie, so he could try to talk some sense into one or the other. Victoria, he'd concluded, was not in the mood to listen to reason. But it became clear that she wasn't going to leave anyone alone in the room with him, and they were leaving any minute.

'You're making a mistake, you know,' he said as Victoria searched among the bedclothes for a missing high heel. 'You should take me to Cuba. That was the plan.'

'Plans change,' she said cheerily. She was wearing a colourful shift and sandals, with a cotton cardigan tied around her neck. In no time she'd transformed herself into a lovely and elegant lady bound for a Caribbean holiday. It was impossible to imagine she was the same woman who'd seduced him, arranged a *ménage a trois* for him, arranged a *ménage a quatre* for him and imprisoned him.

'You can't mean to leave me like this. Victoria? Let me go now. I promise I won't make any trouble for you.'

'Once the plane is in the air, I'll call hotel security and have them come in and release you.'

'I'll tell them what you did. I'll have you charged.'

'I don't think so.' She grinned triumphantly, holding up the high heel. 'Got it,' she called to Penny.

'Let's go!' Penny was backing out of the wardrobe, making sure it was empty.

'Where are the tickets?' cried Lonnie. She'd been hovering over her cell phone since she'd finished dressing, calling on various members of the Posse to do things on her behalf.

'Oh my God, the tickets!' Victoria opened her bag, the gold-coloured one that had up until recently belonged to Penny. Penny had Lonnie's Balenciaga bag now and Lonnie was using Victoria's suede hobo bag. At least, she thought that was the way they'd worked it out. 'With all this purse switching I don't know where they are!'

Ray sighed. There was no doubt Victoria had the tickets somewhere but there was also no doubt that these three would shriek and carry on for a few more moments before she found them. He'd really had no idea that accomplished, talented, sophisticated women were so eager to act like giddy girls. It was worth knowing.

'Thank you for my new friends, Ray.' Lonnie swooped in to plant a kiss on his lips.

The cheek of the woman. His hand opened and closed, grasping nothing more substantial than air.

'I love them,' she added.

Not even thank you for the fabulous fuck? 'Lonnie, come on. From one comrade to another, don't leave me like this.'

'I'm not in charge of this operation, Ray,' she said. 'You know I would like to let you go but more than that I would like to go to Cuba with my new friends. We will be like Charlie's Angels without –'

'Yeah, I know. Without Charlie. But Lonnie, honestly, cupcake –'

'Bye bye, baby,' she said, shutting him up with another kiss.

'Penny, what gives? We had a good time, didn't we?'

'It was the best, Ray. Thanks!' Penny sat down on the bed, at least. Maybe she was his best hope.

'I don't imagine "The Fire of London" wants any of this to get out?'

'I'm depending on everyone's discretion.'

'Let me go and I swear I'll never speak of it to a soul.'

'Victoria promises she's going to get security to release you as soon as the plane takes off.'

'What if she's lying? It isn't safe. I could die here.'

'Don't be melodramatic. You're in a hotel. Even with the "Do Not Disturb" showing, someone would be bound to check in to change the towels or something, within a day or two.'

'A day or two! Do you blame me for being concerned? Penny, I'm chained to the bed!'

Penny stroked his cheek. 'You could have come with us, Ray, but you were greedy. That's OK. No hard feelings. Only, I'm going to stick with Victoria on this. I don't think she's lying. I think she'll call Security and a couple of nice big beefy guys will come right up here, share a few laughs and then let you go.'

She giggled when he groaned and once more his hand clawed at thin air as she slipped away.

'Bye, darling,' cooed Victoria.

'You're a traitorous bitch.'

'Thank you.' Victoria grinned. 'Kiss me, you fool! This really is our very last goodbye.' She put her hand to his mouth but her touch was gentle. She bent close, her incredible moss-green eyes bright.

'Oh, I'll see you again,' he said.

She pressed her lips to his. The kiss was hard and sweet. When it ended he whispered, 'I love you.' She didn't seem to hear.

He didn't even try to grab her as she left him. It was too late. Victoria was free.

25

Dawn had barely begun to tint London with the muted colours of a foggy new day. Penny watched her hometown wake up from her window seat in the taxi on their way to the airport. Lonnie was in the front seat, arguing with their Ethiopian driver about the efficacy of UN embargos. Penny glanced at Victoria, beside her in the back of the cab. Victoria seemed perfectly at ease.

Penny felt a rush of affection for the other woman. Since their meeting a few months ago, she'd wondered, from time to time, if she were getting into a relationship that would be more trouble than it was worth. Sure, she'd always wondered what the card Ray sent from Cuba had said and, yes, she'd imagined from time to time what she might say to the wild Canadian should she ever bump into him, but on her own she would never have come up with a scheme as splendid as the one Victoria had concocted.

It had taken more than money. After all, while she wasn't as wealthy as Victoria, she made a good annual income, although in Penny's business she also lost a good annual income. It was the nature of the game. Still, it really wasn't a question of money, but of intent. Without Victoria's driving desire to be with Ray again, the adventure never would have happened. Somehow, it seemed to Penny, without the Ray adventure, the Bryce Stafford, Junior adventure and the Nobatu adventure never would have happened either. They were interconnected, as if, just by opening herself up to the possibilities that life presented beyond poker, she'd been handsomely rewarded.

She hoped Victoria was as satisfied with the way things had turned out as she was. Come to that, she sincerely hoped Ray would, eventually, look back on recent events with a certain amount of fondness, too. Penny giggled, picturing Ray chained to the bed.

Victoria turned from the window. She took Penny's hand and gave it a squeeze. 'BFF,' she said. It was a continuation of their girly games, but the calm determined way she said it gave Penny a thrill. They weren't girls, they were women, and women didn't make promises like that lightly.

'Best friends forever,' replied Penny.

26

Victoria fastened her seatbelt, although the plane wouldn't depart for a while yet. That was just as well, since she was the first of the travelling companions to board. They'd had to collect Penny's luggage, and it hadn't been as easy as Lonnie had anticipated to change her destination from Hong Kong to Cuba. Victoria laughed out loud as she recalled the high-pitched fast-paced harangue that Lonnie had unleashed upon her Chinese handlers, especially the one called Lo Song. In the end, as Lonnie had expected all along, the unscheduled trip to Cuba was OKed. Lonnie's superiors really had no choice. She was a bright, beautiful, young and popular representative of the Communist Party. They needed to keep her happy.

There hadn't been time for a proper shopping spree but Lonnie and Penny had wanted to check out the duty-free stores. Victoria had decided to board by herself. She could use a few minutes alone to get used to the way her last adventure had turned out before she took off in search of another one.

The weightlessness she'd been experiencing since the *ménage a quatre* in her hotel room was settling now. The cool calm at the centre of her, where until recently a hot coal of obsession had glowed for so many years, remained. But she was already beginning to be able to be objective about the strangely triumphant episode. She realised that her new state of being would take some time to get used to.

The intensity of an obsession is precisely what makes

it impossible to sustain forever. For years, until she and Ray and Penny had ended up in the same city at the same time, her fixation had existed mostly as a deep and raw regret. She'd have to think about that, now. She wondered if she'd brought unnecessary baggage to her marriage, baggage that her marriage might have been better served without.

Still, it had been a second marriage for Gordon and he'd been much older than she, so he'd carried his past with him, too. Together they'd created something new. They'd made a protective affectionate union. Perhaps it was more a case of the grieving widow, which she *had* been, recovering from her loss a little more quickly than might be expected.

Now she'd deal with another loss. Sometime during the night, starting when Ray was fucking Lonnie with delirious delight, making a conquest even while cuffed to the bed, and ending with Victoria's own orgasm, impaled on Ray, she'd understood. With that understanding had come a release that was much more profound than any of the many stupendous orgasms she'd experienced over the last few days. Now she would learn to live with it.

It was sort of like being widowed all over again, except this time it had been her decision to declare a definitive end. Something like divorce.

There was the question, too, of what to do with herself. Perhaps, now that she'd exorcised her personal demons, she could use her remaining time on earth, and her not inconsiderable wealth, to help battle some of the demons that threatened everybody.

She exhaled heavily, as if forcing the last of the air she'd lived and breathed for Ray from her lungs. He wasn't inside her any more, not in any way. But she would never forget him and, though his words had stopped living in her head, she'd probably never forget them, either. Ray had sworn that he'd always loved her, and he always would. She understood that now. Just as she understood that Ray would always be on the lookout for the next new woman.

Victoria felt like she had always loved Ray and always would, too. She hoped just knowing that he was walking the earth, helping the homeless and keeping a sharp eye out for his next female conquest, would make her happy. Victoria was sure that Ray would feel that way again, someday, after his justifiable anger over his present situation subsided. She glanced at her watch. He'd be released soon. As soon as the plane took off, and that was any minute now.

'Last call for Flight 221 to Cuba.'

Victoria unbuckled her seatbelt again. She twisted in her window seat to peer down the aisle. Whenever she'd imagined this moment, and she'd done so many times, she'd never imagined herself departing for Cuba solo. Victoria giggled. Wouldn't it be ironic if that were the way it turned out? She felt a sudden swelling of confidence. She imagined she could go to Cuba on her own if she had to and enjoy it, too. But travelling with girlfriends made it even sweeter.

Their giggling preceded them. Lonnie was wearing bright-red short-shorts, an abbreviated bomber jacket in turquoise silk and a matching baseball cap. She probably couldn't wait to hit the beach. Penny wore khaki capris and a midriff-baring white cotton T-shirt. She was eager to get some colour. When they saw Victoria, both girls grinned and waved and hurried down the aisle, their new straw handbags swinging gaily.

'We can go now,' announced Lonnie, collapsing into the seat beside Victoria. 'Nice big chair,' she purred.

'Don't most chairs seem big to you?' asked Victoria.

'Well, this one is extra big because we're in first class,' said Lonnie.

Penny dropped into the window seat on the other side of the aisle. 'I hope I don't get some bore sitting beside me,' she said. 'As it's first class, maybe I'll get to sit next to a rock star or a politician.'

'If you get a politician, give him to me,' said Lonnie.

'You're just as bad as Ray,' complained Penny. She bit her lip and gave Victoria a guilty glance. 'Oops.'

'We decided we're not talking about that man any more. He's a cad,' said Lonnie. But the look of concern on her face belied her words. 'Victoria,' she said, leaning close to whisper, 'you *will* call the security guards at the hotel to set him free, right?'

'You don't really believe I'm going to do that, do you?' Victoria asked.

Penny said, 'You promised!'

Victoria laughed. 'Oh, he'll be set free, all right, but not by a couple of goons with big mouths. By a discreet member of the housekeeping staff.'

'You scared me!' grumbled Lonnie. She shook her finger at Victoria. 'Ray may be a playboy but he's a playboy whose politics I admire.'

'He'll be discovered on their daily rounds, then?' asked Penny.

'That's what I had in mind at first,' said Victoria. 'But when I saw how attracted Ray was to one of the hotel's housekeepers I fine-tuned my plan. He'll be rescued by a lovely young lady named Cerise, although in some quarters she's known as "The French Twist", and it's not because of the way she wears her hair.'

'You're so good to him,' said Penny. 'I'm proud of you, Victoria.'

'It's easy to be good to him. I've loved him for a long, long time,' said Victoria. 'He's always been the focus of my "should haves" and "would haves"'. My one big regret. I needed to be with him again to remember what I knew as a girl and then forgot.'

'Yeah,' said Lonnie. 'He's hung like a horse.'

'Sssh.' Victoria elbowed Lonnie. 'That's not what I'm talking about at all.'

'But he is hung like a horse, right? I'm saying the expression properly?'

Penny laughed. 'Yes, Lonnie. But I think Victoria's talking about bigger issues.'

'Maybe,' said Lonnie, but she sounded unconvinced.

'With Ray, there's always going to be something that's more important than me,' continued Victoria. 'When he was young it was "The Revolution", now it's "Housing Humanity". Big goals with capital letters. Fair enough. But, along with whatever it is he's doing that's more important than me, there's also the possibility of meeting a New Woman, also a big goal, and also in capital letters.'

'I like a new man every now and then, especially every now,' said Lonnie. 'It never lasts long. I am driven, like Ray, to try to make a difference in this world of ours. The only way I can keep going is by turning it off when I'm not working. It gets easier and easier to do the opposite, as well. Completely forget everything and everyone to concentrate on my work. It makes relationships very difficult. I have always hoped that when I am older I will learn the secret to having a personal life. You know, I'm still young. By the time I'm old like Ray I hope to be a grown-up.'

'You have a good point,' said Victoria. 'I don't think Ray's ever going to grow up. Not when it comes to relationships with the opposite sex. I understand that now. The quest is part of the person. I wouldn't change it in Ray, even if I could, which I now realise I can't.'

'It certainly was fun to try,' commented Penny.

'Yup.' Victoria grinned at her friends. 'It was great fun while it lasted.'

'Ray lasts a long time, huh?' said Lonnie.

'That's not what I meant,' said Victoria.

'He sure does, though,' commented Penny. 'Great staying power, and a great body.'

'Handsome,' said Lonnie, nodding wisely.

'Do you think it's his physical attributes that make him irresistible?' Victoria was taken aback. She'd always been madly attracted to Ray but she'd always assumed the reasons for her attraction were more than skin deep. 'I hope I wasn't obsessed with him all those years just because he's handsome!'

'It doesn't really matter now. Ray's wonderful, we all agree. But he's good for a good time, not for a long time,' said Penny.

'Right!' said Lonnie. 'Good for good time, not for long time. I like that. It can be our motto!' Lonnie started rooting through her straw bag. 'Does anyone have a pen? I'm going to write that down.'

Penny noticed a magazine sticking out of Lonnie's new straw bag. 'Lonnie! I'm surprised at you, buying that trash.'

Lonnie giggled. 'Oh, never mind!' Victoria noted with amusement that this was the first time she'd seen Lonnie clearly embarrassed. 'It has all the scandals and stories and movie stars. I can't help taking a peek when I have the chance.'

'Hand it over,' said Penny.

'It's just for reading on the beach,' said Lonnie, still defending her purchase, but she reluctantly gave the magazine to Penny.

'Anna dumps Bryce at the altar,' Penny read out loud. 'So he was telling the truth. He didn't get married after all,' she mused.

'Those magazines never tell the truth. Do they?' asked Lonnie.

'Sometimes the truth is so simple it's hard to see,' said Victoria. A sense of wellbeing settled over her. What difference did it make, any more, why she'd loved Ray the way she had or he'd loved her the way he had? They'd loved each other the best they could, that was certain. Now that part of their lives was over. Not just until the next time. *Forever*. She stretched her arms and legs to carry the calm to her fingertips and toes. 'I'm free!'

'I'm so glad,' Penny said. 'It means we were entirely successful, in my book.'

'I'm glad too,' said Lonnie. 'I'm much more fun to take on a trip than Ray would have been.'

'I don't doubt that for a moment,' said Victoria. She leant close to Lonnie who lifted her lips for a kiss, but Victoria was just trying to see past her, down the aisle. 'Look who's here! And just in time, too!'

Veruschka strode towards them. She tapped Lonnie's shoulder with a French-manicured fingernail. 'Excuse me, I'd like to sit beside my patient.'

'Huh?' Lonnie gaped at the big beautiful Russian.

'Surprise! My nursie is joining us on our trip,' said Victoria.

'You have your own nurse?' Lonnie hurried to do as she'd been told and meekly sat in the aisle seat beside Penny.

'Victoria has a very bad heart, Lonnie,' said Penny. 'That's the main reason she concocted the plan to see Ray. She could drop dead at any moment.'

Veruschka smirked. She took Victoria's delicate wrist in her hand and tilted up the pendant watch pinned to her blouse so she could calculate Victoria's pulse. 'You're very calm,' she commented. 'Nice colour in your cheeks.'

Victoria knew she was blushing furiously. 'Veruschka, this is my friend Penny and this is my friend Lonnie.'

'Hello, ladies. I hope you are both in good health? Any pain?'

'No, no pain,' said Penny quickly. 'Neither of us is in

pain,' she clarified further when Lonnie remained speechless.

'Good. And you?' Veruschka turned her attention back to Victoria. 'Did you finish your medication?'

'Yes.' Victoria nodded.

'I made sure of it!' Penny said.

'I hope you have more for the trip,' said Lonnie.

Veruschka gave Victoria a scathing look. She dropped the wrist she held. 'Your pulse is perfect,' she growled.

Victoria gulped. 'The truth is – um – there's nothing wrong with my heart,' she confessed. 'I said I had a heart condition to make Ray come see me in my hotel room. I'm sorry, Penny. I decided it would be easier just to let you think so, too.'

'Uh-huh. You really had it bad,' said Penny, shaking her head. 'So the pills were –'

'Candies,' confessed Victoria. She batted her eyelashes at Penny. 'I'm sorry.'

'You scamp!' Penny scolded. 'You should be severely punished.'

'No more surprises! Cross my – um – heart,' said Victoria.

'At least, not until we get to Cuba,' murmured Veruschka. 'Then we'll see.'

The seatbelt light came on and everyone buckled up.

'I'm so excited!' exclaimed Lonnie. 'It seems one adventure barely ends before another one begins!'

Penny took a deck of cards from her bag and started shuffling them with deft hands.

The engines of the plane roared to life. Victoria checked her watch. Yes, right about now Cerise would be letting herself into the hotel room to find Ray chained to the bed. She imagined Ray's chagrin, then his delight at discovering that Cerise was the one with the key to his release. She hoped he was already on his way to forgiving her as Cerise began to work her magic on him.

When they reached cruising altitude and the seatbelt light was turned off, Penny began dealing the cards. 'Who's in?' she asked.

'Me!' exclaimed Lonnie.

'Everybody,' said Veruschka.

'What's the game?' asked Victoria.

Penny laughed. 'Stud Poker, of course. Queens are wild,' she said.

Visit the Black Lace website at
www.blacklace-books.co.uk

FIND OUT THE LATEST INFORMATION AND TAKE ADVANTAGE OF OUR FANTASTIC FREE BOOK OFFER! ALSO VISIT THE SITE FOR . . .

- All Black Lace titles currently available and how to order online
- Great new offers
- Writers' guidelines
- Author interviews
- An erotica newsletter
- Features
- Cool links

BLACK LACE – THE LEADING IMPRINT OF WOMEN'S SEXY FICTION

TAKING YOUR EROTIC READING PLEASURE TO NEW HORIZONS

LOOK OUT FOR THE ALL-NEW BLACK LACE BOOKS – AVAILABLE NOW!

All books priced £7.99 in the UK. Please note publication dates apply to the UK only. For other territories, please contact your retailer.

SAUCE FOR THE GOOSE
Mary Rose Maxwell
ISBN O 352 33492 4

Sauce for the goose is a riotous and sometimes humorous celebration of the rich variety of human sexuality. Imaginative and colourful, each story explores a different theme or fantasy, and the result is a fabulously bawdy mélange of cheeky sensuality and hot thrills. A lively array of characters display an uninhibited and lusty energy for boundary-breaking pleasure. This is a decidedly X-rated collection of stories designed to be enjoyed and indulged in.

Coming in July

THE ANGELS' SHARE
Maya Hess
ISBN O 352 34043 6

A derelict cottage on the rugged Manx coast is no place for a young woman to hide out in the middle of winter. But Ailey Callister is on a mission – to find and overthrow the man who has stolen her inheritance. Battling against the elements and her own desire for sexual freedom, she fights ghosts from her past to discover the true identity of Ethan Kinrade, the elusive new owner of the vast, whisky-producing estate that by rights should be hers.

THE DEVIL INSIDE
Portia Da Costa
ISBN 0 352 32993 9

This is exactly what happens to the usually conventional Alexa Lavelle after a minor head injury whilst holidaying in the Caribbean. And in order to satisfy her strange and voluptuous new appetites, she is compelled to seek the enigmatic and sophisticated doctors at an exclusive medical practice in London. Their specialist knowledge of psycho-sexual medicine takes Alexa into a world of bizarre fetishism and erotic indulgence. And one particularly attractive doctor has concocted a plan which will prove to be the ultimate test of her senses, and to unleash the devil inside.

Coming in August

IN PURSUIT OF ANNA
Natasha Rostova
ISBN 0 352 34060 6

Anna Maxwell is a pixie-like bad girl with a penchant for brawny men, determined to prove her innocence when accused of stealing from her father's company. Los Angeles-based bounty hunter Derek Rowland sets off in pursuit of his fugitive, discovering that Anna's resolve is as strong as her libido. Derek's colleague, Freddie James, is convinced that Derek is being taken for a ride – and not the good kind. Freddie, meanwhile, is engaged in her own rather delicious struggle with a new lover. The sexual stakes rise as desires and boundaries are pushed to their limits.

DANCE OF OBSESSION
Olivia Christie

ISBN 0 352 33101 1

Paris, 1935. Devastated by the sudden death of her husband, exotic dancer Georgia d'Essange wants to be left alone to grieve. However, her stepson Dominic has inherited his father's business and demands Georgia's help in running it. The business is *Fleur's* – an exclusive club where women of means can indulge their sexual whims with men of their choice and take advantage of the exotic delights Parisian nightlife has to offer. Dominic is eager to take his father's place in Georgia's bed and passions and tempers run high. Further complications arise when Georgia's first lover, Theo Sands – now a rich, successful artist – appears on the scene. In an atmosphere of increasing sexual tension, can everyone's desires be satisfied?

Black Lace Booklist

Information is correct at time of printing. To avoid disappointment, check availability before ordering. Go to www.blacklace-books.co.uk. All books are priced £6.99 unless another price is given.

BLACK LACE BOOKS WITH A CONTEMPORARY SETTING

☐ ON THE EDGE Laura Hamilton	ISBN O 352 33534 3	£5.99
☐ THE TRANSFORMATION Natasha Rostova	ISBN O 352 33311 1	
☐ SIN.NET Helena Ravenscroft	ISBN O 352 33598 X	
☐ TWO WEEKS IN TANGIER Annabel Lee	ISBN O 352 33599 8	
☐ SYMPHONY X Jasmine Stone	ISBN O 352 33629 3	
☐ A SECRET PLACE Ella Broussard	ISBN O 352 33307 3	
☐ GOING TOO FAR Laura Hamilton	ISBN O 352 33657 9	
☐ RELEASE ME Suki Cunningham	ISBN O 352 33671 4	
☐ SLAVE TO SUCCESS Kimberley Raines	ISBN O 352 33687 0	
☐ SHADOWPLAY Portia Da Costa	ISBN O 352 33313 8	
☐ ARIA APPASSIONATA Julie Hastings	ISBN O 352 33056 2	
☐ A MULTITUDE OF SINS Kit Mason	ISBN O 352 33737 0	
☐ COMING ROUND THE MOUNTAIN Tabitha Flyte	ISBN O 352 33873 3	
☐ FEMININE WILES Karina Moore	ISBN O 352 33235 2	
☐ MIXED SIGNALS Anna Clare	ISBN O 352 33889 X	
☐ BLACK LIPSTICK KISSES Monica Belle	ISBN O 352 33885 7	
☐ GOING DEEP Kimberly Dean	ISBN O 352 33876 8	
☐ PACKING HEAT Karina Moore	ISBN O 352 33356 1	
☐ MIXED DOUBLES Zoe le Verdier	ISBN O 352 33312 X	
☐ UP TO NO GOOD Karen S. Smith	ISBN O 352 33589 0	
☐ CLUB CRÈME Primula Bond	ISBN O 352 33907 1	
☐ BONDED Fleur Reynolds	ISBN O 352 33192 5	
☐ SWITCHING HANDS Alaine Hood	ISBN O 352 33896 2	
☐ EDEN'S FLESH Robyn Russell	ISBN O 352 33923 3	
☐ PEEP SHOW Mathilde Madden	ISBN O 352 33924 1	£7.99
☐ RISKY BUSINESS Lisette Allen	ISBN O 352 33280 8	£7.99
☐ CAMPAIGN HEAT Gabrielle Marcola	ISBN O 352 33941 1	£7.99
☐ MS BEHAVIOUR Mini Lee	ISBN O 352 33962 4	£7.99

BLACK LACE ANTHOLOGIES

BLACK LACE NON-FICTION

To find out the latest information about Black Lace titles, check out the website: www.blacklace-books.co.uk or send for a booklist with complete synopses by writing to:

Black Lace Booklist, Virgin Books Ltd
Thames Wharf Studios
Rainville Road
London W6 9HA

Please include an SAE of decent size. Please note only British stamps are valid.

Our privacy policy
We will not disclose information you supply us to any other parties. We will not disclose any information which identifies you personally to any person without your express consent.

From time to time we may send out information about Black Lace books and special offers. Please tick here if you do <u>not</u> wish to receive Black Lace information. ❑

Please send me the books I have ticked above.

Name ....

Address ....

....

....

....

Post Code ....

Send to: Virgin Books Cash Sales, Thames Wharf Studios,
Rainville Road, London W6 9HA.

US customers: for prices and details of how to order
books for delivery by mail, call 888-330-8477.

Please enclose a cheque or postal order, made payable
to Virgin Books Ltd, to the value of the books you have
ordered plus postage and packing costs as follows:

UK and BFPO – £1.00 for the first book, 50p for each
subsequent book.

Overseas (including Republic of Ireland) – £2.00 for
the first book, £1.00 for each subsequent book.

If you would prefer to pay by VISA, ACCESS/MASTERCARD,
DINERS CLUB, AMEX or SWITCH, please write your card
number and expiry date here:

....

Signature ....

Please allow up to 28 days for delivery.